Sexy Secrets

A LAKE HARMONY NOVEL

TANJA WALTRIP

ACKNOWLEDGEMENTS

This book continues to bring Lake Harmony and its quirky characters full of love, humor, and charm to the page. I loved writing Bree's story, and it resonates deeply in my heart being a former educator myself and experiencing a loss similar in my immediate family.

Bree is a strong, smart, capable educator that strives every day to bring joy and love to all those she teaches while challenging them to reach for the stars. She is also a character who suffered great heartbreak as a child when deserted by a parent.

To all my readers that have stepped into roles for children that have those gaps-THANK YOU. You may not realize how much those simple actions help fill a void left by someone else.

DEDICATION

This book is dedicated to all my fellow teachers around the world. Keep doing what you're doing. You are appreciated and what you do matters!

Published by Tanja Waltrip

Copyright 2022

Cover Design by: Getcovers

Website: TanjaWaltrip.com

Chapter One

Bree

Driving up to the grand opening of Harte of Harmony, which is my best friend Julia's pride and joy and her new event venue, I stop a moment and admire the majestic old Victorian home as it comes into view through the trees. She's planted flowers in the lush gardens and lanterns glow all over the outdoor porch — it's a big, beautiful yellow home, surrounded by magic fairy dust. Simply stunning.

Harte of Harmony sits on the bluff overlooking Lake Harmony. Graced with bold yellow walls, white trim, and a bright blue door, she insists guests *Please come in*! The house used to be a private home, but Julia and her husband, Jackson, always dreamed of owning the property and raising their family there. The former owners lived in the home for many years but, as soon as Jackson heard it was for sale, he surprised Julia by buying if for her. Instead of living there, they decided to use it for Julia's new business adventure. Her dream was to use the house as a small, intimate event space. The floorplan suited her vision perfectly, and the bedrooms provided a bed and breakfast option for her future party guests.

I park and grab the cute little guest book I found at an eclectic shop while I was in the city picking up school supplies. I know Julia doesn't have a guest book yet; this will be perfect for her grand opening. My hope is everyone will sign the guest book tonight with a short note so she can always remember how important it was to listen to her heart and reach for her dreams.

As I walk through the door, people are strolling around admiring Julia's hard work. Jackson is mingling and answering questions about the remodel and the few events Julia already has on her calendar. He's smiling and sharing his admiration for Julia with everyone. I love seeing them so happy together again — the perfect couple — even after the marital trouble they recently worked through.

Ah, there she is…the woman of the hour. Walking toward Julia, I see the twinkle in her eyes. A smile stretches across her face with utter happiness. Her long blonde hair bounces on her shoulders and a black evening dress shows off her slim, athletic figure.

"Oh my god, Jules, this place looks magical," I gasp.

"Thank you, that's what I hoped everyone would think! I want to make it as magical for everyone else to enjoy as it's always been to Jackson and me."

"I can't wait to walk through and see the final touches to the guest suites. First, though, I brought you a little something. I was in the city last week, and when I was in this cute little shop, I saw this and knew you needed to have it. Here — open it now."

I hand her my wrapped present, and her eyes get a bit teary. She's almost hesitant to open the pretty gift and looks at me with hesitation. "Come on," I say. "Open it so we can commemorate this night."

"Okay, thank you, Bree." She opens the guest book and reads the inscription I put on the inside cover —

Dearest Julia,
You only had to believe in yourself to make it happen. Congratulations on your Harte of Harmony—may it bring magic to all who walk through her doors. I am so proud of you for reaching for your dreams and pushing through obstacles with grace and determination. Love, Bree

Julia wipes a tear away, gives me a big hug, and thanks me for all my help with the remodel and ideas for getting ready to open for business. She takes the book and a pen to the table in the foyer and opens it up for everyone to leave their entry.

"Jules, I think you should be the first one to sign your name in the book. I know you're not a guest, but I think since this is your new adventure, you should put the first note in the book."

Julia writes:

To everyone that walks through her front door,
May the Harte of Harmony bring joy, love, and laughter to
you now and forever.
To many years of wonderful moments — Julia Harte, Owner

"Jules, that is perfect!"

We continue to catch up, the door opens, and *Holy Guacamole — who is that tall, blond, muscular god!* He walks through the doorway, stops, and looks around. When his eyes catch mine, he smiles and begins to walk directly over to me like he's on a mission. Do I know this Adonis? I don't think so, but he's heading this way with long, sturdy strides, and not once has he taken his eyes off me. He stops directly in front of me.

"Hey, Julia, this place is gorgeous. I'm very impressed," he says to my friend, still looking at me.

Lordy, his voice. I think my panties are melting off right now. He's standing here talking to Julia, but he is staring at me. I can't move. I can't even breathe. I stare back. It's like a game of cat and mouse, only I don't think I'd mind if he wants to chase me for a little bit.

Julia is talking to him, thank goodness, because I don't think I even remember my name, let alone how to speak right now. *Ay caramba!* He's still staring at me. Is my mouth hanging open? Am I drooling? Please look away you big, beautiful man candy. I'm a frozen statue and can't find my voice. Julia, please notice I'm dying over here.

I hear Julia talking to him. What did she refer to him as? Was it Noah? Ugh…snap out of being an idiot Bree and pull your big girl panties up. I smile and can finally look away so I can try to control my breathing. How embarrassing. Julia finally senses that I left my brain in the car and says something to me. "Um, huh?"

"Noah, I'd like you to meet one of my best friends. This is Bree. We've been best friends since our childhood."

This man – Noah, is it? – slowly takes my hand into both of his and stares deeply into my eyes. Wow, his hands are big. *Are we both weird? I feel like we are weird. Am I being punk'd?*

"Nice to meet you, Bree," he says. "What is it you do?"

Oh, he smells so good. Would it be weird to lean in a little and smell him better? Probably a bit creepy or stalkerish so I try not to. Come on brain, ya gonna come out and participate here, or are you going to let me continue to look like a ding-dong? Yeah, that's what I figured.

Julia, knowing that I'm struggling with internal chaos, decides she better cover for me. She smiles and chuckles, shares that I teach kindergarten here, and — FINALLY — my brain decides to work again.

"Sorry," I gulp. "Yes, I've been teaching kindergarten here since college. Growing up, I figured I would go away to college and not come back, but slowly we all return to Lake Harmony. It's a great community to raise kids, and I have so many friends here. So, I came back, and I've been teaching here since. How about you? What do you think of Lake Harmony and working with Jackson? I bet it's a big change from living in the city and now living in our quaint little town where everyone knows each other and everything they do. It's fine, though, it makes for an interesting life," I take a deep breath and end my babbling.

Noah's still staring at me and when I finish talking. He has the biggest smile on his face. A smile with a bit of a smirk — that's it — ladies and gentlemen, the butterflies have taken flight in my stomach, I am a body of turned-on lady bits, and I know my face is as red as it feels.

Julia excuses herself to go mingle with the crowd. As she walks away, she turns around and gives me a wink. Now, I'm alone with this beautiful, extremely attractive man, who also, by the way, smells incredible. I can do this. I teach kindergarteners. If I can control a classroom of monkeys, I can speak to this magnificent man standing next to me.

I take a big, deep breath and smile, "Noah, it's so nice to meet you. Are you settling in here at Lake Harmony and getting to know the ins and outs of our little community?"

He looks me over and smiles, "Yes, slowly. I currently have a light schedule at the practice since a lot of the patients haven't decided to see me instead of Jackson yet. That's given me time to get familiar with the town. I enjoy living by the lake as I did in the city, and I've been using the trails to run."

"Oh, you're a runner huh? Me, not so much. I'd rather do some yoga. But I do love to walk the trails by the lake. It's so pretty and a great place to just think."

"It is a great lake, and you can't beat the view. I've gotten to know Julia's brothers through Jackson, and we've been talking about trying to get out on Rob's boat more often on the weekends while it's still warm. You should join us."

"Oh, that would be so much fun. I'll keep it in mind. Thanks."

"Bree, have you had a chance to go look around yet?" Noah asks.

"No, I walked in and was just catching up with Jules when you arrived," I reply. "Do you want to grab a drink and look around together?" *Please say yes.*

"That sounds great. I've never been in here before, so I won't really know what updates they did, but knowing Julia, I'm sure they're perfect."

"Well then, you've found yourself the best tour guide. I have been here throughout the remodel and can fill you in on the changes."

"Great. I feel special getting my own pretty tour guide. Let's go look around the place then."

I head towards the main event space where Jules has the bar area set up and feel Noah put his hand on my low back as we move through the people mingling around downstairs. The minute he touched me, I felt a zing move from his hand through my body. I wonder if he noticed the electricity flowing through us or if it's just me.

We stop to grab two glasses of bubbly and make a toast, "To Julia and the Harte of Harmony!"

"Cheers!"

Chapter Two

Noah

I promised Julia that I would come tonight. She called and invited me herself, even after Jackson mentioned I was included in the grand opening gala for her new business. Julia was adamant about me showing up so she could introduce me to more of their friends. I know I'll get to know most of them eventually since they seem to be such a tight group. Lord knows I need a new group of friends since mine all still live in Chicago and my ex and her new boyfriend, my former friend, are still part of that social circle.

I'm not upset about the divorce — I never really was, which should tell me something. We grew apart because I worked too much, and she wanted a life I couldn't give her. She wanted a family, and I was never home. Do I want kids of my own and a family to come home to after a long day at work? Absolutely. But it wasn't a priority at that point in my life and, well, my ex had it at the top of her list.

We divorced amicably, but she started dating one of our mutual friends, and that's when things got uncomfortable for me and everyone else. Our friends didn't know how to react. Whom do they side with? Could they invite the three of us to the same function without it being weird? Ugh. Who cares?

That's when Jackson, a doctor friend I met during our residency in Chicago, called me. He was in hot water with his wife and kids for working too hard and not being present in their lives. He needed to make some changes and was looking to add a partner to his practice in the west suburbs of Chicago. Then, the magic question – would I be interested in becoming that partner and moving out to Lake Harmony? *Hell yes, I would be interested. Sign me up!*

It didn't take me long to jump on board once I had all the details. I grew up in a small community, and I was excited about the idea of getting to know my patients rather than walking into an exam room completely unfamiliar with the person sitting in there.

The practice I had been with in the city was so big it was rare I saw the same patient twice. There were days that I felt like I was on a medical conveyor belt where patients would trickle by, and I had to examine, diagnose, and prescribe a fix within fifteen minutes before the conveyor belt would continue.

I didn't become a doctor to see how many patients I could see in a year. I became a doctor to help my patients and to get to know who they are instead of just a diagnosis and prescription.

A good doctor knows many outside factors contribute to a patient's health and not having the opportunity to know them more personally was starting to erode my love for medicine.

So, I'm not joking when I say Jackson's call came at the right time — THE. RIGHT. TIME. I gave my notice at my practice in the city, staying long enough to get through the patient load already scheduled for me, then moved out to the charming little town of Lake Harmony.

Lake Harmony sits about forty miles west of Chicago and has a pristine lake for boating, swimming, and fishing. The town is growing rapidly but still has a small-town charm. I was able to find a beautiful home through Jackson's father-in-law, who is a local builder.

Here I was, forty-five years old, single, in a suburb of Chicago, starting over. Instead of dread, I felt exhilaration because I did the city thing, the married life, and it didn't make me happy. Now, I could be a doctor in a nice town, get to know my patients, run outside, and relax without the hustle and bustle of the city and the awkwardness that had evolved in my social circle.

The Harte of Harmony grand opening was going to be fun. I knew a few people already, and I was excited about Julia and her new business. Working with Jackson, I learned all about their recent struggles. I was happy my friends were able to work through their issues, making it to the other side

16

stronger. It still gave me hope that maybe one day I would find that same happiness.

I wore a nice pair of dark slacks and a sapphire blue dress shirt, but I left the tie and jacket at home. My sleeves were rolled up a bit because I didn't want to look stuffy. I did shave and put on some cologne because I am not a caveman — unless asked to be.

A lot of cars were in the parking area in front of the house, and the porch was all lit up with twinkling lights and bright flowerpots. It was all very pretty and inviting, including the front door, which is painted a bright blue. I open the door, and through a few people mingling around the first floor, I see the most stunning blonde standing with Julia. She is comforting Julia and hugging her tight. I can't take my eyes off her. I shut the door behind me and head straight to her. My god. She's gorgeous with her long blonde hair and bright blue eyes. She has the perfect number of curves but is a bit conservative with showing them off. As I approach, I keep observing her, then she catches my eye. Neither of us looks away from the other. It's like two magnets being pulled to each other.

I walk directly over to them, still focusing only on this blonde beauty. "Hey Julia, this place is gorgeous. I'm very impressed."

Julia and I make small talk for a moment, and she introduces me to Bree. The blonde beauty in front of me is Bree. Her name suits her perfectly. As Julia continues to talk, I admire Bree's pretty features: bright blue eyes, heart-shaped full lips, and long blonde hair that falls around her shoulders in big soft waves.

I realize I'm being rude and, after a quick smile to Bree, I turn my attention to Julia, who promptly excuses herself to go mingle with the other guests. Well damn, I didn't mean to be so rude to her.

Bree starts talking. She's nervous. She just rambled on for about five minutes, and I don't think she even took a breath. I smile because I can't take my eyes off her. She blushes and offers to show me the house and the updates

17

that Julia has made. I accept, and as we walk toward the main event space, I put my hand on her low back to guide her. I can't stop myself from touching her. *Why am I so drawn to this woman other than she is absolutely beautiful? Is she throwing off some kind of witchy spell?*

***

As we make our way up the beautiful grand staircase, Bree leads the way and drags her finger along the rail. She is so captivating, and I find myself eager to get to know her better. Once we make it to the second-floor landing, she turns around and looks at the beautiful chandelier hanging over the downstairs foyer.

I hear a deep sigh come from her, "Oh isn't that just lovely? The crystals make little rainbow reflections on the wall. So pretty."
She turns to face me with a smile, "Noah, are you ready to see the Harte of Harmony and its beautiful guest suites?"
I gesture for her to go ahead of me, "Please, lead the way."
She smiles and grabs my hand, "Follow me then," and pulls me towards the guest rooms.
At this point I may follow this woman anywhere she takes me. Not a bad view watching her hips sway as I follow her like a lost puppy.
She shows me all the different guest suites and how each has a flower name like lilac, rose, and lily. I have a hard time keeping track of everything she's saying because I'm so mesmerized by her movements and her charm. I need to snap out of it before I make a fool of myself.
"Let's go upstairs to see the cozy little area that Jules made up there." I follow her up a back staircase, which has us in a tighter space, and again I put my hand on her back. Bree pauses and catches her breath before continuing upstairs. *Am I not the only one feeling this way?* We walk into a huge open space on the third floor.

"Isn't this the cutest space? Originally, it was extra kid space. The former owners had five children and instead of them being underfoot the owners created this big open space for the kids to disappear and have their own area. Jules wanted to make the room a second, more relaxed gathering space. She thought if guests have kids, they may like to come up here. Or, if a wedding party has children, they can use this for the kids and the babysitters to have a place to get away but still be on site," Bree explains.

"Bree, can you imagine growing up in this house? Having this room with that view of the lake. That would have been cool, especially as a teenager."

Smiling and with a giggle, Bree says, "Or sneaking up here with a date when your parents are out."
I look over at her and as I do, she blushes and turns away.
"Bree, were you a troublemaker as a teen? For some reason, that is a bit hard to believe."

"No, I wouldn't have dared get into trouble. I wouldn't have done that to my mom. She had enough to worry about. How about you, Noah?" she asks.
"Oh yeah," I laugh and shake my head at the memories. "My brother and I were complete troublemakers and not afraid of anything. We would always dare each other to do stupid shit. Usually, we got away with it, unless one of us ended up with an injury. Man, my parents would get pissed at us. I think that's one of the reasons I went into medicine. I was never afraid of the doctor, and I thought it was such a cool job."

"Your poor mother! How old is your brother?"

"We're Catholic twins. Hunter is a year younger than me."

"Wow, your mom must have been busy with the two of you. I can't even imagine."

"Yeah, and I have a sister too, Shannon, who is three years younger than me. At least, mom had a little bit longer break with her than between my brother and me," I tell her.

"I always wanted siblings," says Bree. "I guess that's why Jules, Hillary, Sam, and I are so close. Plus, I've always been considered an adopted Stone. Julia's family always

19

included my mom and me with holidays and big celebrations. Our mothers grew up together and stayed friends all these years."

"Is your dad not in the picture?" I ask.

"Nope. He left when I was nine and never came back. We don't even know where he is anymore. He never wanted to be a husband or a father."

"I'm sorry, Bree. That couldn't have been easy. I'm happy you had close friends and the Stones to provide an extended family for you and your mom. At least, you weren't completely alone."

"True. But let's talk about something more exciting than my past. That isn't anything fun."

I grab Bree's hand and look into her eyes, "I don't really know what's happening here, but I want to get to know you better. Would you like to go out to dinner with me?"

"Yes, I would like that," she says.

Raking my hand through my hair and feeling a bit flustered, I say, "Bree, I'm so drawn to you. I can't really explain it, but I want to kiss you. Is that okay?"

Bree puts her hand on my cheek and steps into my chest, "Kiss me, Noah."

I lower my lips and gently move them against hers and feel her take a quick inhale when they touch. She slowly moves into my arms and opens her lips for more. With a gentle kiss, I move my hand to the back of her neck, gliding my fingers through her golden hair that feels like silk. I pull away from her, and we both just stare at each other.

Bree blushes, and she quietly whispers, "Why do I feel like I can't let you walk away from me?"

"I don't know, but I feel the same. I know we just met, but from the moment I saw you downstairs, I knew I had to get to know you, kiss you, and hold you in my arms. Have you put a spell on me?"

Giggling, Bree blushes, "No, but isn't this crazy, Noah? I feel the same way."

"Maybe it's crazy, but I don't care." She licks her lip and I lean back down and kiss her again. She wraps her arms around me, and we stand there kissing like those teenagers we were joking about just moments ago.

Pulling back and putting my forehead against hers, I say "We better head back down before someone comes looking for us. It's taking everything in me right now to be a gentleman. Go to dinner with me tomorrow, Bree. I don't think I can wait longer than a day to see you again."

"I'd like that, very much," she says.

22

Chapter Three

Bree

As I open my eyes Sunday morning while still laying in my bed, I reach up and touch my lips and think about Noah. Wow, did that really happen last night? He's so handsome and charming and kisses like a prince.

We exchanged phone numbers and we agreed to meet tonight for dinner. *Oh, my goodness, I have a date tonight!* Ugh, as exciting as that is, why do I still have this sense of dread? *Don't get your hopes up, Bree, to just be disappointed in the end.* I grab my cell phone to check the time, the weather for the day, and any emails or messages. I have a couple of texts, one from Mom, another from Noah, and another from Jules.

MOM: Looking forward to brunch today with my beautiful daughter. See you at the diner at 1030 am.
Me: Can't wait!

Jules: Thank you so much for the beautiful guest book for Harte of Harmony. I love you so much B *Heart emoji* and SPILL whatever happened between you and NOAH>OMG!!! Sparks were flying!!!
Me: I am so glad you liked it. Noah-very nice, handsome, date tonight
Jules: ...
Me: Need coffee before I call *smiley emoji*
Jules: FINE *sad emoji*

Noah: Looking forward to our date tonight. Pick you up at 6?
Me: That sounds great. Not picky-you choose the place

Okay, time to jump in the shower and make some coffee. I look over to the other side of the bed and Mr. Franklin, my tuxedo cat, is looking at me, "Hi Franklin, are you hungry?"

He replies with a "Mew," because he is broken and doesn't know his alphabet. Of course, to him, I just said Franklin let's go grab your delicious food and please meow and head butt me until I get out of bed! Silly cat.

"Come on, mister. I'll start the coffee and get you some breakfast before I jump in the shower."

On my way into the kitchen, I decide to put some music on, "Alexa, play the best of Pink."

Dancing in the kitchen to Pink singing about giving her a reason, I stumble — good words to live by — talking about not being broken. *Okay, Universe, I am not broken, and I can learn to love again. Maybe? I promise I'll try.*

I mean. I just met Noah. One date doesn't mean we'll live happily ever after in a cape cod with a white picket fence and have two kids and a golden retriever who is best friends with Mr. Franklin, the cat. Why do I always put that happily ever after dream into play with every guy I meet? Nothing like dooming something before it even has the chance to happen.

Picking up my phone, I text Jules.

Me: You free for a call?

She doesn't reply to my text because my phone is already ringing in my hand. Smiling, I answer, "Hello Jules, good morning."

"Tell me right now! I'm dying. Jackson and I talked about you guys last night. I saw the sparks flying as we watched the two of you walk away together. Oh my god, Bree. Come on — dying here!"

"Well, if you would take a deep breath and give me a minute to answer you, I promise I will."

"Okay, go. I am going to be quiet now. I mean, you were in a fog after he walked over and didn't say anything. You were just standing there staring at each other like

24

statues. For a minute, I didn't think either of you were going to talk or even notice I was standing right there next to you too. It was so funny! Okay, I promise, I'll be quiet now."

"Jules, you're killing me. You and I were standing there talking about the guest book and all emotional when I saw him open the door and walk in, and I just froze. He is the most beautiful man I have ever seen, and holy fireworks…he smells delicious, and his voice was so sexy! I may have to ask him to read me the phone book and record it for when I need something fabulously romantic. Mmm…he is so dreamy."

"Bree…you have to give me more than that. Where did you leave things? Are you going to see him again?"

"Once I got myself out of being a ding-dong and could talk and you ran off and ditched me, we grabbed a glass of bubbly and went upstairs. He was a perfect gentleman. I asked him if he was getting settled from his move to Lake Harmony, and we talked a little about what he likes to do in his free time. Then, we walked through the guest suites, and I shared the room names and the special touches you put into the house. Oh, I took him upstairs to see the big open lounging space, and when we were up there, he kissed me. So that's it."

I knew she was going to go crazy, so I gave her a few seconds for that to register.

"Wait — he kissed you? That's it! Oh no, girlfriend, I want the deets. That isn't fair, and you know it."

I could just see her standing there with her hands on her hips frustrated with me. Laughing, I knew I better give her more information. "Yes, he kissed me, Jules. He even asked me first if it was okay for him to kiss me. It was so romantic, but it was also like the two of us had to kiss. Like it wasn't really an option for either of us. So magical, mmm."

"Oh my god! I'm dying over here, Bree. That's awesome! I love Noah, and we've been trying to get him over to meet everyone, but he's been so focused on getting settled in his new place and the practice. So, our timing hasn't been very good with getting everyone together but —

25

don't be mad — I just knew you guys would hit it off. Jackson was completely in the dark because you know men can't think that far ahead, but I just had this feeling that the two of you would be good together. And I was right!"

"He is very handsome and such a good kisser. So charming too. We got along great once I stopped acting like an idiot. Thank goodness he looked past my moment of being paralyzed. So funny."

"So, what's next, lady?" Jules asks.
"He's taking me out for dinner tonight. He said he didn't want to waste any time before he got to see me again."
"Oh, that's so sweet. Do you know where you are going?"

"Nope," I say. "I told him to pick the place and let me know."

"This is so exciting. Remember to relax and be yourself. Obviously, he's interested in you and wants to get to know you better. Noah is a great guy, and I trust him. Just go with your gut. It seems like chemistry isn't the problem, so just have fun tonight."

"That's my plan, Jules. I need to remember to not put too much pressure on myself and enjoy the night. Now, if my head would follow my heart that would be easier for me to do. But I'm going to try my best to just get to know him and enjoy the food and company," I tell her.

"Okay. I'll let you go because I know you're probably meeting your mom for brunch. Give her my love, please."

"Will do — talk soon."

"Yes. I will need date details."

"Bye, Jules."

***

After getting ready and locking up the house, I head to the diner to meet Mom for brunch. We try to do this at least twice a month. Just time to catch up and enjoy breakfast together.

Walking in, I see Mom already has a booth, and she smiles and waves at me as I walk over. "Hey, Mom. How are you today?"

26

"Good" she replies. "I'm happy to see you. You look pretty this morning."

"Thank you, I had a good night," I say.

"I'm sorry I missed Julia's grand opening. I had promised Mrs. Gardner next door that I would come for dinner. She's so lonely since she lost her husband," Mom shakes her head. "Was there a good turnout? I'm sure the place was beautiful and ready for her first event. She has a small wedding next week already, right?"

"Yes, and she is so excited. It's a second wedding, and the couple is keeping it small and immediate family only. They have the whole house reserved for overnight guests too!"

"That's amazing. I am so proud of Julia. Now, what's new with you?" Mom asks.

Before I could even answer, my phone went off with a text message. I tried to ignore it. It went off again.

"Honey, I know we have a rule about no phones at the table but why don't you make sure it isn't something important," Mom says.

"Thanks, Mom. I'll make it quick." I read the texts. All from Noah.

Noah: I can't wait to see you
Noah: I can't get you off my mind
Noah: Dinner at the Italian restaurant – Bella Roma's?
Noah: You aren't avoiding carbs, are you?
Me: I love Italian, and all carbs are welcome *smiling emoji*
Noah: Looking forward to it — Have a great day!
Me: U 2 — see you then!

I look up, and my mother has a big smile on her face. "What?" I ask, feigning innocence.

"Don't give me that 'what,' because when you looked at your phone, your face just lit up. Are you going to tell me who he is?" She asks.

"His name is Noah, and I met him last night at Julia's grand opening. He's taking me to dinner tonight. He works with Jackson."

"Hmm, is this the doctor that moved from the city to be his partner?" Mom raises her eyebrow.

"Um, yes? How do you know about Noah?" I ask.

"Honey, Ruby told me all about it when Jackson and Julia were having issues. You know we discuss our children and what's going on in their lives when we get together for our coffee talk afternoons. Ruby shared what was going on between Julia and Jackson when they were reevaluating their lives and marriage. She said Jackson found a doctor friend that went through his residency with him who was also looking to make a change, and it was all perfect timing. I heard the doctor he found moved out to Lake Harmony from the city, but I haven't really heard anything further — unless Gertie posted about it on Facebook in Harmony Hears."

"Oh. Okay... I met him last night. He came to the grand opening, and we got to talking. He seems nice, so I agreed to a dinner date tonight, but I am not getting my hopes up. You know how it goes," I say.

Bringing her hands over to hold mine on top of the table, Mom gives me a cautious smile, "Honey, trust yourself. I know you have hesitated to put your heart on the line, but you have to know that not all men are going to be like your dad and walk away. Look at your two best friends and their marriages. Julia had trouble with Jackson, but they didn't walk away from each other. Instead, they fought to make their marriage stronger together. Your friend Sam has been married to her husband, Paul, for a long time and they also seem to be very happy. You're friends with a lot of young couples that are still together. Not one of them has divorced or left the other. Is marriage and being in love perfect? No. But if you don't allow yourself to take that risk, you won't ever find it. Go on your date, get to know Noah, and see where it goes."

"I know," I say. "And I understand not all men are like my father. I know there are decent men in the world that love their families and their wives and don't just leave and never come back. But I'm happy, and I don't feel like I need to get married. I have my teaching and great friends in my life."

"Bree, just go out on a date and have fun. If there's no chemistry or you don't feel like there's a reason for a second date — then you don't have to kiss at the end of the night and promise a future together."

I can feel the heat on my face, and my mother sees the blush too, because she gets a bigger smile.

"Oh... or maybe there is some chemistry there?"

Dropping my head into my hand, "Ugh, Mom, I hate that you see right through me."

"Of course, I do! I'm your mother and you're not good at hiding what you're feeling from showing on your face. So, are you going to tell me, or is that too private?"

"There is a lot of chemistry there. I'm not sure what's going to happen, but both of us are drawn to each other." Cautiously and biting my lip I share, "We kissed last night." Smiling at me and giving me that *it will be okay look*, mom says "Oh, honey, it'll be fine. Take your time but give yourself permission to see where this goes without setting expectations. Don't focus on the future. Focus on the now. Can you do that? Don't put so much pressure on yourself. Just enjoy the moment."

"I'll try. He's taking me to dinner tonight at Bella Roma's."

"That's lovely, honey. Enjoy a nice evening with delicious food and time to get to know one another better. What are you going to wear?"

"Mom, I love you but don't stress me out over this. I'll probably wear a cute dress — not too fancy, not too casual. The last thing I want to do is feel uncomfortable in my own skin. I'm going to treat this as if I was going out with the girls. Otherwise, I'm afraid I'll talk myself out of enjoying the night and focusing on everything that could go wrong."

"From what I've heard, Noah is a very nice man and very easy on the eyes."

"You are completely right about that!" I exclaim.

29

30

Chapter Four

Bree

I have about an hour or so to get ready before Noah picks me up. I decided to take a shower, not a bath so that I have more time to do my hair. Obviously, I will still use my sugar scrub and primp a little bit, but I can manage that in a shower while I have a conditioning mask on my hair.

I already laid out my outfit on the bed, so that I can slip into my clothes and heels. I'm going to put on my favorite feel-good dress I wear when I'm feeling happy. It's so cute! It's a pink geo-patterned mini with three-quarter length bell sleeves. It's sexy, sassy, and comfortable. I will pair it with silver sandals that tie up the ankle and some bangle bracelets and a necklace.

After my shower, I throw on my satin robe and start with my hair. My hair has gotten long again, with long layers that give me some bounce around my shoulders after I put some curls into it.

I don't usually wear a lot of makeup, so I apply my basics: under-eye concealer, soft pink eyeshadow, mascara, and lip gloss. Teaching kindergartners means sometimes I don't sit all day unless we're having carpet time, and I can sit and read a story or give a lesson. Otherwise, I like to joke and tell everyone I helicopter through my classroom all day. I mean, have you ever tried herding cats? Because that's what it feels like some days in my classroom with five and six-year-olds. They are adorable at this age, but they don't always listen or follow directions. But I love my job, and I love my students.

With my hair and makeup done, I check the time; I still have about fifteen minutes before Noah should arrive. I drop the robe and put on my pretty pink lace bra and panty set. One of my guilty pleasures is expensive lingerie, even though I am usually the only one that sees it. I deserve it, so

I splurge on it — actually, all of us girls do. It's one of the things we love to treat ourselves to.

I put on my shoes and my jewelry, slip my dress over my head, and spritz perfume on. Another guilty pleasure — but a girl needs to feel beautiful inside and out, right?

I head to the kitchen to make sure Franklin has food and water. "Hey buddy, let's get you a treat." Once he hears the baggy with his cat treats shake, he's next to me, pawing my leg and meowing like a crazy tiger. "Here little man. I love you. Be good while I'm out tonight."

I grab my regular, everyday purse, pull out my license and credit card, and stick them, along with my lip gloss and phone, inside a little clutch that matches my outfit. Before I even shut my clutch, there's a knock at the door. I take a second and check myself in the mirror. *Looking good, Bree!*

Opening the door, I smile at Noah. *Jumping Jellyfish! Noah looks dreamy.* "Hi."

He's standing there looking me over from head to foot with a huge smile on his face. While he takes a moment to appreciate how I look, I do the same. Boy-oh-boy. This man is simply gorgeous. He's tall, probably six foot four, with a muscular body, dark blond hair he wears shorter on the sides than the top, high cheekbones, full lips, and arctic blue eyes. He has a light blue dress shirt on with the sleeves cuffed up his forearms, which look strong, a Movado watch on his wrist, dark grey tailored slacks with a belt, and what looks like Cole Hahn wingtip oxfords. *Hello, Mr. GQ! This man is yummy!*

His eyes move back to my eyes then settle on my mouth. I pose, arms akimbo, and one hip out, "Do I pass go and get a delicious dinner at Bella Roma's in your company this evening?"

Noah leans in to give me a kiss just shy of my lips. "Absolutely. Although, you look mighty delicious yourself. You are beautiful."

He hands me a small bouquet of pink gerbera daisies — my favorites — and smiles. "These are for you. How was the rest of your day?"

Leaning into him more, I inhale and say, "Mmm…you smell good! Thank you for the beautiful flowers. My day was good. I spent some time with my mom and then worked on lesson plans for the week. I try to go in Monday morning with a good plan for the week. Let me quickly put these in water before we head out."

"Okay. But I'm going to stay right here by the front door while you do that so that we can head to dinner before I get other ideas and we never get out the door," he says.

I go into the kitchen and put the flowers in a vase I have from my mom. I love fresh flowers in the house. *These are so pretty*. I head back out to the front door, "All set. Thank you again for thinking of me and bringing me flowers. That was very thoughtful."

"You're welcome. A beautiful woman deserves beautiful things." Grabbing my hand, he guides me to his car, which is a beautifully sleek, black Audi SUV. He walks me to the passenger side and opens the door for me.

"Thank you. Such a gentleman," I murmur.

"My mother made sure we knew how to treat a woman with respect." Leaning into me he whispers, "I can dance too."

He comes around to the driver's side and gets in. "I'm so hungry," Noah says. "I haven't been able to try this restaurant yet, so I'm extra happy that I get to do so in your company."

***

Arriving at Bella Roma's, Noah once again comes around to open the car door for me and escorts me into the restaurant. I love this place and the food is amazing. The owners, Maria and Lorenzo, are a cute middle-aged couple that opened an Italian restaurant to share their family recipe. They don't have a set menu; instead, they serve five main meals each evening, and when they run out, that's it. Everything is fresh, homemade, and delicious. The restaurant has twenty small tables, and the atmosphere is Tuscan-style romantic with exposed wood beams, stone, and plaster walls in warm yellows.

After being seated, we look at the dinner menu and consider all the mouth-watering options. "Noah, what do you think you're going to order? I'll add that anything you choose is going to be amazing."

"I can't decide if I should go with the lasagna or the seafood risotto. I was also looking at the Ragu Alla Bolognese. Help a guy out here, please. Which dinner are you leaning toward?" He asks.

"They all look good, don't they? Let me ask you a question first." I look at him with my best teacher's serious stare. "Do you share?"

He studies me and a smile forms on his face. "Yes, I share. I think I know where you are going with that question, and if you're open to getting different things and sharing with each other, that's a solid yes to sharing with me."

Leaning into him, I say quietly, like a secret between the two of us, "But, which two do we choose?"

Noah whispers back, "I think we go with one pasta and the risotto."

"That's probably a good way to go. If it helps, I've had the lasagna, and it was delicious. But I haven't tried the Ragu Alla Bolognese."

"Then, I think we have our selections. Let's get two we've not tried so it will be a new experience for both of us," he says.

"Perfect."

Maria comes over to our table. "Hello, Bree. It's so lovely to see you tonight." She looks over at Noah, "Who is this handsome man you have here with you?"

"Maria, I'd like you to meet Noah. He recently moved to town to partner with Jackson at the medical practice."

"Welcome to Lake Harmony, Noah," Maria says. "I know Jackson and Julia very well, and most of our residents. I hope you like our town as much as Lorenzo and I love being here."

Noah says, "It's very nice to meet you too, Maria.

Bree is gracious enough to spend her Sunday evening with me before a Monday with her little kindergartners, so I feel very fortunate to be here with her. Your restaurant and the menu are wonderful. I will most likely become a regular here."

"Wonderful. Can I start you two off with some wine?"

Noah looks at me, "Bree, do you have a preference?"

"I'd love a glass of red wine," I reply. "Maria, I'll let you choose since you know what I like."

"I'll try whatever Bree is having. I trust I can't go wrong with your selection either. Thank you."

"Would you like a bottle or just a glass?" Maria asks.

"Bree, we could do a bottle since it will only be about two glasses each. Does that sound okay with you?"
"Yes, if you promise not to let me drink more than two glasses," I tell him, "because I cannot go to class with a wine headache. Those little boogers will take me out if I show any sign of weakness."

"No problem. I'll stop you after your two," he promises.
Maria says, "I'll bring your bottle in a moment then take your order."

One of the restaurant staff comes by our table with fresh bread, olive oil, and ground parmesan. We each grab a piece of bread, dip it, and moan. Both of us, with our mouths full, just smile at each other.

"That's delicious, and I'm hungry," Noah says.

"Me too. I'm so happy to be here right now, Noah. The food's delicious, the atmosphere is wonderful, and my date for the evening is very easy on the eyes," I say.

Laughing, he takes my hand, "I don't know. I think I have the better end of the deal. You're charming and kind to everyone around you. You're so beautiful, you take my breath away, and you're willing to share your dinner with me. See? I think I got the better deal."

"Flattery will get you everything," I say as Maria comes with a bottle of wine.

"I brought you one of my favorite reds," she says. "A Renieri Rosso Di Montalcino, Sangiovese. It's a medium-bodied cherry-spiced red. Very elegant."

Maria pours the wine for Noah to taste first. When he accepts the bottle, she pours my glass.

"Maria, this is delicious. Thank you for choosing this one for us. I think Noah and I are ready to order if you are ready for us."

"Of course, what would you both like to enjoy this evening? We have all selections still available," she tells us.

I say, "We are going to try the seafood risotto and the Ragu Alla Bolognese."

"Very good choices. Would you like a salad with your meal? We have garden salad or Caesar salad."

"I would love a green salad with your house dressing. What about you, Noah?" I ask.

"I'll take the same. Thank you again, Maria. I am looking forward to my dinner," Noah says.

"I hope it meets your expectations," Maria says as she walks away with a wink.

While we wait for our food to come out, we start talking about our day and the week to come.

"Thank you for inviting me for dinner," I start. "I'm enjoying myself. It feels like I have known you for a long time, yet we just met last night. This isn't a stressful date where I feel like I can't be myself and eat what I want."

Noah smiles at me. "I'm happy to hear that. I want you to feel comfortable with me. I'm enjoying getting to know you too. Let's see…we don't want to make this awkward so instead of the usual stressful date questions, let's make this more fun. What do you say?"

"Okay. I love this idea. How about we ask each other a random question and we both have to answer it? Does that sound like a good plan?" I ask.

"Yes, and since ladies go first, you can ask me the first question."

I take a sip of my wine and act like I'm thinking up a hard question, tapping my finger on my chin, "Noah, first question. What is your favorite holiday and why?"

"Easy. Thanksgiving, because I love eating all the food that comes with it and spending time with family. Now, your turn."

"I would say Halloween. I love to see all my students dress up and all the kids in my neighborhood come trick or treating. It also gives kids some social and emotional development because it can help build self-esteem and how to work with others."

Laughing, Noah leans back in his chair. "Bree! My answer now sounds ridiculous. You gave a well-thought-out answer, and I am all about the food! Okay, my turn to ask you something. Where is the one place you would love to travel if money or time was no concern?"

Before I can answer, our salads arrive at the table. That's fine. It gives me time to think about it. "I have always wanted to go to Greece. From all my reading and watching the traveling pants stories and there are a lot of interesting historical locations there. I'm also fascinated by mythology and that seems like a neat place to go. What about you?"
"I've always wanted to go to Africa and go to a safari lodge where I can see the animals roaming in the wild. I had a chance to do something in Africa with Doctors Without Borders, but the timing wasn't right, so I didn't go," Noah says a bit sadly.

"Oh, that would be an amazing trip. Maybe one day the timing will be right, and you'll get to go," I say.
We finish our salads and one of the restaurant staff comes by to grab our empty dishes. I take a sip of my wine, "Next question. If you could have dinner with anyone famous — dead or alive — who would it be?"

"Oh, that's an awesome question. I could go so many different directions — sports, a dead president — but I was just thinking about David Bowie today during a run when one of his songs was playing. I would love to ask him about his music, all the people he worked with in the industry, and the choices he made about crossing genres and being Ziggy Stardust. Okay, your turn. Who would you like to meet and talk to?"

I consider for a moment. "I would love to be in a room with Princess Diana. I find her fascinating. She obviously didn't marry for love, or at least I don't think he ever loved her. She probably hoped he loved her and realized he didn't. She was a means to an end for him, and he used her to have children. She was shy and quiet and married the wrong man. He treated her poorly and broke her spirit, but then before she died, I felt like she found her voice. She was taking personal risks and getting stronger. I would just like to tell her that I understood how she may have felt giving her heart to someone who broke it. Plus, I'd really love to ask her about Harry's father."

As I finish my spiel about Princess Di, Maria brings our food to the table. "Bon Appetito," she says.

"Thank you, Maria. This looks delicious." She put the seafood risotto in front of me and the pasta in front of Noah. I look up at him, and his eyes keep going back and forth from my plate to his with some hesitation.

"Bree, we are still sharing tonight, right?" he asks.

Looking at him, I think he'd rather have both plates in front of himself. "Yes, we can still share. How about if we just eat a little and trade plates? I know I can't eat as much as you, so feel free to dig in and eat more than half of that pasta."

"I want to be a gentleman and ask if you're sure, but I don't think I can be right now. This all looks amazing. I almost want to order more to take home."

Laughing, I put my hand on him, "You can do whatever you want. No judgment here. Enjoy your dinner. I don't think you'll be able to stop once you start eating anyway."

After Noah takes a few bites and groans about how good the food is, I ask the next question, "Do you believe in ghosts?"

"The science guy in me says no but being in medicine I have seen and heard things that I hope are true."

"What do you mean?" I ask him as I keep eating my delicious dinner.

"There have been situations where a patient will tell me they see someone they love, and later, I learn from their family that person is deceased. I don't know if they truly have visits from loved ones from the other side, but in my heart, I hope they do and that when our lives are coming to an end, we have someone from the other side to help us cross without fear."

"That would be lovely, wouldn't it? I do believe in ghosts. I think I've seen one before. It wasn't like seeing Casper or a floating white sheet, and it wasn't scary. More like a calm, peaceful feeling. I thought I saw someone that I know has died and I know it wasn't my imagination."

"Okay, let's switch plates," he says. "We can always switch back later, but I'm dying to try that risotto."

We trade plates while giggling a bit at Noah's silly pun. He takes a bite of the risotto and groans again, while I taste the pasta. His love for food is adorable. I knew he would be in heaven once he got a taste of Maria's food.

Noah stops eating and puts his fork down, "Before I can't stop myself from finishing my plate, I want to make a toast."

I grab my glass and lift it up, "I'm ready."
He holds his glass and looks into my eyes, "To delicious food, wonderful company, and new beginnings. I hope this is just the first of many evenings together. Cheers!"
"Ditto! To us and making memories." And we clink our glasses together. "I think it's your question."
He takes a couple more bites and refills our glasses. "That's our second glass, and we've finished the bottle, so you are now cut off from further alcoholic beverages this evening."

"Perfect. Thank you for keeping my two-glass max rule tonight. I don't know what I would do without you sitting here." I smile and wink at him. *Is that a blush on his cheeks? Cute.*

"What's the greatest risk you have ever taken and do you regret it?" he asks me.

39

"That's probably not a good question for me because I feel like I haven't taken a big risk — ever. The one I need to take seems too big for me to handle. So, I keep it on the procrastinator's to-do list."

"What do you mean?" Noah says. "Why does it seem like too big a risk?"

Feeling a bit insecure I share, "I've always wanted to write a book, a romance novel, but I just haven't committed to it."

"Why do you think it's a risk? Because you're a teacher? You aren't a good writer? Why do you think it's an unattainable goal?"

"This probably sounds silly, but how am I supposed to write a good love story if I haven't ever allowed myself to be in love? Won't I look like a fake?" I ask.

Noah sits there just looking at me for a second and not saying anything. He puts his fork down and takes a sip of wine. "Bree, maybe you need to do some research?"

"What?"

"Hear me out…what would you tell a student that doesn't want to do something because they feel they don't know how to do it and are afraid to fail?"

"I always tell them practice makes perfect or not to be afraid to try something new because we can't all be perfect at something the first time we try something new. Ah ha! I see what you're doing — you clever man." I take a sip of my wine and continue to look at him. "So, this research, Noah, what does it look like exactly? How does one research love?"

Noah grins at me. "I may have some ideas on that. Would you like a study buddy? I would like to offer my time to help you with this big risk."

***

We're finishing our dessert, a shared piece of tiramisu, and enjoying an espresso when a shadow falls over our table. I look up and Gertie is standing there with a big smile on her face. Gertie our seventy-five-year-old resident gossip who runs the Facebook page Harmony Hears.

"Good evening, Bree. Dr. Roarke. It looks like you two are enjoying a wonderful evening out together. I was just sitting over there with Roxie, Jane, and May enjoying our monthly Sunday dinner when I saw the two of you, so I wanted to come and say hello."

Wishing we would have bumped into anyone but Gertie, I take a breath, "Hi Gertie, it's so nice that you and the ladies get out together. I hope that I'll always have Jules, Hillary, and Sam to enjoy nice dinners with too."

She stands there looking at both of us hoping for more, but Noah probably doesn't know Gertie is waiting for one of us to spill some secrets and worried that he is going to say something, I kick him under the table. Instead of understanding that I would prefer he not say anything, he provides exactly what Gertie was hoping for.

"It's nice to see you, Gertie. Bree and I were just enjoying a nice evening together before the busy week starts."

Looking like she just won the lottery with her eyes lighting up, Gertie replies, "Well, I don't want to take any more of your time during your date. Enjoy your evening together — tootles."

She walks away. I let out a sigh and my shoulders sag.

Noah looks like he got caught with his hand in the cookie jar. "From your reaction right now, I'm guessing I just did something wrong."

I shift my gaze to his guilty face. "You've met Gertie before, haven't you? Because she knew exactly who you were. I'm guessing, though, no one has had the chance to fill you in on her hobby of being our town gossip. I kicked you under the table to warn you."

"Shoot. I thought that was so I'd carry on the conversation. I'm sorry. No, I'm not aware that she gossips, but how much harm can that little old lady do?"
I laugh and shake my head, "Oh, Noah. You'll find out soon enough. Have you heard of Harmony Hears on Facebook? If

not, we better get you up to speed and make sure you know how to avoid being on the town gossip page."

TWO TAKEN - NIGHT ON THE TOWN

Two of Lake Harmony's favorite singles were seen having a cozy dinner at Bella Roma's last night. Sorry ladies and gentlemen, but two of our most eligible singles may be off the market. Better luck to those of you still out there searching for your forever love.

Chapter Five

Bree

It's Thursday afternoon, and I'm cleaning up my classroom so I can go home and prepare for book club. Julia, Hillary, and Sam, my three best friends, are coming over, and Ellen, who is Julia's younger sister and a good friend, is also coming over.

Julia is married to Jackson and has an event business. Hillary is a caterer and has her own business in town and is the only other single one in our group. Sam is married to Paul, and they own a garden and landscape design business. Ellen is married to Scott, and she owns Harmonious Bites the coffee shop downtown.

We get together every month and rotate houses for book club. Whoever hosts is the one that chooses the book we discuss. The guys joke that we should call it "wine club," because we all bring a bottle of wine to share and some form of food.

While we meet for book club, the guys head to Garrett's house for poker night. Garrett is Julia's older brother and the town sheriff. They sit around gossiping like women, just as badly as we do.

I haven't seen the girls since my date Sunday with Noah, so I know they're going to harass me and want details. It's been a good week texting Noah. We both have busy schedules and haven't had a chance to see each other, but I think he wants to see me again this weekend.

I better get home, shower, make my taco dip, and get together the ingredients for mango margaritas. We decided to ditch the wine and go with tequila and Mexican food. We read a book that takes place in Mexico, so we thought it fit the mood. Obviously, I picked a rom-com love story; if I had chosen the type of book I really read for myself, I would be afraid of what the girls would say.

It's about time for the girls to show, and I'm looking forward to spending time with my friends. Julia arrives first a few minutes early. I open the door, "Hey, how are you doing?"

"I'm good. Busy with work. I'm more interested in how you are and what the current situation is between you and a sexy doctor I know."

"Nope. I'm not saying a word until everyone gets here, because I know all of you are going to bug me about Noah. You're going to have to wait. While you're patiently waiting, though, can I make you a mango margarita?" I ask.

"Yes, please!"

I walk into the kitchen with Julia hot on my trail. She sits on a stool at the island while I whip up a frozen margarita for her. Just as she sits, the doorbell rings and Hillary walks in. "I'm here bitches, where are you?"

Laughing, Julia and I just roll our eyes. "We're in the kitchen Hill, come on back."

"Hey girls, Ellen and Sam just pulled up as I hit the front door so they should be walking in shortly. I brought some mini tacos with shredded chicken and cilantro."

"That sounds delicious." Watching Hillary unwrap the serving dish full of mini tacos that smell heavenly, I hear the rest of our crew walking in the house. "Back in the kitchen, ladies."

Ellen and Sam walk in, their arms loaded with bags. "Oh, my goodness, what all did you bring?" I ask.

Ellen starts digging chips and salsa out of her bag and some Mexican beer. "I know you're making margaritas, but I wanted to provide an option. I also made some salsa and brought beer and limes."

"Yum," I say and look over at Sam. "Sam, what did you bring?"

"I figured since we had tacos and salsa, I'd bring guacamole and dessert. I ran to the market and got Tres Leches cake," says Sam.

"Oh, I love that cake. Now that everyone's here who wants a margarita or beer?"

Hillary smiles big, "Yes, now that we're all here sweet cheeks, time to spill about what's going on between you and sexy Dr. Noah. All I know is that the two of you looked rather chummy at the grand opening of Harte of Harmony. Then I heard from Jules that you went out on a date Sunday."

Ellen gasps, "Oh my god, please tell me you're the couple Gertie wrote about in Harmony Hears. Please — was it about you and Noah?"

"Oh, I saw that post too and wondered whom Gertie was writing about," Sam says.

"God bless it! Yes, Noah and I went to Bella Roma's and at the end of our date Gertie walked over to us, and instead of Noah taking the hint NOT to talk and give her something to write about, he opened a can of worms and gave Gertie exactly what she was looking for."

Jules smiles, "We've all been on the receiving end of Gertie's gossip at one point or another, but what I want to hear is how the date went and what's next. Are you seeing him again?"

"We had a great time together both nights, and we got to know each other over dinner. Noah is charming and funny and so handsome. I like him, a lot, but you know me guys, I get myself talked out of dating or making time for someone because I just can't put myself out there," I sigh.

"He is hot, Bree; I'll agree to that. Is there a spark? Do you have any chemistry?" Hillary asks.

"Oh, there is quite a spark. It isn't that. Not at all. It's me."

Julia puts her arm around me, "Bree talk to us. You know whatever you share with us is never repeated. What's on your mind? What's your hesitation with Noah?"

"We've been texting all week and still asking each other random questions. That's what we did at dinner, and it opened communication so that it wasn't your typical awkward first date. We asked each other fun get-to-know-you questions, biggest fears, favorite things, that kind of

45

stuff. I already feel like I've known him longer than I actually have, and he feels the same way. I think we've both been really honest with each other so far. He knows a little bit about my past and my life history. But all of you know me and how when I start to feel something for someone I tend to put on the brakes and hesitate to let someone in. If I let them in, I give them the opportunity to hurt me."

Sam smiles at me, and I see the concern in her eyes. "Bree, I think I can speak for most of us that have been or are in a relationship when I say we have all felt the same way. Being in a relationship means you have to put your trust in someone else, but I think you know when your gut is right or not. What's it telling you with Noah?"

"It's telling me to take that leap and trust that he will hold my heart carefully in his hands," I say.

"Then, I think between listening to your gut and Jules and Jackson knowing that he's a good guy," Sam says. "Noah isn't just some stranger you met. He's a mutual friend, so there's some unspoken awareness of how he needs to treat you."

Hillary with her typical snarkiness adds, "Plus, I always have your back. If he does hurt you, I will make sure he feels just as bad. I promise."

Jules hugs me a little tighter. "Bree, I know this all stems from your dad leaving you and your mom when you were a little girl, but not all men are selfish and walk away. Give yourself permission to see where this goes."

"Okay, you guys are right. Mom said the same thing. I really like him, and I enjoy his company, so I promise I will be brave and put my big girl panties on and go for it."

"Bree, instead of your big girl panties, I think you should put on that blue silk set you bought our last shopping spree at the boutique and wear that on your next date," Hillary adds with a chuckle and sparkle in her eye.

***

46

Noah

Poker night with the guys is becoming one of my favorite nights of the month. There's nothing better than sitting around with a bunch of friends, playing poker, drinking whiskey, and taking their money.

I got lucky moving into a community with a friend already in place. Even luckier he has a cool group of guys he hangs with, especially when their significant others are all at book club.

They're a small group of friends that do a lot together. I've known Jackson since our residency at the hospital in Chicago. Two of his brothers-in-law are also in this group, Garrett, the town sheriff, and Rob, who runs the family construction company. Cooper is Garrett's best friend from the army and owns Cooper's Corner, the local bar. Scott is an architect for Stone Builders and married to Ellen, Jackson's sister-in-law. And Paul is married to Sam and owns a landscape design company.

As we're sitting around the table playing our next hand, Garrett says to me, "So, Noah, rumor has it you're spending time with our Bree. Any truth to that?"

"We spent some time together over the weekend. We had a great time, and I'm hoping to get to know her better. Does that answer your question?" I say.

"Wait what? You and our sweetheart Bree are an item? How did I miss this?" says Rob, the sarcastic one of the group. "I always had a thing for Bree. She's so sweet and pretty. I loved when Julia and the girls hung out when we were kids. Bree always let me be part of whatever they were doing at the house. Of course, Julia always tried to get rid of me because I was the annoying little brother, but Bree would say, *just let him hang with us* — because I was already so charming, even as a little boy. What can I say, I've always had it with the ladies."

As we chuckle over Rob and his lady's man attitude, Garrett says, "Yeah, Rob, you were a pain in the ass, but she did always let you tag along. Probably because you were so needy."

"Hey now — bite me — you're just jealous you don't have my charisma," Rob says.

Jackson pauses and speaks to me in a very serious tone, "Noah, I know you're a good guy, but just know, Bree is special to all of us around this table. We don't want to see her hurt. She's had enough hurt in her past, so we're all a little protective of her."

"I know about her dad walking out on her and her mom. We talked about that a little bit. I can sense that she still has some issues from that experience that affects the way she handles things." I take a deep breath and look around the table. "Guys, I'm not just looking for a hook-up here. I'm not interested in that. I've been married, and, no, that didn't work out as I had hoped. But I do want to have a wife and family in the future. Is that Bree? Who knows, but I think there's something between us worth exploring. I enjoy her company; she's absolutely beautiful, and she's smart and kind. Those are things that really draw me to her."

The guys give me a sort of nod of approval, and we continue with our poker game and shooting the shit. A little while later, it comes out that the Facebook post from Gertie's Harmony Hears was about Bree and me. Then the harassment really starts coming at me from left and right.

"You know, having a Gertie Harmony Hears post about you is as good a town initiation as you can get. How in the world did you pick somewhere for your first date that had Gertie there?" Jackson asks.

"I met Gertie when went to the 1-Stop General store to grab things after the move to town. I had no idea that sweet little old lady was the number one gossip queen of the town. Honestly, I'm a bit insulted it took her so long to gossip about me," I laugh.

"Oh, that wasn't the first time she wrote you up," says Garrett.

"What? Oh man, I think I better get on Facebook and join this group, so I know what the hell is going on around town."

Rob laughs, "Yeah, buddy, it's the only reason most of us are on Facebook these days. It's best to know exactly what's going on, and Gertie is in the know about everything and everyone."

"True. I pay attention to her posts because half the time she knows who's caused a problem that ends up on my sheriff's to-do list," Garrett says.

Rob looks at his phone, laughs, then hands it to me, "Here, this was probably the day you moved to town — look at the date."

LAKE HARMONY GETS ITS OWN DR. MCHUNKY

As our town grows with the expansion of Stone Builders, our needs grow as a community. We are lucky enough to have another skilled doctor join our current practice with Dr. Harte. Please welcome the new addition, Dr. Noah Roarke, to town if you see him. He is one doctor very easy on the eyes ladies, plus I hear he is single!

"Jesus, really? This is like the day after I moved to town," I groan.

"Yep, she moves fast Noah. Better have your guard up around her if you don't want everyone to know your business," Garrett says.

49

Chapter Six

Noah

Friday morning while I'm drinking my coffee before work, I send Bree a text. I want her to know I'm thinking about her, and I want to make sure our next date is on the books.

Me: Hope you have a good Friday
Me: Thinking about you and can't wait to see you
Me: It's been a long week
Bree: Good morning, Noah-TGIF finally!
Bree: Kids were rowdy this week!
Me: Do I need to come and tell them to be nice to Ms. Daniels?
Bree: No, silly *laughing emoji*
Bree: Looking forward to our date tomorrow
Me: Me too!!!
Me: Lady's choice. Go out to Cooper's Corner or pizza and movie in?
Bree: Pizza/Movie in. No interruptions/noise
Me: Are you planning on taking advantage of me?
Bree: Yes *wink emoji*
Me: I'm all yours

All day I'm in a good mood, and, apparently, everyone notices, because at lunch Jackson walks into my office and leans against the door frame. "Okay, spill. You have been smiling and buzzing around the office all day. Even patients have asked me what's up with you?"

"No way, they haven't really — have they?" I ask.

"No, but Paige was in my office just now asking between patients. So, it's not just me noticing that you're in a great mood today."

"Not much to report other than I'm looking forward to my date with Bree tomorrow and thinking about some texts we shared this morning," I say.

"Oh yeah? Good, I assume?" Jackson asks.

"I'm not sure what happened at book club with the girls, but I'm sensing a bolder side of Bree coming out. She was a little more outgoing this morning."

"Ah, yes. What the girls call *book club* is more them getting together each month and drinking and gossiping about everyone and everything. I'm sure they all asked Bree about your date. Who knows, maybe they gave her some encouragement about you."

"Thanks? Do I need some encouragement?" I ask.

"I didn't want to say too much last night with all the guys around, but Bree tends to spook and run away from relationships. It all stems from her dad walking out on them."

"Listen, Jackson, you know me, and I'm not out to hurt her. I am honestly very attracted to her in more than a physical way, but I don't want to push or screw up something that I think could be good. I like Bree. A lot."

"The best advice I can give you, Noah, is to be honest with her and patient when she starts to pull away. Reassure her that you're staying. Oh. And don't fuck it up. Jules will kill you, and the guys won't be very forgiving either. We all grew up together, and the girls are all adopted Stones. Just remember that."

"I hear you and thanks, Jackson," I say.

***

Bree

Thank goodness today is Friday and the kids have been well-behaved. I gave them the option of story time on the carpet with me or center work to end their day. They chose story time, so we're wrapping up with a story and our Friday sendoff song before they all go put their items from their cubbies into their backpacks to take home.

"Okay, kiddos, please push your chairs in and come to carpet time. Make sure you're wearing your walking shoes… three, two, and one. Good job listening everyone.

Today, I picked a story to read about my friend, Geoffrey. Let's look at the cover picture. Who can guess what kind of animal he is?" I ask my class.

They all eagerly raise their hands, "Tyler, what kind of animal do you think Geoffrey is?"

"A giraffe," Tyler says.

"Good answer. The cover has a picture of a giraffe wearing a bow tie and overalls, so that's a good guess based on the picture. Let's read this story about a clumsy giraffe who likes to make friends with other animals like birds and monkeys. Before we start our book, I would like everyone please sit crisscross applesauce and remember to keep your hands in your lap."

After I read the book to my class, ask questions about what they predicted, and share all the pictures, we do our end-of-day silly song singing, *It's time, it's time, to say goodbye…oh yeah.* Then, I excuse them to pack up their cubbies and line up for dismissal.

Little Charlotte runs over to me and throws her arms around me. "Ms. Daniels, I am going to miss you SOO much."

"I will miss you too, but I bet you're going to have a great weekend with your family. Monday will be here before you know it. Go ahead and line up so we can get ready to walk down to parent pick-up."

Heading to the parent pick-up area, my students all walk with their hands to themselves and are quiet. *Thank God!*

After handing the kids off to the team working the pick-up line, I head back to my classroom. I need to grab my planner and some things to work on for next week's lesson. I always like to set the calendar and certain things for the next school day before I head out.

As I am straightening up, I think about Noah and smile and remember the text I sent him earlier. It was a bit flirty and out of my comfort zone, but after talking to the girls last night and thinking about it, I'm going to tell Noah that I accept his proposal of being my research buddy. *He is going*

53

to help me research all kinds of sexy things. He just doesn't know it yet.

I'm going to allow myself to feel all the good things and fall into this new relationship with everything I've got. No holding back! The girls said to trust it, trust him. And I will. First things first, talk to Noah and be open and upfront with him, then let him be my muse for research purposes so I can start writing my book. *Can I really do this? Ugh, stop it, Bree. You can't already set roadblocks. Be brave. Be strong.*

Tonight, the plan is to relax, binge a little bit of Schitt's Creek, and enjoy a glass, or two, of wine snuggling on the couch with Mr. Franklin. Tomorrow morning, I have yoga in the park, then I'll clean around the house and do laundry before getting together with Noah. Sunday, I can focus on my lesson plans for the week after brunch with Mom.

I get home and as I'm about to throw a salad together for dinner, my phone rings. I close the refrigerator and grab my phone. *Noah calling...* "Hello."

"Hi. Hope I'm not interrupting."

"Hey. You're not. I'm about to make dinner. What's up?"

"I'm just home from an after-work run. I was restless and figured I'd try to run some energy off."

"Hmm...did it work?"

"Yes and no. I'm not as restless but it did give me time to think about nothing but you while I was running, and I wanted to see what you're doing tonight."

"I'm just going to relax and hang out with David and Alexis."

"Oh, well I don't want to interrupt. Have a good night with them and we'll talk tomorrow."

I laugh, "Noah- David and Alexis are two characters on a show I like to binge. Not real people I'm going to see, except for on the television."

"Ah, Schitt's Creek huh? I love that show. I'm a big Eugene Levy fan."

"Well, I'm being super lazy and wearing yoga pants and a sweatshirt. But if you don't care about that, and you want to join me, I'd love to have you over."

"Really? I don't want to interrupt a night in to recharge after the week, and we have plans set for tomorrow."

"Noah, come over, please. Wear couch-comfortable clothes and please join David, Alexis, and me," I tell him.

"What are you having for dinner?"

"I was just going to throw together a salad."
"Instead of salad, can I bring some Chinese food? I'm dying to eat some food out of little square cartons with sticks. What can I bring you?" He asks.

"You're so funny, but that does sound better than a cold salad. I'd love some chicken with veggies and an eggroll if you want to bring me something. Thank you."

"On my way — save me a seat."
"Will do. See you soon."

The evening just took an interesting curve. I know I said I was in casual clothes, but I quickly get up and brush my hair and make sure I don't look like a zombie after the week with my students. I straighten up the couch and pillows a bit and go into the kitchen to grab another glass for Noah and some ice water.

Less than thirty minutes later, Noah's knocking on my door. I hurry over to let him in, "Wow, that was fast."

"That's the best thing about Chinese food. It only takes like fifteen minutes to be ready. I ordered it from home, drove there, picked it up, and now here I am. Are you hungry?"

"Starving! Come on in. Do you want to eat in front of the tv or at the table?"

"I bought a lot of food. We can eat from the box or grab plates and share everything. Up to you."

"Let's sit at the table. We can watch tv and relax while our food settles."

We head into the kitchen. The food smells delicious. I love Chinese food, but if I order it for myself, I usually have three days of leftovers because you get so much. Again, Noah's hand is on my lower back guiding me, and I smile.

"I ordered some beef and broccoli and sesame chicken with fried rice. Please help yourself to whatever you want," he says.

We fill our plates, I pour him something to drink, and he asks me how my day was with the kids. I tell him about little Charlotte and how she's going to miss me so much over the weekend.

Noah chuckles, "I remember being young and thinking that days were so much longer than they truly were. Remember summer and winter breaks and how they felt like they dragged on for years? I was always so happy to go back to school in the fall so I could see my friends that didn't live in my neighborhood or played sports with me through the summer because it felt like I hadn't seen them in forever."

"The nice thing about growing up in Lake Harmony is we would all see each other often because our moms would take us to the beach at the lake to swim. I spent a lot of my time at Julia's because my mom had to work. Julia's parents always told my mom not to worry — what was one more kid when they already had five of their own to watch over?" "The guys told me at poker night that everyone is really close because you all grew up together," Noah says.

I nod. "Small town. You know everyone and everything they're doing. Jackson was good friends with Garrett and Rob. Sam, Hillary, and I were always best friends with Julia. Julia's sister, Ellen, wasn't much younger, so she'd be with us most of the time. Stella, the youngest Stone sibling, wasn't with us quite as much unless we were babysitting her. Cooper moved here when he retired from the service. He's from somewhere in Iowa but went through the service with Garrett, and I think that's how he ended up moving here and becoming one of the crew. Sam married Paul, and Ellen married Scott, who works for her dad and Rob at Stone Builders."

"I feel a bit like I won the friend lottery when I moved here," Noah says. "I'm lucky to be friends through association with Jackson. It's hard to make friends as adults unless you find people through work or social activities. I moved here and I feel like I have a group of friends that just welcomed me in like I've been here all along."

"Yep. I agree. I don't have the same experience since I grew up with everyone but once you fall into our crew you're stuck with us." Laughing I grab his hand, "But I am really glad to be stuck with you."

"Same."

"I'm also glad you came over tonight."

"Me too. I just want to spend time with you."

"Let's finish dinner and go watch some tv."

***

Wrapped up in Noah's arms could be the best thing that's happened to me in a long time. We're snuggled up into the corner of my couch with my back to his chest and his arm around me.

"We forgot to eat our fortune cookies." I lean towards the coffee table and grab the cookies, "Here. One for me. One for you."

We open our cookies, and I read mine first, "You will become great if you believe in yourself. Wow."

"Bree that fortune was completely meant for you," Noah says.

"What does yours say?" I ask.

Noah looks at me with a twinkle in his eye, "You will meet a beautiful woman and fall in love."

I turn around and look at him. "What? Does it really say that?"

"Yep," he says trying to hide the fortune.

I grab the fortune out of his hand, laughing, "You are so full of bologna, Noah. Give me that fortune right now!" I read Noah's fortune and start laughing so hard I'm bent over, gasping for breath.

"What? That's what it said," he looks at me innocently.

"Mister, you are so full of shitake mushrooms. Your fortune says *Fortune favors the brave*."

"Same difference," Noah shrugs.

"It is not. To me, this says, *look out buddy because you better be really brave to be in a relationship with Bree*."

"Nonsense, I am the luckiest bastard alive to be in a relationship with you and nothing will make me feel any different."

I lean into him and give him a kiss, "I think I'm lucky too."

While we watch and laugh along to the television show, he rubs my arm or plays with my hair. I'm getting so turned on by him constantly touching me that I have no idea anymore what's going on in the show, "Um, Noah?"

"Hmm?"

"I've been thinking about what you said at dinner last week, and, if you're still interested, I would like you to be my research partner."

I feel like I'm holding my breath, his hand has stopped moving, and I can tell he isn't breathing. "Noah?"
He turns me so I am facing him on the couch and instead of an answer he pulls me into his chest and the next thing I know his mouth is on mine and he is devouring me. This is no gentle kiss; this is a kiss that means business. His hands pull me closer, and he tilts my head so he can plunder my mouth. *Oh my god, this is amazing!*

He pulls back and takes his thumb and runs it along my lower lip, both of us breathing hard, smiles, and looks into my eyes, "Bree, I would love to be your research partner. What do you need from me? I'll do it. Anything. I am completely under your direction."
Biting my lip, I try to put my thoughts in order. "Last night when I was with the girls, I talked about you. Us. They told me I should accept my feelings and take a leap of faith — that it'll be okay. So, I want to let you know that I will try to not be hesitant, and I will try to be open to seeing where this will go."

58

I look into his eyes and pause, and he brings his hand to my face. "Go on."

"I want to let you in, Noah. I want to explore what I'm feeling. And I'm going to trust you to lead me a little bit and be patient with me. Can you do that for me?"

"Bree, I will do anything you need me to do or be. I want to be someone you can trust, and I want to see where this will lead too. I haven't met someone with whom I have had this instant attraction and chemistry. I don't think I could walk away from you right now, even if you asked." We both smile, and he kisses me softly on the lips.

"What does your research partner need to do? The goal is for you to focus on letting yourself feel so, ultimately, you can write your book, right? So, you want me to be your research partner and your muse?"

Smiling big, I look into his eyes and nod. "Do you want to be my partner and muse?"

"Absolutely."

He gently pulls me in and starts to kiss me again. He turns us so that we are now laying down across the couch with him holding himself above me. I open my legs and allow him to lower himself, and I can feel his erection against me. *Oh my god, this amazing man is turned on — by me, and hello there huge erection!*
We continue to kiss, and I allow my hands to roam his shoulders and down to his butt. Oh lordy, this man's butt is muscular and firm. I pull him into me harder and his erection hits me right where I need him. I may orgasm dry-humping him right now like a teenager, and I don't even care.

"Don't stop, Noah. Please."

I hear him growl in my ear and he shifts us a little bit and pulls my leg over his hip while he is pressing against my center. I feel the orgasm building, "Fuck, don't stop, don't stop," then it hits and all I see are stars. *Jiminy crickets!*
He continues to move against me and kisses me as my orgasm slowly fades and I become aware that he is looking at me with a smile. My face is probably red from embarrassment because who has an orgasm dry humping

after like two minutes? "Hi. I guess it's been a while and I wasn't expecting that."

"You are beautiful, and I love watching you come apart for me."

I feel myself blush even more if possible, and I look away.

He pulls my face back to his, "No, don't get shy with me. We promised we would do this together right? So, you are going to accept that orgasm and all your future orgasms. Think about how you are feeling and own it."

He starts to sit up and pulls me onto his lap, "Noah, don't you need to finish? I can feel you and..."

"No, tonight was all you. I'm going to be a gentleman now, give you a kiss, and say goodnight. You've had a long week, and since I invited myself over tonight and it's nearly midnight, I'm going to go."

"Are you sure?"

"Yes, sweetheart, I'm going home but I will see you tomorrow. Okay?"

We get up and I walk him over to the door. He pulls me into his chest and gives me a kiss, "Sleep good tonight. I'll see you tomorrow at my place." He walks through the door, takes a few steps, turns around, and says, "Remember, I'm your research partner and muse. You get to direct me all you want." Then winks and walks away.
Ooh, that makes me start thinking, and the story starts to appear. Noah walks to his car, gets in, and drives away. I shut the door and run to find my notebook where I write all my story ideas down.

Chapter Seven

Bree

I wake up Saturday morning excited and a little exhausted. After Noah left, I grabbed a notebook and started writing down some ideas for the book. *Maybe he is my muse.*

While I was up last night, I got some storyline ideas down and created my two main characters. The story is going to be about a woman who takes on a dominant lover. I secretly love to read these types of stories. If anyone would ever take a minute to look at my bookshelf in my bedroom, they would see a lot of these paperbacks — or maybe not, since I turn the spine of the book with the title towards the back. It's my guilty pleasure to lose myself in books, and the hotter the better.

I stretch my arms above my head knowing I need to get up and feed Franklin, start cleaning the house, and do laundry today. I want to have enough time to shower and get ready before I head to Noah's house. He isn't going to be allowed to stop himself tonight. I am going to make it impossible to refuse me.

Enjoying my morning coffee, I have my notebook in front of me looking over my thoughts for the book I scribbled down last night. My phone is charging over on the counter, and I hear a text come through. It's from Noah.

Noah: Morning beautiful – sleep well?
Me: Yes, when I finally could sleep *smile emoji*
Noah: Oh, restless? Me too
Me: Why didn't you let me fix that?
Noah: last night was for you
Me: I'm going to need more from you
Noah: Tell me

Ugh…. I type and delete, type, and delete, different ways to respond. *Come on Bree! Be Brave! Here goes nothing.*

Me: research- I'd like to begin tonight
Noah: Anything you want
Me: I need to research feathers and silk

I see texting bubbles, then nothing, then texting bubbles. *Oh no, maybe that was too much?*

Noah: You are making me hard again

OH! Well then …

Me: um- sorry?
Noah: LOL can you elaborate?
Me: How they feel
Me: Against my skin
Noah: Got it. I will be prepared for research purposes
Me: *wink emoji* thanks Noah
Noah: I need to go for a run now or a cold shower
Me: I will help YOU research later *smiley emoji*

Holy cannoli! Did I just say that to him? I giggle to myself. I sure did and it feels kind of good. "Alexa, play morning acoustic."

Better get this laundry started and clean up the house before I get distracted and start to daydream. Lots to do today and I want time to get ready for dinner. I throw in a load of laundry and decide to do some quick yoga to get my body stretched out and moving. Not having a lot of sleep, I may need to take a nap later before heading out. *Right! Like that's going to happen.*

I pretty much gave Noah the go-ahead on us having sex tonight — all in the name of research of course. It's been a while, so, as Hillary would say, "Clean out the cobwebs" and get it on. I'm going to do as she suggested and put on my new blue silk and lace lingerie set. It is so soft and pretty. I want to knock his socks off.

I'm laying here on my yoga mat, and I've done more *shama-lama-dingdong* and daydreaming than any real yoga poses. Oh well, good intentions and all that. Better start cleaning the house.

Putting away the yoga mat and cranking up the tunes I start dusting and vacuuming the house. I'm singing along to the music and swaying my hips. I need to go outside and water the flower boxes too, but I can do that just before I clean up.

I hear my phone ringing in the kitchen. It's Julia.
"Hello."

"Good morning, how are you today?"

"Hey, I'm good. Just cleaning the house a bit. What are you up to?"

"I have an event over at Harte of Harmony, so I'm just about to head over there but wanted to see what you and Noah are up to tonight. Date two, right?" She asks.

"Three," I correct her.

"Huh? When did you see him since Sunday?"

"He came over last night and brought Chinese food for dinner, then we snuggled on the couch and watched Schitt's Creek," I say.

"That sounds nice," Julia says. "Are you still having a date tonight?"

"Yes. And I listened to what you and the girls told me, and I followed your advice and talked to him about dating and seeing where things could go."

"Oh, and he was probably happy about that right?"

Giggling, I say, "Oh, he was VERY happy about that, Jules."

Julia gasps, "Bree, did you guys get naked last night?"

"No, but he took care of me and said last night was for me and he wanted to be a gentleman. Oh my goodness, Jules, I had the best orgasm, and he left and was probably miserable."

63

"So, what's the plan for tonight? Still pizza and a movie at his place?"

"Yes, I believe so. I told him I want to do some *research*."

"BREE! I am so proud of you. I need to go, but I want you to relax and just have some fun, okay?"

"I will. Promise. I plan on having lots of fun!" Hanging up the phone, I continue to clean and hear my phone again. *Jiminy Crickets!* Who is texting me?

Hillary: Research? Is this code for getting naked?
Me: Maybe — did Jules tell you?
Hillary: yep, she's busy — told us to keep you MOTIVATED
Sam: Ooh, details *wink emoji*
Me: I listened to you guys, ok
Hillary: and....
Me: Told Noah I was ready to see where things go
Sam: YAY!!! *Fire emoji*
Hillary: so tonight – naked time?
Me: Oh yeah *wink emoji*
Hillary: he's so hot!
Sam: ^^^what she said
Bree: I KNOW! and big *eggplant emoji*
Hillary: Figures *fire emoji* and big *Eggplant emoji*
Sam: Lucky girl — have fun!
Hillary: Blue silk set!!!
Bree: Yes to all of the above *smiley emoji*
Julia: ^^^ what you said!!! *kissing emoji*

My friends are the best. Love them!

***

House is clean. The laundry is finished and put away. And I am showered and heading to Noah's house for the evening. I'm trying not to be nervous, but I am very nervous. I have a bottle of wine, and some brownies, and in my purse, I brought a feather boa and silk scarf. Just thinking of those things makes me warm.

Pulling up to Noah's for the first time, I sit and look at his house from the car. He has a brand-new modern farm-style house built by Stone Builders. It's white with black trim and a beautiful dark walnut-colored front door. A pretty porch in front only has a doormat. Men, don't ever add any plants or potted flowers. Taking a deep breath, I get out of the car, smooth out my dress, and walk up to the house. Before I can even knock, Noah opens the door and smiles at me.

"Hello, beautiful. I heard your car when you pulled up. I was out back starting the grill."

"Oh, no pizza tonight?"

"No. Since we had take-out last night, I thought I'd whip up some steak and baked potatoes with a salad. That okay?"

"If you want to cook for me, I won't say no. What can I do to help?" I ask.

"I haven't made the salad yet. Do you want to cut the veggies for that while I put the steak on in a few minutes?"

"Sure, I can do that."

Walking towards the kitchen I put the wine on his counter with the brownies, and I feel him come up behind me.

He turns me around, puts his hands on my hips, and looks into my eyes, "I haven't given you a kiss yet." He leans down to kiss my lips. It's gentle and sweet, and we get lost in it. Slowly he pulls away, "I better get the steaks ready. You look beautiful tonight."

"Thank you. You look handsome yourself and smell good."

His eyes twinkle with mischief and he smiles, "I wanted to look and smell good for you. I figured the better I smell, the closer you'll get. I love when you try to sneak a sniff."

"What?! What are you talking about?" *Oh, my goodness. Does he notice that?*

"I've caught you a few times when you lean in. Once, I thought I heard you moan."

"As much as I'd like to deny that — guilty. There's nothing better in this world than a good-smelling man, and you, sir, do it very well." Noah stares at me. He isn't saying anything, but I can see his wheels turning. Then he just smiles and goes to the fridge to pull out the makings for salad.

"Here are the veggies for our salad. While you do that, I'll put the steaks on. How do you like yours?"

"Medium, please."

Noah heads outside, and I start to wash and cut up the veggies for our salad. He walks back into the house and opens the wine I brought. "This okay for tonight?"

"Yep. It's one of my favorite local wines from Harmony Winery. Have you tried it yet?"

"No, but I've heard of it, so I'm looking forward to trying it."

***

We finish making dinner, eat, and clean up the kitchen together. Our conversation tonight has been easy and fun, and we're enjoying getting to know each other more. We talked about his family and the shenanigans he and his brother, Hunter, caused. The two of them sounded like big troublemakers when they were young. His sister was always a good girl and well-behaved and the apple of her dad's eye.

I shared more stories of growing up around all the friends we have in common now here in Lake Harmony. We both laughed at how Jackson was a rowdy kid and got into a lot of trouble with Rob and Garrett, who's now the sheriff. Jackson is a respected doctor, and Rob runs the family construction company since his dad, Edison was semi-retired. The girls all have their own businesses, except for me since I went into teaching, but we've all stayed in Lake Harmony.

After dinner, we walk into Noah's family room. On the table, I see a notebook with a pen and what looks like lists written down. "What are we watching tonight?"

"That's up to you. Come here."

66

He pulls me over to the couch and puts his glass of wine down. "I did my own research for our movie selection and figured I would let you decide what we watch."

I move over to the couch and sit down. I place my wine glass on the table and start looking at the list of movies. One column is labeled Greece: Momma Mia, Big Fat Greek Wedding, and Sisterhood of the Traveling Pants. The second column is labeled Mythology: Clash of the Titans, Percy Jackson, and Hercules. *This man!*

I look up at Noah, who is smiling. "You pay attention," I say.

"I listen. You said you've always wanted to go to Greece because you enjoy mythology. Knowing that I decided to give you a choice of both tonight. If there isn't something there that you want to watch, we can check Netflix."

"You would really sit through some of these chick flicks for me?"

"If it means I can hold you in my arms, touch you when I want, and kiss you — then, yes."
"You make this all too easy for me. What if I say I don't want to watch a movie anymore?"

I see his mood shift and a sense of disappointment come over him, "Are you tired? Do you want to go home?" Noah asks.

"No, I think I'd rather begin research for my book."
His eyes lift, and he smiles, "Does this research involve the silk and feather? Because I think I could handle doing some research."

"Yes, it does, and I have both with me."

"You do? Well, then let's not waste time when we could be learning new information for your book."

I pull the feather boa and the silk scarf out of my purse, hold them both in my hand, and watch his reaction.

He walks toward me and takes my hand, "Follow me." We walk into his master suite, which is on the first floor of his home. "Bree, since this is the first time I make love to you, I don't want to rush things. I want to take my time and enjoy your body. Will you trust that I know how to make you feel good and that my sole purpose here tonight is to make sure you feel nothing but pleasure?"

I bite my lip. That is the hottest thing a man has ever said to me. "I trust you, Noah."

"Good, now let's take off your dress."

I slowly pull my dress over my head and stand in front of Noah in nothing but blue silk and lace. I study his eyes as they roam over me and watch as his breathing gets faster and deeper. Looking down I see that he has an erection, and I can't wait to see him naked. He is beautiful, standing there trying to control himself. I can't believe this gorgeous man is so attracted to me, but it is empowering my current mood.

"Do you like what you see, Noah?"

"I like it very much. You are beautiful Bree. Simply stunning. And I'm one lucky man."

"Your shirt needs to go." I move my hands to his shoulders and run my hands slowly across his collar bone. I lean in and kiss his jaw and slowly start unbuttoning his shirt. As I unbutton, I run my fingers over his warm skin. Finally, I push the shirt off his shoulders, and it falls to the floor with my dress.

"Good girl. Now, unbutton my pants and touch me." I do as he says, and as I pull the zipper down, I feel his erection pushing against my hand. I brush against him, hear his deep intake of breath, and look into his eyes. They are darker than normal and dilated with desire.

I push his pants and boxers down and he steps out of them. He's standing in front of me completely naked. The man is magnificent. Strong muscles in his legs from running. His arms are strong and lined with veins. He has defined abs that are like an eight-pack. As I look and feel my way up his body, my own body is reacting. My nipples are hard, my breasts feel heavy, my center heat is expanding, and I know if he touches me, he will feel how wet I am for him.

I reach down and move my hand back and forth over his erection. I feel the wetness already leaking from him. I

68

smile knowing I'm responsible. His breathing is heavy, and he groans.

"Bree, sit on the bed."

I walk over and sit on the edge of the bed and wait for further instructions. He walks over and drags his finger from my lips down my chest and across my nipple.

"You are beautiful, but I need you completely naked." He moves his hands around the back of me and opens the clasp of my bra and slowly drags the straps down my arms before dropping my bra on the floor. Looking at my naked breasts he leans forward and licks my nipple, moves to the other breast, and licks. "Beautiful and pink."

He grabs the silk scarf and holds my wrists together, then looks at me, "Trust me still?"

I can't even answer. I just nod. I am so turned on right now I'm ready to combust. He ties the scarf around my wrists, lays me down, and puts my wrists above my head.

"Keep them there."

Next, he looks down at my panties and runs his finger over my slit. I blush because I know they have a wet spot. I try to look away from him.

"No," he says. "Look at me."

I turn back and look at him. "Sweetheart, you're going to own this. You're in total control right now. I'm here as your research partner, and I promised to make you feel good. Do you trust me still?"
"Yes, I do."

"Good, now focus on what you're feeling and what you need. Can you do that for me?"

"Yes. Take off my panties, Noah, and touch me."

He slowly pulls down my panties and drops them on the floor. His eyes again roam my body. "I need to taste you," he says before lowering down between my legs. I feel his breath against me before I feel his tongue lick me from the bottom all the way up to my clit. I lower my hands to touch him, and he stops. I see him look up at me.

"Hands back above your head honey. Don't make me tie them to the bed."

The wetness is slowly dripping down my legs just imagining him tying my wrists to the bed. *Oh no, he is going to know that I fantasize about those things.* I hear him chuckle before he moves back to licking me with long strokes. He slowly pushes a finger into me and there may be a benefit to sleeping with a doctor because it doesn't take him long to find where I fall into almost an instant orgasm. He licks and uses his fingers until I'm done spasming and moves up my body to give me a kiss. I taste myself on his lips, and I don't shy away from it.

"When can I touch you, Noah?"

"Not yet, sweetheart. We need to try the feathers first."

"Oh fiddlesticks, okay."

I hear him chuckle, "I love your cuss words."

He gets up and grabs a condom and the feather boa. "I want to be ready for you because I won't be able to stop myself for much longer."

He takes the feather boa and starts running it up and down my body, lightly brushing it over my nipples and down over my stomach and back. "Close your eyes and feel."

He leans down and pulls a nipple into his mouth, sucking hard and using the feather on the opposite nipple. I feel him nip me, pull away, and blow on the same nipple. He switches sides and repeats the nip, blows, feather. It feels so good, and I need more, but he just keeps repeating and switching sides. I open my eyes and look at him.

"Tell me. How does the feather feel?"

"Amazing. Everything you're doing feels amazing." "Do you need more or is my research with the feather a success?"

"The feather is amazing, but now I need you, Noah. I need you to be inside me. Right now."

"And the silk scarf? How does that feel? Do we have enough research for that today?"

Smiling, I look at him, "Yes, and if you would please allow me to touch you, I think we can untie my wrists."

"For now," he answers me and removes the scarf from my wrists dragging it down my arm and across my breasts.

My hands move down over his back to his hard ass. My goodness, you could bounce a quarter off his ass. I want to take a bite of it.

He grabs the condom, rips it open, and slowly pull it down his erection. God, that's a turn-on, watching him touch himself like that. He comes back between my legs, "Look at me, Bree. I want to look into your eyes as I fill you," and slowly pushes inside me.

We stare into each other's eyes as he pushes into me. He takes his time allowing me to adjust to his size. I feel so full that I barely need to move to orgasm. I already feel it starting to build. He begins moving slowly in and out of me and I wrap my legs around his calves pulling him into me so that I don't know where he ends, and I begin. I know I'm groaning and saying crazy things because this feels *SO GOOD*. The base of his penis is hitting my clit perfectly. He shifts us and pulls my knees up so he can penetrate even deeper. His eyes remain on me and watch my reactions.

"Right there. There. Don't stop."

"Never."

He brings his hand to my clit and applies pressure and I fall over, "Oh my god, holy crap, fuuccck!" I scream as I orgasm so hard that I can barely catch my breath. Noah starts pumping into me harder and faster. My body is still spasming through the orgasm when I finally hear Noah groan and stiffen and I feel his orgasm. We just lay there breathing heavy, sticking to each other, catching our breath as our bodies settle down.

"Stay here, I'll be right back," he says kissing my nose and getting up.

Noah walks into the bathroom suite, and I hear him turn the water on. He walks back out, comes over to the bed, and pulls me into his chest. "Do you think we concluded our research on silk and feathers?"

"Maybe."

"Well, we can always try again. Practice makes perfect."

He starts chuckling, and I look up at him, "Care to share what's so funny, mister?"

"You." He smiles and kisses me. "Do you know you swear like a sailor when you orgasm, Ms. Daniels?"

"What? No, I don't."

"Oh yes, I believe I heard a 'holy crap' and 'fuck' come screaming out of you just now."

"Well, I suppose you bring out the bolder side of me."

"Stay the night with me, sweetheart. Let's see how much bolder you can get."

Chapter Eight

Noah

I wake up with a beautiful woman wrapped around me. I slowly move my hand down to her hip. She is amazing and so open in bed. We made love two more times during the night. Using the scarf as a blindfold, and she even used the feathers on me. She allowed herself to explore her sexual desires with me last night.

I took it easy with her since it was our first night being intimate. I usually have a little more kink in my sexual appetite, but she surprised me, and I wouldn't be surprised if she wouldn't enjoy a little bit more eventually.

"Hey, are you up already?"

"Sorry, honey, I'm usually up early for a run, but there's no way I am leaving you this morning. You have a couple choices: get up, have coffee, and breakfast. Or… stay in bed and figure out something to do."

"I think I have an idea," she says as she pulls the sheet over her head and starts to move down my body under the covers.

She kisses her way down my stomach and my erection grows even bigger. I feel her lick me from the bottom to the tip and put just the crown of my erection in her mouth then groans. The vibration makes me even harder, and I bring my hand down to her hair. I want to remember to be gentle with her. She starts sucking and moving her mouth up and down my erection. She uses her hands to move up and down what she can't fit in her mouth. She is giving me one damn good blowjob and as much as I want to take control and start fucking her mouth, I won't. I will let her own this and be in charge. She moves her hand to my balls and squeezes. It's taking more effort not to go over and explode in her mouth.

"Bree, honey, I'm close." I want to give her a heads up I'm about to shoot down her throat. She doesn't ease up or pull away instead she starts deep-throating me and sucking even harder. I feel the tingling and heat start to form and come hard. She continues to suck and swallow then pops out from under the covers smiling and wiping her mouth.

"Now let's go have some coffee."

"Oh no, not yet. Now, it's my turn." I grab her and move her under me. I kiss her gently and touch her breasts and begin to work my way down her gorgeous body.

"Noah, you don't have to. I still owed you one from Friday."

I pause my descent and look up at her, "You don't owe me a thing, but I want you to start your day off just as good as I have, so let me please."

Blushing and smiling she says, "Well if you want to start my day off on a good note who am I to stop you."

I smile and continue kissing my way down her body.

***

After another hour in bed and breakfast together, Bree left to work on her lessons for the week. We made plans to get together again, and both said we would try to be more available throughout the week. I felt bad she canceled her standing brunch with her mom, but we were running late, and she didn't want her mom upset with her being a no-show.

I like this woman — a lot. I never had this connection with my ex-wife. We met, got along, dated for a few years, and figured we should get married. That is what you do right? Meet someone, date, marry, have a family, etc. I know I wasn't madly in love with my ex, but we had things in common and enjoyed each other's company. It worked, at the time.

Now, having been with Bree and spending time together, I can't get enough of her. I want to be with her any time I can. I want to call and hear her voice at lunch. I want to send her text messages letting her know I'm thinking about her. I want to be buried deep inside her and hear her

74

use real cuss words when she orgasms. Which she still doesn't believe she does.

After my run around the lake, I come home and shower and decide to surprise Bree with dinner. I know, three days in a row, but who cares? I'll run by the 1-Stop General store and grab some of Gertie's potato salad, sandwiches, and some beer. I'll be quick and try not to spill any information to Gertie. I don't need another Facebook post in Harmony Hears.

Walking up to the deli counter I hear, "Good afternoon, Dr. Roarke. How are you today?"

"I'm doing great, how are you, Gertie?"

"As good as can be with my old bones and tired mind. What can I get you today?" Gertie asks.

"I'd love some of your potato salad. Can you give me a big container and two turkey club sandwiches?"

"Sure. I can do that quickly for you. I wouldn't want to make you late for your date," she winks at me.

"Oh, it's not a date, just dropping by to feed Bree while she does her lesson plans for the week." *Shit, why did I just say that?*

"That's nice, dear. I love Bree. Such a nice girl."

"Yes, she is. While you get those together, I'm going to grab some other things." I quickly walk away and act like I'm browsing the shelves. *Great Noah, you just gave Gertie even more ammo. Maybe it's nothing and she won't write about it.*

I pay and head over to see Bree. I knock on the door, but she doesn't answer. Hmm, I text her.

Me: Are you home?
Bree: Yes, doing lesson plans — remember?
Me: At your front door
Bree: OH! Come around back — on the porch

I walk around the side of the house and push through the gate and see her sitting at the table with her lesson book and a pile of other things. She has on yoga pants and a t-shirt, and her hair is piled on top of her head.

"Hey. Hope I'm not interrupting, but I know you had a lot to get done and I wanted to surprise you and bring an early dinner. I promise I'll leave after so you can finish what you need to do."

"Hi there, handsome. Miss me already?"

I drop down in the seat next to her and give her a quick kiss. "Honestly? Yes, I did. So, I decided to come by and see you for just a little bit. I figured you need to take a break to eat. Is that okay?" I watch as a smile appears and lights up her eyes.

"I can give you an hour, but then I need to kick you out of here. I'm running behind because when I got home my mind was racing, and I sat down to write some notes down for the book and fell down that rabbit hole."

I lean in, "Come here and give me a real kiss first." Bree gives me a sweet kiss and her hand comes up to my cheek.

"What's for dinner?" she asks.

"I stopped by the 1-Stop General Store and grabbed turkey clubs, potato salad, and this six-pack of beer. How about I grab plates and you make room for us at the table?"

"Perfect!"

I head into her kitchen and see Franklin, the cat, sitting there looking at me. "Hey buddy, how are you today?" He slowly winds around my leg. I bend down and pat his head while he purrs. "I know, I can't stand to be away from her either. What can we do about it? She has total control over me."

I wash my hands at the sink, grab some plates, head back out to the table and sit down.

As we eat our early dinner I ask, "So, research was successful, and you got some writing in?"

She blushes, "Yep!"

"What's next? Leather? Chocolate sauce? Or something more daring? You're the boss. Just let me know."

"You are so accommodating, Dr. Roarke." She says with a big smile.

We finish eating and go inside to throw away our garbage. Looking around in the daylight now I can see a little more of her home, "Your home suits you, Bree. It's warm and welcoming and has a lot of colors."

"Thank you, would you like a quick tour?" she asks.

"Sure. I'd like that."

Bree takes my hand, and we walk through the house. She has a charming cape cod bungalow with three small bedrooms. One is a guest room. The other is what she refers to as her craft workshop. Being a kindergarten teacher means Bree's always crafting or sewing things for her art projects, so she decided to make one room for all the mess. Her bedroom has soft fluffy curtains and a down comforter in white. There aren't a lot of colors in this room, and I wonder about that. She has a big queen bed and dresser and a bookshelf that is almost overflowing with books.

"Your house is bursting with color except in your bedroom. Why's that?" I ask her.

"This probably sounds silly, but I need a place to turn off my thoughts and imagination, and figured, the calmer my room, the better. I try to keep it very muted in here so I can tune out and sleep and get my rest before the munchkins attack at school."

I move back over to her bookshelf because some of the books are turned backward. I go to fix one, and I hear her gasp and turn around. "What's wrong?" She's standing there, her face red and biting her lip looking nervous.

"I'm just embarrassed that you pulled that book off the shelf, that's all."

Looking more closely at the book in my hand, I see the image is of a nearly naked couple with handcuffs. I pull another backward book down. Again, a nearly naked woman with "tied up" in the title. Just to make sure, I pull the third book down and look at a Highlander having his way with a woman. *Interesting, is she into bondage? Be careful how you handle this, Noah.*

77

I put the books back into their spots on her bookshelf, sit on her bed, and pat the spot next to me. She slowly sits down next to me, fidgeting with her hands on her lap.

Turning toward her with my knee bent on her bed, I take her chin in my hand. "Bree, honey is this what turns you on? Because if it is we can explore this together."

Her eyes quickly meet mine. "I am so embarrassed, Noah."

"Why? What's there to be embarrassed about? Would you feel better if I shared that I enjoy a little kink myself?"

Surprised she looks into my eyes, "You do? You didn't show that last night. Not really."

"I was being cautious because I didn't want to be too aggressive. Not the first time I had you in my bed. But yes, I can be a little more aggressive with our research if you want me to be." She thinks about this and stares into my eyes. *Is she going to step outside her comfort zone and be honest?*

"I would like to try some things. I don't want pain or anything like that, but I must be in control of my life at work, and at home, and I don't always want or need to be in charge of everything. Does that make sense?"

"I understand completely. I'm not a true dominant, but I do like to take control and be in control during sex. If you want me to explore that with you I will. Don't be embarrassed. You never have to be shy about what you want with me. In this type of role-playing, the submissive partner is actually the one in complete control. If you don't like something, you tell me, and we stop."

"Okay," she smiles at me, "Let's do it."

Chuckling I lean over and kiss her, "Oh, we're going to do it a lot. I'm heading out now so you can prepare for the rugrats tomorrow."

"Can we get together for dinner tomorrow, Noah? I want to see you again, and maybe try some research techniques?"

"You won't be able to keep me away." I get up and head home with a smile on my face. Tonight, was the perfect end to a great weekend.

At home, I get a group text from the guys.

Rob: Another one bites the dust
Garrett: Dude! Avoid Gertie at all costs
Jackson: Noah — look @ Fb I think Gertie got you again
Cooper: Better you than me!
Paul: So, things are going well w Bree?
Scott: Thanks for taking one for the team
Me: Do I want to look?
Jackson: Not too bad, better to look than not to
Noah: Fine

Pulling up Facebook, which I only use to keep track of Gertie's town posts, I see the newest post.

IT'S OFFICIAL- MCHUNKY AND TOWN SWEETHEART A COUPLE
Dr. McHunky was seen in town buying dinner for his sweetheart so she can focus on preparing for her work week. This is how real men court a lady. Doing things to make her life easier while getting to know each other and developing trust. You, youngsters, should be taking notes!

Shit. How is it I keep giving her dirt to use for her gossiping? I better let Bree know. Instead of a text, I call her.
        "Hello."
"Hi, I know you're busy, but I just got hounded by the guys. I messed up again with Gertie."
        She starts laughing, "Oh, I know you did, because I just got off a group text with the girls, Dr. McHunky."
        "Ugh. I'm so sorry. She just catches me off guard, and she's like this sweet little old lady. I forget she uses everything she hears to gossip about the town on Facebook!"
        "Noah, it's fine. Really. It's just Gertie, and, honestly, I'm flattered. I mean little ol' me was able to catch Dr. McHunky! I must have mad skills."

"That you do, honey, that you do. All right, I'll let you get back to schoolwork, but I wanted to make sure you saw the post and weren't upset with me."

"Nope, she must really like you, though, because you're getting a lot of headlines lately. Better watch your back, Dr. McHunky." She's giggling.

"You're laughing at me, Bree."

"I'm laughing because you're so upset over it. Trust me. It will pass. She'll be on the lookout for something else to post by morning. Don't let it bother you. I'm seriously happy you're mine."

"Okay, honey. Sleep tight, and I'll touch base tomorrow."

"Night, Noah. See you tomorrow."

Chapter Nine

Bree

I'm at my desk eating lunch, and my phone starts buzzing with texts. I just spoke to Noah, so maybe it's the girls. I grab my phone and see a group text blowing up my phone from Cooper. Huh?

Cooper: Starting Tuesday Trivia Nights @Cooper's Corner
Cooper: need you all tomorrow for the trial run 7pm
Cooper: Beer-Wings-Fries on the house
Rob: Cool-I'm in
Garrett: Me too
Hillary: Oh fun!
Jackson: Julia and I will come w the kids, ok?
Cooper: ok *thumbs up emoji*
Scott: Ellen and I are in
Stella: I'm coming to co-host w Griff
Sam: Paul and I are coming too
Griffin: Be there with my sexy pants *fire emoji*
Cooper: Thanks for hosting Griffin
Cooper: Bree? Noah?

I get a text from Noah:

Noah: Trivia?
Bree: Ok
Noah: Go early for a drink first?
Bree: Yes please *Wink emoji*
Noah: Ok, call me after work

Our group text pops back up:

Noah: Bree and I are in
Rob: OOHHH!!! RSVPing as a couple-INTERESTING *wink emoji*

Julia: Love it
Hillary: About damn time
Sam: *heart eyes smiley emoji*
Bree: You guys stop
Cooper: Thanks guys *laughing emoji*

I finish the day and head home. My workday ends way before Noah's does, so I know I have a few hours to work on my book.

At five-thirty my phone rings, and I see, *Noah calling*. "Hey, how was your day?"

"Pretty good. Now that I've been here a couple of months, people aren't so hesitant to see me instead of Jackson and that's helping balance out the patient load for us. How was your Monday? Are the kids less crazy this week?"

"They were better. Probably because it was a nice weekend and a lot of them go to the lake, so their parents try to wear them out."

"Anyone make any comments to you about the post from Gertie yesterday?"

"Only the girls. I don't think too many people have connected me to Dr. McHunky yet."

He groans, but then laughs, "I guess she could have called me worse. Anyway, I'm in the car heading home. I took some chicken out I was going to grill. Want to head over whenever you're ready? I just need to jump in the shower and wash the day off me."

"I can bring some veggies and rice to go with the chicken if you want."

"Perfect, and I also stopped and grabbed some of that local wine on my way home. I will leave the door unlocked in case you come while I'm in the shower."

"That's some risky business there, Dr. McHunky. What if I wander into the master bath while you're in the shower?"

"We may never eat if you do that, and you're always welcome in my shower."

82

Laughing, "Okay, Okay. Don't make those kinds of threats when I'm hungry. I'll see you in a bit but don't hurry on my account."

"See you soon, sweetheart."

I've barely hung up with Noah and my phone rings again.

"Hey, Mom, how are you?"

"Hi, honey. I'm good. How was your day?"

"Pretty good. No crying, fighting, or wet pants."

"I love how you can use those three things to describe your day. I happened to look at Facebook today because all the ladies at Harmonious Bites were gossiping about Dr. McHunky. Is that supposed to be Noah?"

"Ugh, yeah. Gertie saw Noah and me out on our date at Bella Roma's, then he told her he was picking up dinner for me yesterday. So now everyone in town knows he's dating someone. They haven't quite put it together with me yet, though. At least, I don't think they have."

"No, they're still trying to piece it together. Gertie cracks me up. She just has nothing better to do than gossip about everything she sees and hears."

"I know, but it's fine."

"Speaking of Noah. It seems like you two have been spending a lot of time together."

"I guess you could say we're dating, Mom. He's a great guy and treats me well. I've decided to see what happens, and I'm trying to go with the flow."

"I'm happy to hear that, honey. You deserve a nice man in your life, and as long as you're enjoying yourself, I'm happy for you."

"Thanks, Mom. I don't want to be rude, but I'm heading over there for dinner right now. Can I call you another time?"

"Go enjoy yourself. I'm here if you need me."

"Love you."

"Love you too, Bree."

***

I arrive at Noah's, knock on the door, then poke my head in and yell out, "Noah? I'm here and let myself in." He walks around the corner from the kitchen, fresh from the shower, smiling. He's in jeans, bare feet, and wearing a fitted t-shirt that clings to him, showing off his strong upper body. *Yummy! Why is a man in jeans and bare feet so hot!?*

"Hey. Just got out of the shower and was starting to prep the chicken. Come on back."

He leans in and kisses me, takes the bags out of my hands, and guides me into the kitchen with his hand on my low back.

"Can I pour you a glass of wine? I got some from that local winery you like."

"Yes please, that would be great. Can I help with anything?"

"I was just about to season the chicken and get it ready for the grill, do we need to do anything with the sides you brought?"

"They just need to be reheated a bit, that's all."

"Then relax and let me get these on the grill. Do you want to sit out on the deck or in here? It's a nice night. We should enjoy them before it gets too cold to be outside at night."

I follow Noah outside. He puts the chicken on the grill, and we sit on the outdoor couch he has near the grill. His arm is around me, and I lean my head on his shoulder as he plays with my hair. I could stay like this forever. It's so peaceful. Noah listens to me and hears me. So far, he hasn't run in the other direction. I like him a lot. I like, like, like him.

I look up at him from my spot on the outdoor couch, "I like this. I like us. You make me feel like this is exactly the place I need to be."

He turns a little so he can face me. He studies my eyes for a minute and gives me a soft kiss, "I like this too. A lot. Thank you for coming over tonight."

"Thank you for having me."

He is still studying me with a smirk on his lips, "I have something in mind for later. Do you still want to do some research?"

"What do you have in mind? No, you know what...don't tell me. I told you that I trust you and that I'm open to research. Well, no, I actually think I would like a small hint."

"All I will say is this research may involve a blindfold and some ice cubes."

I feel my smile gets bigger, "Okay, Dr. McHunky — I agree to let you have your way with me all you want." Smiling, he kisses me again, "Then let's get our dinner started so I can take you to my bedroom, strip you naked, and begin our very important research."

Chapter Ten

Noah

Typical Tuesday. My schedule is full, but, over lunch, Jackson walks into my office with a smile and sits down opposite me, "Hey. So, things with Bree are progressing nicely?"

"When did you turn into a teenage girl, and do we need to pass notes in the hall?"

"Come on man, don't be that way. Bree is like a sister to me. I care about her, and I like you together. Watching the two of you find your way and become a happy couple makes Jules and me very happy."

"I'm glad my dating life makes you happy." Laughing and shaking my head, I look over at my good friend. Jackson knows me. He knows how my marriage fell apart, and he also knows Bree from childhood. "All right, yes. I really like her. Getting into this relationship with her makes me also realize I didn't have this with my ex. That part makes me feel kind of shitty, but also makes the divorce seem unavoidable. It's different with Bree. I want to be with her as much as I possibly can. We've spent the last couple of evenings together, and it just keeps getting better. She was hesitant to let me in at first; that seems to be gone, and now we try to be together as much as both of our schedules allow."

I'm just looking at my buddy who is smiling at me. A stupid smile on his face. "What?"

"I'm enjoying this. Just give me a moment to enjoy it."

"Don't be a dick, Jackson. I like her, okay? I could see this turning into a lot more."

"Really? Okay, wow. You've known each other like a month."

"Doesn't matter. I feel like I've known her forever and it's just easy. It's so easy to fall more every time I'm with her."

"Does Bree feel the same way?"

87

"I think so, but she's still holding a small piece of herself back. I'm not pushing her; I'm letting her find her way. I'll wait however long it takes."

Standing up, Jackson gives me a friendly smack on the shoulder, "Well man, I'm happy for the both of you. I'm glad you're willing to be patient and let her work through her doubts and fears. Her asshole of a father put her and her mom through the wringer. I don't know how any man can walk away from his family. I would die if I lost Jules or either of my kids. But to willingly walk away and never see or talk to them again — no fucking way."

"Yeah, I don't get it either. I can't imagine ever giving up on my family. No matter what."

Jackson heads back to his office, and I grab my phone. I know my lunch doesn't line up with Bree's schedule today, so I just send a text.

Me: Thinking of you
Me: Pick you up at 6 for Trivia and an early drink
Bree: *Smiley emoji* *Thumbs up*
Bree: Kids working on letters have 2 sec
Bree: Thinking of you 2

***

Bree and I head to Cooper's Corner for Trivia night. The whole crew will be here so that'll be fun. It's never a dull night when we get together. There's something fun and interesting watching people who grew up together still hang out and remain friends as adults. They have a commonality among them and a deep level of friendship. I am one lucky guy to be able to call them all my friends now.

"Have you done a trivia night before or is this your virgin voyage?" Bree asks.

Laughing, I glance over and she's looking at me with her eyebrow raised. "Growing up my family had game nights, but we never really did much trivia."

88

"Mm…good to know. How smart are you on trivia from let's say one to ten?" she asks me.

"Well, I was pretty smart with books growing up and through med school. Does that count?"

"How 'bout celebrity, movie, or music trivia?"
"Oh my god. Are you sizing me up to see if you want me on your team tonight?"

"Hey, a girl must be prepared. Just because you're good at many other things doesn't mean that you'll be a strong trivia partner. I don't like to lose when I'm playing against the crew. No offense, Noah, but if you aren't good with trivia, we can't be on the same team. I can't float you if you're the weakest link."

I start laughing so hard I'm glad we already parked because I'm dying. "I'm glad you like me overall but during games, I can't be the weakest link. Come here." I pull her over towards me and give her a kiss. "You are a funny, smart, and beautiful girl, and I will try to keep my trivia up to your standards."

"Noah, I'm serious. Trivia is a big thing, and we're all VERY competitive. Do you really want to be on the losing side of Rob? Or Hillary? I don't know who is worse with their mockery."

"I promise to never embarrass you if we are on the same team during any games in the future. Deal?" She thinks about it. I mean she is really debating if this is a good deal or not. I'm trying hard not to laugh.

Finally, she smiles, kisses me, and says, "Deal. Let's go before the rest of the loons arrive."

We head into the restaurant and Coop waves at us from behind the bar and starts making his way toward us. "Hey, you two know that trivia doesn't start for another hour, right?"

"Yeah, we thought we would come and have a drink alone first while we wait for the crew to show up," I answer with a grin.

"Sounds good, let me get your tables set up. Should we do two big tables or a few couple-size tables, Bree?"

89

Bree smiles and says, "It's going to be boys against girls tonight. Noah hasn't shown me his trivia skills yet, so I'm playing it safe." Then she looks at me and winks. This woman kills me.

"She doesn't want me to embarrass her with poor trivia skills. So, I guess the guys and I will have to show her I'm capable of not being the weakest link, right honey?"

She leans in and gives me a quick kiss on the cheek, "Exactly. Glad you understand."

Coop shakes his head and laughs, "Let me get the tables set up. I guess about six each since everyone is coming. Give me a sec."

Coop calls over to one of his staff, and they move tables around in the middle of the room to accommodate our large group for trivia tonight. Since trivia wasn't announced outside our group, the restaurant probably won't be too busy. Just the regulars will be here. Once the tables are ready, Coop puts a reserved sign on them, and we head over.

"For now, will you please sit by me?" I say to Bree.

"Of course, but when the others get here you are going to need to shift to the boys' table."

We each order a beer and about then, Griffin and Stella walk in. Griffin is Hillary's right hand at the catering company she owns. He's also best friends with Stella, the youngest Stone sibling. Griffin is tall and always looks like he stepped out of a fashion magazine, and flirts shamelessly with all the guys. He's harmless but would probably fight someone to honor his friendships. He's also part of our group of friends through Hillary and Stella. Not always present, a lot younger, but entertaining and funny as hell.

"Hello there, pretty people. Aren't you here a little early?" Griffin says.

Bree smiles, "Hey, Stella, Griff. We figured we'd come a bit earlier for some alone time and have a drink until the rest show up."

"I see. Aren't you two just the cutest new couple? OOHH!" Griff practically squeals. "Now I get it…McHunky and Sweetheart…mmm. Interesting."

"Stop! Griff, you know Gertie can't help herself and Noah hasn't learned to not share information with her quite yet."

"No worries. I like it." He looks me over for a long minute, "You sure are one Dr. McHunky. Ms. Gertie does have that right." He winks at me and walks away.

"So, that was funny," I say to Bree chuckling.

"Aw that's just Griff," Stella says. "You'll get used to him. My brothers get a kick out of Griff flirting with them all the time. Once they realized that he knows they aren't gay, and he isn't trying to really go after them, I think they enjoy the ego boost and they treat him like an adopted Stone now," Stella shares.

"I didn't mean to make that sound like an insult, Stella. I'm sorry. I mean it's nice to see he can be himself and not worry. Things are sure different now than when I grew up. I like that society is more open and understanding. You shouldn't judge a person by whom they love."

Bree leans in and grabs my face, "That just scored you big brownie points for research mister." She kisses me and smiles.

The rest of the group trickles in and gathers around the two tables. Griffin walks over and asks us to decide how we're going to group for trivia.

Bree smiles and says, "Boys against girls, of course!" The girls all give their significant others a smirky smile. The guys all look back and give their best mantastic smile back. *Let the games begin!*

Griff is up in front on a small platform with a microphone, "Good evening, lovely customers. We hope you're all enjoying your evening nourishment. Welcome you to the premier of Trivia Tuesday at Cooper's Corner. For those of you in the house enjoying a meal or a drink at the bar, if you would like to participate, please get my attention as I walk around the room with the directions, scorecards, and rules. Single or group players are welcome. Please keep your team family-friendly since I'm sensitive to bad words."

The room laughs. They must all know Griffin well. He walks around dropping off the rules and trivia sheets. The guys are deciding what our team's name should be. Griff hears this and comes to an abrupt stop, "Boys, you have already been named by me — so stop this insanity."

Garrett looks up at Griff. "What? Do I dare ask what you named us, Griff?"

"Only the best name handsome— Harmony Hunks." He winks, blows a kiss, and walks away.

"I'm good with that. Wonder what name the girls will come up with," Garrett says, sipping his beer.

The girls are laughing and talking up a storm. Bree glances up like she feels my eyes on her, smiles at me, and winks.

"That's so cute, Noah," says Rob with a snarky smile on his face.
"What?" I ask, feigning innocence.

"Oh, just watching you two love birds make googly eyes at each other. So sweet."
I lift my eyebrow, "Googly eyes huh? Well, it's better than her telling me I can't be on her trivia team because she was afraid I was going to be the weakest link."

The guys bust up laughing at that. Most are laughing so hard they're wiping tears from their eyes.

Jackson looks at me, "Shit. Does that mean that we now have the weakest link on our team? Crap!"

Shaking my head at all of them, "Thanks a lot guys, you have no clue if I am bad or not. For all you know, I'm the reigning trivia master, and I'm going to put you all to shame."

Rob stops laughing, "You are?"

"No. Maybe. I don't know. But at least give me the benefit of the doubt." They continue to laugh and make fun of me.

Coop walks over and joins us, "I'm bringing out wings, fries, and more beer. Let me know if you need anything else."

He tells the girls the same. Griffin and Stella are walking around and collecting the teams' name cards and making sure everyone is ready to go.

Garrett leans over to Stella, "Hey, what name did the girls pick?"

Smiling, Stella answers, "She's Out of Your League." She laughs and walks away.

Garrett looks around the table at the ladies and says, "Game on, little ladies."

Griff states the rules and tells us the three categories: Disney, Music from the Eighties, Movies & TV.

The first category is Disney, and the question is: Name the Seven Dwarfs in alphabetical order. We have ten minutes to complete this trivia and turn the answer sheet in with him or Stella.

The girls immediately put their heads together and start whispering while we sit around trying to remember the names of the Seven Dwarfs. "I know Dopey was one. He had big ears. Oh, and Doc!"

Jackson shares, "Grumpy, Sneezy, there's two more."

Rob shares, "Bashful."

Garrett laughs, "Surprised you even know what that means, Rob."

"I don't see you offering up any dwarfs, big shot," Rob says.

From across the next table, we hear Hillary say, "Garrett should know Dopey since he is the human version."

He responds with, "Too bad they don't have Princess Know-it-all Dwarf."

Hillary lifts her middle finger at him while taking a sip of her beer, "Yes, that is too bad isn't it."

Julia moves into distraction mode, and their bickering stops. Those two are always at each other's throats. It's so strange. They're always together but can't stand each other.

"Does anyone know the other two so we can put this together?" Jackson asks.

I'm thinking about the movie from growing up and trying to remember the scenes...oh, I've got it. "Sleepy and Happy! Cool, now someone put those in order and turn it in."

Trivia night continues for another hour, and, of course, the girls beat us by at least one hundred points and are walking around like proud peacocks until we all head out for the night.

Chapter Eleven

Bree

My week continues to be busy with Drama Club after school, writing, and seeing Noah as much as possible. We've spent almost every evening together again this week, and I'm falling more in love with him every day. I haven't told him how I feel, because I'm not ready to share that quite yet. That's a huge boulder I need to climb. I promised myself I would let myself enjoy this relationship but telling him I love him is something I'm not quite ready for. He hasn't said it to me yet; he either doesn't feel that way or he's worried about my reaction. I guess we need to take that leap of faith together but, again, not yet. Just thinking about it makes me want to take a big step back, and that's not fair to Noah.

I have Drama Club tonight with the kids. We're voting on the next play, which is between The Wizard of Oz and Grease, so attendance is mandatory. I'm happy with whichever we choose. Either will give us the opportunity to cast everyone involved. That avoids any hard feelings or anyone feeling left out.

I love Drama Club. It was always something I was involved in growing up. Julia, Sam, and Hillary were more sporty girls, whereas I shined with drama and choir. When I got the opportunity to be the Drama Club director, I took it because I wanted to help kids shine just the way it helped me growing up. I also get to work with former students, which is always fun.

After school my phone rings, *Noah calling*. "Hey. Are you in-between patients or is your day over early?"

"I had a short break and wanted to hear your voice. Will I see you later?"

"I have Drama Club until about seven, but then I'm free. Your place or mine tonight?"

"Since you're running later today, come to me, and I'll have dinner ready for you. Have a good rest of your day. See you later."

"That sounds great, honey. See you later."
It's like we're both holding back those three little words. Maybe one of us will slip and say it. "Or, maybe, Bree, you should put on your big girl panties and tell the man that you are absolutely crazy about him!" *Oh, ship, that's so scary!*

I head to the small theater where we hold Drama Club. Some of the older kids are there already. "Hey guys, come on in and help me set up the room with the chairs, please. We need to get ready to vote on our show tonight."

One of my high school boys, Darren, says, "Ms. Daniels, do we have to be a good singer for this? I mean I like to sing along to the radio, but I don't know how good I'd be singing solo on stage."

"Darren, that's the easy part. Once we perform the show you'll feel confident no matter what I promise. Will you go out and win a Grammy? That's going to be up to you!"

He laughs and smiles, "Ms. Daniels I love how you never show fear. You see a problem and you tackle it as I do in football."

Darren walks away and starts setting up the room with the others. *If you only knew, Darren. I don't always tackle my problems.*

***

As I head to Noah's, I go over and over in my head what Darren said to me. How can I seem so confident to others when I constantly have so many doubts? I need to suck it up and be brave. No hesitation — just tackle that darn problem, Bree!

I park the car and march up to the front door and knock.

"Come on in, Bree," Noah yells.

I walk in, and he yells that he's in the kitchen and to come on back. "Hey, you." I walk over and see he has his hands in some meat and marinade. He leans over and kisses me and continues to mix whatever he's got in front of him.

"Sorry, I'm hands deep in this steak marinade and couldn't answer the door. How was club? Did you decide which play you're going to do?"

I sit down on the island stool across from him. "Yes. They voted on The Wizard of Oz, which I think is the better choice because of the various ages and not so much singing. What are you making there?"

"Steak and veggie kabobs with rice. Sound good?"

"Delicious. What can I do to help?"

"How about pouring yourself a glass of wine and sitting there and talking to me? Is there a reason you seem fired up tonight?"

"One of my older students said something to me and it's bugging me a little bit. He said that I tackle my problems and don't show fear. Now I feel kind of like a fake."

Noah studies my face. "Bree, I agree with him. Once you decided to talk to me and be open to a relationship, not once have I felt you holding back or afraid to put yourself out there."

I quietly say, "But I have, Noah."

Noah stops what he's doing, washes his hands, then walks around the island to stand next to me. He wraps his strong arms around me and kisses me, "What are you holding back or afraid to tell me, honey?"

I look up into his beautiful eyes, "That I am falling in love with you and that it scares me."

"Honey, if it makes you feel better, I am in love with you too, and I am scared too. I am scared of you walking away and not letting me love you forever."

I pull back so I can look him in the eye, "You love me?"

"I think I have been in love with you from the moment I saw you at the grand opening, but I wanted to give you time and not pressure you."

"Okay, then I won't be scared anymore if you won't."

"Deal. You feel better now?"

"I do and thank you for letting me be me and being patient with me. I know it's not easy."

"Oh, Bree, loving you is the easiest thing I have ever done."

"Then don't stop loving me, Noah. Don't ever stop."

"Not in a million years."

***

Tonight, when we made love it was different. After we both declared our love for each other, our connection felt deeper. We put our research on pause for the night, and it was more intimate than before.

Wrapped around each other and about to fall asleep, I asked Noah, "Does it seem crazy that we fell in love so fast, or do you think that fate put us together and we just needed to meet at the right time and place?"

"I think everything happens for a reason. If we met earlier, maybe I would have still been married, or you would have been too busy with becoming this amazing teacher and Drama Club director. I think fate put us in each other's paths at the right time so that we'd find each other and be open to falling in love."

"I do love you, Noah."

"I love you too, sweetheart. Now let's get some sleep."

Chapter Twelve

Bree

It's Saturday morning, and I'm meeting the girls at Harmonious Bites, our usual hangout, and the coffee shop in the town square that Ellen owns. We try to meet on the weekends when time allows. They've no idea I'm sharing my book draft with them. Honestly, I haven't even told them I'm writing a book. They probably don't even know that I want to write a book. Man, what a bad friend I am not bringing that into our trust circle. Anyway, I'll share an electronic draft as soon as everyone is here. I don't want anyone to get a head start on reading it.

I walk into the shop and greet Ellen behind the counter, "Good morning, Ellen."

"Morning," she replies. "What can I get you? Coffee? Scone?"

"I'd love a hazelnut latte and lemon scone if you have it."

"Of course. We haven't sold out of scones yet this morning. Do you want to head back to our table, or do you want to wait and chat up here with me?"

"I can stay up here. Do you have time to join us too? I want to share something with all of you at the same time."

"Yes, I have enough helpers in this morning. I can take a break and join you girls."

I make small talk with Ellen while I wait for my coffee and scone. She hands them to me over the counter and walks around to sit down with me.

"I just saw Jules and Sam park, and I think Hillary is walking over from her shop. Is everything okay with you, Bree? I hope so, honey."

"Oh yeah, I'm good. Really good. I will fill you all in at once. I promise."

Jules, Sam, and Hillary put their order in, and we all walk to our table in the back of the shop.

"Good morning!" Jules says.

"Morning. I'm so glad you all are here this morning. I have something to share with you."

Hillary leans onto the table, "Is it about McHunky and all the sexy times you're having?"

"Oh my god, Hill, you're starting to sound like Griff," I laugh.

The girls laugh too and agree with me. "I have something different to share. But yes, I'm having a lot of sexy times, and we both said I love you to each other. So, I'm trying to keep calm and not be afraid. We talked through it and I'm okay."

They're all looking at each other, smiling, and having a silent conversation. *She told him she loves him. He loves her back! She isn't running in the other direction. She looks happy, so I don't think we need to worry. Do you know what she wants to talk to us about? Oh my god, is she knocked up? No, Hillary, stop it.* Then, they all look at me.

"No, I am not knocked up, Hillary."

"What! It's a legit question. I'd love you and support you anyway. But okay, that's good. What's up?"

"Do you all have your phones on you?"

I watched as they all pull their phones out of their purses and pockets and show me.

I take a deep breath, "Okay, I'm going to share something with you. Up to now, I've been afraid, but I've decided I'm not going to be afraid anymore. With a lot of support from Noah, I started writing a book."

"Support? Oh! RESEARCH?" Hillary whisper-yells.

"Shh, yes, that research. Anyway, you know I love to read romance, but what I haven't shared with you was exactly what type of romance. Being with Noah and being open to what I'm feeling, I finally got the courage to write my own romance novel and not come off as a fraud. I mean, how could I write my own book when I wasn't sure I even knew how to love someone romantically? So, yes, he has helped me work through some of my fears."

"I am so proud of you," Julia says to me.

100

I look across the table at my best friend. "Thing is, I don't know if I'm any good. I mean, I've shared my writing with Noah, but he could be biased. He's helped with some of the scenes, but I really need a female opinion."

Hillary has a huge smile on her face, "So, Bree, just curious... has the research been acting out these scenes?"

Turning red, I answer, "Yes, some of it, and what we haven't researched is still on his to-do list."

Sam says, "Holy crap, girl! He's both sexy and hot in the sheets. How did you win this fabulous lottery? But honestly, good for you!"

I laugh along with them. These women — this is the reason they're my best friends. "I want to share some of my book with you today. I'm going to send it to your phone. I want you to read it at the same time, and when everyone is done, I want to talk about it." *So, here I am, being brave and putting myself on the front line.* "Be gentle, okay." I forward the file to them, and they all begin to read.

Pure torture! This is absolutely the worst feeling watching my best friends read my words. I put my heart into those words in that book. Now, watching them and waiting for their reactions, I'm an anxious mess. *Do they love it? Do they hate it? This was a horrible idea. What the H-E-double hockey sticks was I thinking?*

Slowly, one by one, they finish reading, sit back, and look at each other.

"Oh, for Pete's sake, you guys! Please. Tell me it doesn't suck. Or be honest and tell me to stop this insanity."

Julia asks, "Can I start the discussion?" They all nod and look at her and me. "Bree, why have you been keeping these sexy secrets? First, if this is the kind of book you read, why aren't you sharing your book choices with us in our book club? Second, this is HOT. I'm so turned on right now I am going to go home and have hot sweaty sex with my husband. God, I hope the kids are out. Third, where is the rest of this book because I need it — Now."

I may need to pick my jaw off the table. "Seriously? Do you like this type of book? You liked my book?"

Julia smiles and laughs, "Do I like my mother's lemon squares? Hells to the yes!"

Laughing, I look at all my friends whose eyes are wide with shock. "Girls, do you feel the same way?" They just all nod.

Hillary leans in, "I feel like you've been holding out on us, and I'm a little insulted. Why the hell would you think we wouldn't like this type of book? It's fuckin hot. I don't have a husband, but I have a battery-operated buddy that needs some recharging before I go to bed. Holy shit, Bree, this is like sixty shades hot!"

Relieved I sit back in my chair, take a sip of my lukewarm coffee, and ask, "Seriously, though, at any time did you feel the writing was gross, or yucky? Did you make an 'eww' face? I didn't want to watch you guys too closely."

They all shake their heads and smile with big, round eyes and eyebrows disappearing into their hair.

Ellen looks at me, "Bree, I thought it was really good. Until you finish this one, do you have any books like this that you could recommend? I could use a little research myself."

My best friends laugh and congratulate me on stepping outside my comfort zone, writing my first book, and allowing Noah into my life. They all continue to tell me how proud of me they are and that they know with the right motivation I will push myself and keep writing.

We finish our coffees, and I've been informed that I have the next book club choice and it better be similar to what I just teased them with. I laugh and agree to find them a very good book with a lot of research possibilities.

Chapter Thirteen

Bree

The next couple of weeks go by, and Noah and I spend most of our time together in the evenings and weekends — basically, all our free time. Of course, Noah's favorite thing is continuing our research, ensuring I have enough ideas for my book, and, occasionally, I surprise him with some research ideas of my own. He even went and bought Mr. Franklin a bed and cat dishes so when I come and stay for the weekend, Franklin comes with me. We turned into a family once I was able to get over my fears.

Noah has also been included in my weekly brunch with Mom. Either she comes to his house, or we all go to the diner. I've never been this happy in a relationship before and watching Noah and my mom become friends warms my heart.

We've also spent a lot of time as a couple with our friends. For once, I'm not the single girl on the outside looking in. Work is going great, and when I'm not focusing on my classroom, I'm working with the Drama Club on the production of The Wizard of Oz. I secretly finished my book a week ago, and another teacher is working on the edits for me before I self-publish. Noah continues to push me. He is an amazing man and a wonderful influence on my life and routine. Life is great. I constantly want to pinch myself to know I'm not dreaming.

Tonight, we're heading over to a Sunday BBQ at the Stone's house. They have a standing Sunday dinner for their kids and their families, but tonight they extended the invitation to the adopted Stone family members. We're looking forward to a nice afternoon together before the cold weather hits, and I'm hoping Ruby made her famous lemon squares. Those lemon squares are the most desired food at any Stone gathering that includes the matriarch, Ruby. I've watched the Stone siblings literally fight over who gets to eat their mom's lemon squares, even though I know Ruby makes extra for each of her kids to take home. She can run her family circus with her eyes closed.

It's Sunday morning, and, since Mom is also going to the BBQ this afternoon, and we're not brunching, Noah and I take the opportunity to stay in bed and be naked and lazy a little bit longer than usual.

Noah gently runs his hand up and down my arm, "Honey, have you heard back from your teacher friend about the book? I wasn't sure how long it'll take her to make edits for you, but I can tell you're on pins and needles waiting. I haven't wanted to ask all week because I didn't want to add to your anxiety."

"She thinks she can get it back to me in two weeks, so I should hear something soon. We've both been busy at school and haven't had a chance to talk. I know she's using her lunch hour to read and make edits for me. All she shared is that she loves it and didn't know I had this in me."

"I wouldn't have thought my sweet and pretty Bree had such a mind either, but I'm so happy she does," he says before rolling on top of me. "Let's see if I can help you brainstorm for your next book."

"I may have to write a whole series, Noah because you're very good at brainstorming ideas."

***

Arriving at the Stone's house for a group BBQ means fighting for a parking spot with the other ten to fifteen Stone family cars. We finally find a place to park and head around to the back of the house. Some of our friends are already there, drink in hand, hanging out by the fire pit. It's fall and we're enjoying a sunny, slightly cooler day that requires jeans and a sweater. But any time is a good time for the fire pit in the Midwest.

Noah asks, "Honey, what can I get you to drink? Beer or wine?"

"I would love a glass of wine if there's a bottle open, otherwise, whatever you're having. Thank you."

"Be right back," he says after leaning in for a quick kiss.

Jeez, he is so sweet. I walk over toward our friends and sit down with a sigh.

"That's quite the sigh you've got there, Bree. If I look closely and squint my eyes, I see little hearts floating around your head," says Hillary. "Oh, to be in love and have a gorgeous man doting on you."

Garrett snickers, "Enjoy it from a distance Hill — that's probably all you'll get."

"You wouldn't know the first thing about doting on a woman since you are such an arrogant caveperson. Careful, or your knuckles will drag when you walk."

Julia pipes up quickly to avoid their tempers escalating, "Anyway, I am glad that you and Noah could make it. Your mom is in the house with my mom. As usual, she refuses to just sit and relax. She's helping Mom prepare the food. They kicked us out of the kitchen, so don't even attempt to help."

Noah comes back with two glasses of wine and sits in the chair next to me, "Here, sweetheart."

"Thank you."

Jackson sits down with Jules. "So what's new with everyone? I haven't seen some of you since Trivia Night at Coops. I've been taking some of the last couple of on-call shifts. Oh, hey Coop, how did Trivia Night turn out? Are you going to continue to have it?"

Cooper replies, "Feedback was good. And Griffin brings a lot of entertainment. Since everyone seemed to enjoy it, I think I'll make it the first Tuesday of the month for now and see if the buzz grows. If it does, I'll make it weekly, but for now monthly and I'll make some info cards I can attach to the menus."

Rob stands up and stretches, "I still can't believe the ladies beat us. I want a rematch."

"Bring it," Hillary says. "Always happy to remind you that our team, She's Out of Your League, is happy to show you how trivia is done."

Garrett, as usual, must have the last word, "You act like you're the trivia master when we all know the ladies on your team had to float you to win. You always talk a good talk Hill, but you never walk the walk. Pfft." He walks away shaking his head.

"Asshole," Hillary whisper-shouts.

We try to push their bickering under the rug and continue to talk about life and whatnot. Noah and Jackson end up talking about the office and the next steps as the partnership continues to grow. They're thinking of bringing on a third nurse to help their current staff with minor surgical needs.

Julia has had several events at Harte of Harmony and word is getting out to those looking for a nice intimate setting in the countryside. I'm not sure you can refer to Lake Harmony as the country, but it's a lot greener with its landscape and the lake compared to the city. She thinks she may even need to hire someone full-time to live on-site soon since she's so busy and has a lot of overnight guests.

Sam and Paul have a new program at the landscape design gardens where they help teenagers and retired veterans with job placement. This seems to be growing and bringing a lot of veterans into town for work.

Rob is busy taking over Stone Builders for his dad, who is retiring and is talking about putting a new development in next year. He and Scott, Ellen's husband, have their heads together discussing the best design and use of the land they have to work with on the west side of the lake.

Ellen is talking about hosting small groups that like to use Harmonious Bites for their gatherings. She hired some high schoolers to oversee the counter, giving her more time to work in the office.

Hillary and Griffin have been catering all the events at Julia's, which has increased their workload. Griffin has taken on a larger role with the company and that allows Hillary to focus on the menus and food prep for her customers.

Stella's essential oil line, Blooms, continues to grow, but she has kept it online or sells at her farmers market booth. She decided that going into business on a larger scale at this time would be too much for her. She's happy and continues to help Griffin when he needs servers.

Sitting around the fire and talking to my friends, it seems like everyone's life is in a good place. There are no pranks being pulled in town, no crazy arrests, or issues, so even Sheriff Garrett isn't being pulled into anything crazier than speeding tickets or accidents.

We all enjoy the delicious BBQ. The guys took turns at the grill to allow Edison to relax with Ruby and Mom. Everyone has their belly full, and a couple of drinks to enjoy, and we fought over making sure we all got our lemon squares. We're just about to head out for the night when I get a text. I reach into my back pocket and pull out my phone. *Why in the world do I have a text from Diane Sullivan, my principal?*

Diane Sullivan: Sorry to interrupt your Sunday evening. Can you please stop by my office in the morning before class?
Me: Sure, I will come in early-7:30.
Diane Sullivan: That would be great. See you then. Enjoy your evening.

I glance up and Noah's looking at me with concern, "Is everything okay? You looked at your phone and your smile dropped off your face and, instead, you have a look of panic."

"That was a text from my principal, Diane. She wants me to come to her office tomorrow, and she didn't say why. It just seems odd. I don't normally get called to the principal's office."

"I'm sure it's nothing. Don't let it upset you. Maybe she needs to ask you to cover something. Don't let it ruin your evening."

"You're probably right." But I continue to be anxious about the text. I guess it doesn't matter how old you are. If you're called to the principal's office, it always feels like you're in trouble.

Chapter Fourteen

Bree

It's early Monday, and I hurry with my morning routine so I can make it in to see Diane before class. Noah stayed over last night because I'm sure he could sense that I was a wreck worrying about why Diane wants to see me. He kept telling me to relax, that it was probably nothing crazy, but my gut is turning. I barely slept, and now I feel like I'm going to throw up my morning coffee.

I park my car and take a deep breath. I pull down the mirror on my visor and look at myself. "You're a big girl, Bree, and it's probably nothing. Relax, pull your big girl panties up and march in there with your head held high." *Ugh...here we go.*

I push through the office doors and see the staff quietly shuffling around to get their Monday morning started. "Good morning, everyone. Is Diane in her office?"

"Morning, Bree. Yes, she's in her office — go on back," says Amy, our front desk person.

"Thanks."

I walk toward Diane's office, knock, and take a deep breath.

"Come on in," Diane says.

I open the door and walk in, "Morning, Diane. Here I am. What can I do for you?"

"Morning, Bree. Can you close the door please and come have a seat?"

OH, Pluck it! I was right. Always listen to your gut is what my mother says, and I did, and now I am freaking out because I knew to worry. Noah was sure it was nothing, but I knew. I KNEW. But what am I in trouble for? Huh?

I nervously ask Diane, "Is everything okay? What did you want to see me about? I feel like I've been called into the office because I'm in trouble."

Diane takes a deep breath and leans forward. Her eyes go from normal to a deep concerned looked. "Bree, I've known you for many years. I wanted to come to you first and hear your side of things. There has been a complaint that you're writing porn and sharing it on the school campus."

I gasp and fall back hard against my chair, my eyes about to pop out of my head! *MOTHERSUCKER FUDGE BERRIES!!!! WHAT? I don't understand! What the frack is she talking about and who in the world would be evil enough to say those things about me?*

I'm breathing rapidly and starting to feel sick, "Diane, I'm not writing THAT! Who would be so cruel and tell you those lies about me?"

"Bree, they didn't come to me." She pauses and sits back in her chair. "They went to the district office. I've been notified by the district superintendent. This complaint went straight to the top."

"Son of a biscuit! Who would say and do such a horrible thing? I don't understand. Is this about my book?"

"Possibly. Can you tell me about this book and how it's the school's involved? I know you, Bree, and you are a well-loved teacher at this school and in the community. I'm here to listen and help figure out what's going on so I know how to handle it moving forward."

I shake my head to acknowledge her because I'm barely keeping it together right now. I'm embarrassed that someone thinks I write porn and worried about what other people might think about me. That's not who I am. Why is someone being so hurtful?

"Diane, I just finished writing a draft of a romance novel. It's not porn. I mean, there are some romantic scenes in it, but nothing that any other romance book on the shelves of any of the chain stores wouldn't sell. One of the other teachers does editing for supplemental income, and she's been editing my book for the last couple of weeks. That's it. I don't know how anyone else would know. Not even my best friends know the book is finished. I don't want to get this teacher in trouble because of me. Can I please talk to her and see if she knows how this got so out of hand?"

"I need to get back to the superintendent by the end of the day with an update. Do you want to bring me in for support with this teacher? Do you think she is the one that went to the district?"

"No, she would never do this. But I do want to go talk to her. I'll come to see you as soon as possible today. I'm so embarrassed."

"Bree, I will support you the best way I can. Because we aren't a union school district where you would have back-up with this, we need to figure out what is happening and fast. I wasn't given a name; the complaint was made anonymously. But you know that being an educator, you are held to very high standards. Let's try to get a handle on this quickly."

I stand up on shaky legs with a fake smile. "Thank you, Diane, for trusting me and believing in me. I will try to fix this, I promise." I turn and focus on walking out of the front office without falling and without the tears leaking out.

Once outside in the hallway, where it's still quiet and too early for kids to be arriving, I head to Reagan's room.

Her door is open, so I knock, and poke my head in, "Reagan, are you in here?"

"Hey, Bree. Come on in. I'm just setting up for my first group."

Reagan is our special education teacher and does small groups for the elementary school. She is also an editor in her spare time. Since she's editing for me, I need to start with her to find out who else might know about my book. I close the door to keep our conversation private.

"Morning. Do you have a second to talk? This is important."

She turns around with worry on her face. "What's up? You okay?"

"No, I am definitely not okay. I just left Diane's office because someone went to the district superintendent and

111

told them I'm writing porn. I need your help. Who knows that you're editing my book?"

"Are you fucking kidding me!? Someone went to the district and turned you in for writing porn. Who the hell would care if you are? Which you aren't! This pisses me off. I'm so sorry, Bree. This is so hateful. But I haven't told anyone I'm working on your book."

"Do you have any idea how anyone would even know that I wrote a book? I haven't told many people outside my circle. Only Noah and you know that I finished it."
"You know I've been working on it at lunch and at home. OH MY GOD! Those bitches!"

"Oh, frack! What?"

Reagan sits on a child's desk and is looking like her dog just died. "Bree, I think I fucked up. I am so sorry. One day last week I was reading one of your spicy scenes at lunch in the faculty break room. When I was done eating, I went to rinse out my dish. I left my editing copy face down on the table. When I came back, Melanie and Robin were standing there. I didn't think anything of it, but they asked what I was reading, and I said that I was editing something for you. They must have turned the book over and read a bit of that scene while I was at the sink. That is the ONLY thing that I can think of where anyone would have had exposure to your book."

I feel sick to my stomach and now the tears are streaming down my cheeks. "Reagan, it's not your fault. Those two have been out to get me since we were kids. They've always been the mean girls, and they're still mad that I took over Drama Club. I can't believe they would stoop that low. Stupid fart knockers!"

Reagan comes over to hug me, "I will do whatever I can to help you, Bree. I am so sorry I was working on it at school. It shouldn't matter because who doesn't do more than just be an educator around here? I'm going to run up to talk to Diane right now. Okay. It will all be okay."

Still hugging Reagan, I give her a little squeeze and wipe the tears off my face. "I think I'll go with you and talk to

Diane; the kids won't be here for another thirty minutes, and I need to get her the information. Part of me feels broken like I just got buried in muck, and I just want to go home and pull the covers over my head for the next couple of months."

Reagan grabs my hand, "Come on, let's go talk to the principal and get you out of trouble."

***

The kids are gone for the day, and I'm sitting at my desk. Noah has been texting all day, and I haven't had the energy to reply, but I know I need to. Reagan and I went to talk to Diane before class started. Reagan told Diane what happened, and who we think made the comment to the district. I had to tell Diane about the book and that it is definitely not porn.

I'm mentally exhausted. I just want to go home but that means getting up out of my chair and driving home. I pull out my phone and look at all the texts from Noah. I know he's worried, but there's nothing he can do. I can't take him down the porn trail with me. *I knew things were too good to be true in my life.*

Noah: What happened with your meeting?
Noah: thinking of you
Noah: Please tell me you're ok
Noah: I know you @ lunch now-please talk to me I'm worried about you
Noah: Honey-please.
Noah: If I don't have a text from you by 4 pm I'm canceling the end of my day and coming to you

It's almost four o'clock so I better respond to him before I screw up his day too.

Me: Hey, the meeting wasn't good. The district got notified that I'm writing porn at school (my book). The district is upset, and

Diane needed details to help me set things straight. Typical mean girls causing problems because they have it out for me. For now, it's handled the best it can be.
Me: Going home but I just want to be alone
Me: Love you-sorry to make you worry-talk soon

There, that should at least calm him down. I don't really want to be alone tonight. The girls will ask too many questions and I don't have it in me to explain the situation. There's one person that will make sure I'm okay and be there when I need her — Mom.

Me: Mom-had a bad day. Can Franklin and I come home tonight and just hang with you?
Mom: Of course. I will make your favorite chicken and noodles. Love you honey. Whatever it is, it will be okay. *Smiley emoji*

That decided I collect my things and head home.

Chapter Fifteen

Bree

I'm camped out at Moms with Franklin. After Mom makes my favorite dinner and we share a bottle of wine, I'm beginning to feel better. I just want to go to sleep and wake up with this mess over. I am so humiliated that those darn girls did this to me. I have never gone out of my way to hurt either of them, but they sure have it out for me. Those horrible shnookerdookies!

"What does Noah think about this?" Mom asks. "I'm sure he's upset and worried about you. I'm flattered you'd rather be with your old mom than in his arms tonight."

"Mmm, he doesn't need to worry about this mess. We spend almost every night together. Sometimes it's nice to come home and be here with you. I'll talk to him soon."

Noah is not happy with me right now because he wants to make this all go away and make me feel better. But I can't. I just can't bring him into my mess. He doesn't deserve this, not that I do, but it isn't his mess to fix.

I tell Mom, "I know who did it and why. Remember Melanie and Robin from school?"

"Those girls that always made you feel bad. They haven't outgrown being jerks by now. You have got to be kidding me!"

"Lucky me! You'd think the mean girls from my childhood could have picked a better job than education. They should have been lawyers because they are all full of mean bones. How they are teachers for elementary students I will never understand, yet here they are, in my school, still harassing me!"

"What happened after you and Reagan went to speak to Diane? I know Diane, and she has always been a very fair administrator. I hope she's supporting you as best as she can. There's no reason writing a romance book should hurt your career. It's not like your students will read it."

"I know, and she was supportive. Poor Reagan feels horrible, but it's not really her fault either. I should never have written that darn book. If I hadn't, none of this would have happened."

"Bree, look at me. You did nothing wrong. You did this outside of the school, not during teaching hours. This book is something that you've wanted to do for many years. It shouldn't make a difference if you wrote a romance novel or not. Just have some faith that things will work out okay in the end. Try to stay positive sweetheart. We've suffered enough, haven't we?"

"You're right, Mom. I will try to stay positive and not focus on what I can't fix right this minute."

"Are you staying here tonight? You can if you need to. I made up the guest room for you."

"Yeah, just tonight, Mom. I need to forget this day ever happened. Thank you. I love you so much." I give Mom a hug and go to what used to be my old room and is now the guest room.

I check my phone as I get into bed. I have a couple of texts from the girls, but I can't even go there right now. Another text from Noah. I need to call him back because I owe him that much.

He answers the phone right away, "Hey, honey. You, okay?"

"No, but I'm getting there. I'm at Mom's and I'm going to stay here tonight. I just didn't want you to worry about me. I needed to disconnect a little after today. I hope you aren't mad."

"No, not mad, honey. Worried, but not angry. Is there anything I can do?"

"Not right now. I spoke to Diane, and told her about the book and now she needs to go back to the superintendent and determine what the next steps will be. I'm exhausted, so I'm going to go to sleep, but I'll talk to you later, okay?"

"Go rest. Tomorrow will be a better day. I love you."

"You too, night." Then the tears slide down my cheeks again. He doesn't deserve this. He doesn't deserve the baggage I'm bringing into his life. He's going to hate me after this ruins his reputation too. No one is going to want to see the doctor that dates the lady who writes porn. I can't do that to him. I love him too much to make him hate me and leave me.

**

Noah

She's pulling away from me. I can feel it in every word she says and doesn't say. She didn't tell me she loves me tonight, and she went to her mom — not me — when something was wrong. I can't lose her now! She needs to realize she can lean on me in good and bad times. What can I do to make her realize that we're a team and that when she's hurting, I'm hurting? I need to reach her before she pulls too far away. I text Julia. She'll know what to do.

Me: Julia, I'm worried about Bree. Can you touch base when you have time, please?

I barely put my phone down when it rings. *Mamma Julia to the rescue. Thank god!*

"Hello, Julia, thanks for calling so quickly."

"Noah, what's going on? What's wrong with Bree?"

"She's in major trouble at school about her book. She's pulling away from me and going into isolation. She ignored me all day, then, instead of coming to me, she went to her mom's tonight and is staying there."

"Noah, I'm putting you on speaker so Jackson can be on this call because he may be of help too. Hold on so I can catch him up." I hear them talking about what I just said, then I hear them shut a door. "Okay, we're up in our

117

room on speaker. Jackson is caught up. What exactly happened."

"All I know is she got a text from her principal last night while we were still at your parent's house asking Bree to come to see her before school today. The principal told her someone went to the superintendent at the district office and turned her in for writing porn. She thinks she knows who did it and that they did it intentionally to hurt her. Now she's worried but instead of letting me in, she's pushing me out. I don't know what else to do. She ignored my texts all day today, at least until she couldn't because I threatened to cancel my afternoon and come find her. She said she would rather be alone tonight than with me. I can't lose her you guys; I am in love with her."

I hear them say to each other, "Yep, she's running." "Noah, hey man, stay calm and just relax for a minute," Jackson says. "We've known Bree most of our lives and this is normal Bree behavior when she gets scared. Remember when I said that if you want Bree in your life, you're going to need to be patient and keep proving yourself to her? That's still the best advice I can give you. Her dad messed her up big time. Made her feel like she isn't worth making an effort for. Do not let her push you away. Fight for her. Show her you are here to stay. If that's what you still want."

"Jackson, I just told you both I am in love with her. Of course, that's what I want! I want to marry this woman and have a family with her."

Julia says, "Hey, buddy, that's great, and I love you both together as a couple, but I agree with Jackson. You need to put actions into play right now. Bree needs to see that no matter what shitastic mess happens that you love her, and you are here to stay. She's most likely expecting you to think this is too much to handle, and that this is going to tarnish your standing at the practice. What she never realizes is that she's well-loved in the community and the school. I have an idea of who could be behind this if it's someone from school, and they'll get what's coming, but for

Bree, right now you need grand gestures. Make loud, obvious gestures that you are not leaving her. Ever."

"I will do anything to keep her in my life. If I have to write, *I love you, Bree,* in the sky with an airplane I'll do it! Julia, I know she's in hiding tonight, so maybe give her the night to calm down and get her feet back under her. Please let the girls know what's happening. Once I get my head wrapped around my next steps, I'll reach out to everyone. Right now, we all need to show her that we are here for her. Thanks, guys, I feel better. I appreciate both of you. Now, I need to go and start putting things in motion."

"Back at you, Noah. Friends are there for each other. During the good and the ugly. We'll all be here for Bree; she just needs a little help remembering that she isn't alone. See you at the office tomorrow."

"Thanks again, guys. Night."

I hang up the phone and ideas are already starting to connect. Time to put a plan in place and get the ball rolling. Time to get my woman back and happy in my arms. Team Bree. Be prepared because we are going to fight like hell for our girl and teach the teacher that she isn't alone. She will never be alone again.

I grab a pen and start writing down my next steps. My beautiful girlfriend is going to see that she's loved and supported and that no matter what she does, I am not going anywhere.

Chapter Sixteen

Bree

How is it only Tuesday? I barely slept at Mom's last night. I got up extra early because of it, grabbed Franklin, left Mom a note, and headed home to shower and prepare for my day.

As I'm getting ready for the kids to arrive, Diane pops her head in my door. "Bree, do you have a second?"

I exhale. This feels almost like the movie Groundhog Day and this is day two of starting my school day by being scolded by the principal. "Sure, come on in. I'm just getting the classroom ready for our first lesson."

"I wanted to talk to you early enough that you can prepare for the day and before you head out to Drama Club. I've spoken with different people at the district office about this book issue and somehow it has even gotten the attention of the school board. Whoever is out to hurt you have done a good job. That being said, the school board is asking you to temporarily step down from Drama Club. They've asked Melanie Mitchell to oversee the club for now."

My heart shatters. I feel defeated, "Are you serious? They are pulling me off my club because of this and giving it to the person I think is responsible for all this mess. Diane, this is complete bullspit!"

"I know, Bree. Somehow, they managed to really get their claws in you, and I haven't even figured out how yet. I promise, I'm on your side and I'm fighting behind the scenes for you best as I can. I just need to ask you to stay away from Drama Club for now. Don't make waves. Don't act guilty because you are not. And just give me time to sort this out. Melanie will pick up where you left off, and she'll continue to prepare the kids for when the show opens."

I look at her and I'm sure she knows I am defeated, "I will do whatever you need me to. Diane, I need to ask, is my job in jeopardy?"

She stands up tall and looks me in the eye. "Not if I have anything to say about it. Bree, you are one of the best teachers in my school, probably in the district. I know this is a hurtful, completely unfair personal attack. We will get through this, and I will support you all the way."

**

I barely got through teaching today, but I guess the good news since I'm in trouble, is I didn't have to go to Drama Club tonight. Instead, I get to go home. "Hey Franklin, you ready to eat ice cream for dinner and drink some wine and pretend that life is still perfect?"

"Mew, mew," he meows without the second syllable. Sweet but broken, my cat loves me no matter if I write porn or not. *You don't write porn Bree, stop it.*

I change out of my work clothes and throw on my ratty sweatpants and the big sweatshirt of Noah's he left here. He has texted me all day and even sent flowers to school for me. My favorite gerbera daisies again. At least he loves me and made me smile today.

I'm about to sit down when there's a knock on my door. "Open up right now, or I'm breaking down this door. I know you're home. I saw you through the window." I guess Hillary is here. I open the door and there are my three best friends, with Hillary in the lead.

"What are you guys doing here? It's barely after work for most of you."

Hillary pushes past me, and Julia and Sam follow her in. Julia hugs me. "We're here because you're hurting, and instead of reaching out to your best friends for comfort and support, you're hiding. That is not how we operate, and you know it."

My face turns red with embarrassment. "Oh my gosh, Gertie already found out and it was in Harmony Hears? Does everyone think I'm writing porn?" I break down in tears and fall back onto the couch. "I will never be able to leave

122

my house again. I am so humiliated. All because of this stupid book."

"Knock it off, drama queen. We're here because lover boy called Julia and Jackson in a panic last night and told us what happened. He's worried sick about you and called in your support system since you seem to have forgotten that you have one," Hillary says with her usual sarcasm, but toned down to a level four.

I wipe my tears away. "What? What are you talking about? Noah is fine."

Julia sits down next to me and in her comforting mom voice says, "No, Bree, he isn't fine. He was scared last night that you were running and leaving him in the dust. That man is in love with you, and, no matter what happens, he isn't going anywhere. He could only share the little bit of what he knew from you, but for Hillary to go kick some ass like she's gearing up for, we need to know all the details."

Sam sits down on the coffee table in front of me and grabs my hand, "Think you can tell us what exactly happened so we can help?"

I wipe away more tears and nod, "Yeah, but it isn't going to be pretty. I still can't believe this is happening to me."

I share with them everything that I know from Reagan. They are a little upset I didn't share that I had finished the book. I explained that I wanted to surprise them. Then, the girls get angry when I tell them Reagan and I put the pieces together and believe Melanie and Robin are behind this insane rumor and attack on my character. They're familiar with the mean girls from our high school days. They're happy that Diane at least seems to have my back since she is my principal.

After I explain everything, I sit back, exhausted. "I just don't get how as adults they can be so vicious; you know? Aren't you supposed to mature and grow out of being mean girls? Plus, how would they even get to the superintendent and school board so easily and so quickly? Reagan has only had the final draft for a little bit, and she thinks this all happened last week."

Hillary stands up with her hands on her hips, "I know exactly how she got to your superintendent. Is he the guy that has a bald head and wears those black-rimmed glasses?"

I nod yes. Hillary's face screws up with a combination of concern and anger.

"They were together at a function I catered a few weeks ago. I thought it was strange because she was barely divorced, but that was him. He looked like a peacock with his feathers fanned out having her on his arm. Looks to me like she is sleeping with the superintendent. He'd probably do anything to keep her happy."

Julia and Sam's mouths drop open. "Seriously? Do you think she's sleeping with him and that's how she was able to easily stab you in the back and rat you out to the district for something you didn't even do, Bree?" Julia is shocked and angry. "I can't believe after all these years that woman is still such a bitch!"

"Once a bitch always a bitch," Hillary says. "So, how do we fight this without getting you in even more trouble?"

"I have no idea except I need to be me and keep pushing forward. I can't believe they pulled Drama Club from me. I love those kids, and they expect me to be there helping them. Now, Melanie is in charge, and I know she's going to be impatient and cold. Those poor kiddos."

Julia leans forward and hugs me. "Bree, we're here for you and will be by your side supporting you in any way we can. Don't push us out. Do not push Noah away. He loves you. He is just as angry and hurt by this because it is hurting you and he can't fix it. You have so many people that love you. Just don't give up and hide."

I look at my best friends and try to smile, "I'll try not to. I promise. It's just hard not to think that all of this is going to be too much for him. What if it hurts his reputation? He's just starting to feel like part of the community. This could hurt the practice. I don't want to make him feel like he has to stick around out of guilt."

"Enough, you worry wort. That man is over the moon crazy about you! He is a big boy, and if he didn't want to be involved with you or standing next to you, do you think he would be? Come on, even I think you need to give a little credit where credit is due," Hillary says.

"It's true. He was going on and on about how he sees a future with you to Jackson and me. He isn't going anywhere, sweetheart, you'll see. Give him the chance to prove it to you." Julia smiles at me and gives me another one of her mom squeezes. "It will be okay. Keep your chin up. You are not at fault here."

***

The girls left after an hour or so. Before I know it, there's another knock on the door. I open it and Noah is standing there with his arms full of what smells like dinner, a bottle of wine, and a big smile.

"Hello, beautiful. I come with a delicious dinner and your favorite wine, and I am not leaving until I see a real smile on your face and know you are okay."

"Hi. Come on in." I move out of the doorway and let him walk into the house.

We walk to the kitchen and as soon as his arms are free, Noah pulls me close and rests his chin on my head, "I love you, honey, and I know you are upset and angry about what's happening but don't shut me out. If you're sad, I'm sad. And if you need time to think or get through this at your own pace, that's fine, but I don't want you to do it alone. I'm here for you. This is what men do for women they are in love with. I'm not leaving you. This is not too much for me to handle. This is not going to hurt me in any way unless you push me away." He leans away from me so he can see my eyes. "The only way this is going to hurt me is if you walk away from me and don't want to love me anymore. That, that would destroy me, honey."

125

I'm hurting this man and making him miserable by pulling away and not letting him love me. I'm acting like a coward, like my father, and that is not acceptable. Oh, criminy, I'm the one leaving just like I was left. I'm acting out my biggest fear and not even realizing it. *Son of a biscuit — I'm being the coward.*

"I'm sorry for making you worry. I can't even believe any of this is even happening. I should have come to you, but I needed a night to just be sad and figure out what the heck I need to do to keep moving forward, not lose my job, and not feel like a guilty person. I haven't done anything wrong."

"No, you have not done anything wrong, and you need to remember that when you don't have the energy to fight is when you lean on me a little bit more, and I will fight for you and keep reminding you that you are going to be okay."

He gives me another long hug and a kiss, "Come on, let me feed you. I went by Bella Roma's and mentioned to Maria you were not feeling good. I think she loaded me up because all I ordered were two dinners, but those bags were heavy." He starts taking container after container out of the bags.

"Holy smokes. What all did she give you? There are like four dinners here and this looks like dessert. Let's open these babies up and see what our choices are."

We both stare at the delicious dinners Maria gave us. "Lordy Noah, how are we going to eat all this? There's lasagna, ravioli, risotto, and what looks like lemon chicken with capers. We need to leave room for the tiramisu too."

Noah has a serious expression on his face. "Bree, don't laugh at me, but I'm going in. I'm taking a little bit from all of them. Whatever is left over, we can eat tomorrow for lunch or dinner. Sound good?"

I laugh at him because he looks like a cute little boy in a candy shop, rolling up his sleeves, and he's already piling food on his plate. This man. At least he's good at bringing laughter into my life. I do the same and add delicious food to

126

my plate. Noah grabs two wine glasses, pours us each a drink and we sit at the table.

With this man at my side, how can I be anything other than happy? We enjoy dinner and talk about plans for the weekend. He is exactly what I need in my life, and I was foolishly pushing him away. Having him by my side and in my life makes me believe that I can handle anything else that comes my way.

"Thank you for coming over, honey, and for not letting me push you away. I know I was in panic mode, but after talking to the girls and knowing you've got my back, I feel a bit more settled."

"I will always have your back, your friends will always have your back, and I think the entire town has your back. You need to realize and accept that when you need us, just ask, and we will be here for you."

"I know and thank you for reminding me. My life is so much better with you in it. Don't let me push you away ever again and in case I forget, remind me or ignore me please."

Chapter Seventeen

Bree

Time moves forward slowly, and word is spreading that I'm in trouble for writing a dirty book. Thankfully, the gossip modified the book from porn to steamy romance, which I guess isn't as terrible. Why this is even an issue is getting on my nerves. I can't walk around town without someone either telling me they support me or whispering and giving me dirty looks behind my back.

Last night, Noah and I were grabbing ice cream at the Freeze Hut, and we ran into some of my high school kids from Drama Club. They're upset I was pulled off being the director of the club, and they are very upset about being under Melanie's rule. She's making changes to some of the main scenes, causing major frustration, and the kids aren't enjoying being involved anymore. They were begging me to please come back and take over. It broke my heart, but I tried explaining to them that it wasn't going to be that easy.

I've also been notified that Diane will be completing an evaluation of my teaching. It was also requested that someone outside of our school sit in with her during the evaluation because it needs to be completed without bias. She was not happy about that, but her hands are tied, and she wants to stay in control of the school procedures without issue. That is scheduled for next week.

I've been asked to not have parents volunteer in my classroom for the time being, which means I have more prep to do for lessons. I loved my parents coming in and helping cut out pieces for our craft projects. Now, all that work is also on my shoulders. Thank goodness the girls were helping me last night.

I found out from Reagan, who overheard Melanie whispering to Robin, that the older kids are all dropping out of The Wizard of Oz production and boycotting all rehearsals until I come back. I love that they're supporting me, but not at the cost of them enjoying this experience and missing out on making amazing memories. I need to figure out how to get them back to rehearsal to show them that's how they can support me best.

Noah has been amazing and continues to keep me positive and won't accept that this is a burden and that he should walk away. *I know, I know, but old habits die hard.*

It's been a long week, and I get myself a treat on the way home from work. I walk into the 1-Stop General store for some ice cream. Gertie is behind the counter, and she's watching me as I walk around. I make my way to the counter to pay, and she continues to stare at me. "Hey, Gertie, how are you?"

"Young lady you look like what the cat dragged in after a shakedown with the neighborhood alley cat. I'm fine, but I am more worried about you."

"I'm okay, Gertie. Life doesn't give you things you can't handle, right?"

Her lips are pushed into a tight line. "Young lady, I think what the district is doing to you is ridiculous. I am also very angry about how some of our community members are behaving. I want to smack them all upside the head."

"It's okay, really. I just need to keep moving forward and hold my chin up."

"It is not okay. What you do on your own time has nothing to do with the kids. You have been the best kindergarten teacher this town has had for the last twenty-odd years or so. What do they think they're going to achieve by bad-mouthing you for writing a romance novel? I bet some of them read romance novels and, if not, they should! I am insulted for you!"

"I appreciate your support, Gertie. Thank you for having my back. That is so sweet of you."

"We are going to stop this nonsense and soon. You trust me on that, Bree. Ice cream is on the house today. Go home, snuggle up with that gorgeous man of yours, and remember that I'm on your side."

"Gertie, I can't just take this ice cream. What do I owe you?"

"Nonsense. Now go on and get out of here before it melts."

"Thank you. I appreciate it."

Gertie is one woman you want on your side — her voice travels far and wide. On my way to the car, my phone buzzes with a notification. Sure enough, Gertie is back at her Facebook posting. Let's see what she's posted in Harmony Hears now. I get to my car and before I drive away, I read the post.

TREAT OTHERS AS YOU WISH TO BE TREATED
Since some of this community has forgotten the golden rule, I will be happy to remind you! If you have nothing nice to say-shut it. Lake Harmony is a community of kind-hearted people that support each other in good times and bad. If you find yourself on the wrong side of that mindset, you'd better go see a doctor and get fixed. Shame on those of you hurting our own. It is unacceptable and you should all be in detention!

Well, she's made her statement for me and at this point, I will take any support anyone wishes to give me. *Thank you, Gertie, for having this girl's back.*

Time to go home and relax with my book edits. Since all this nonsense with the district started, I have gotten my book back and I'm working on some minor edits. Once that's done, I need to decide if I am still publishing this book or not. Is it worth the hassle? Noah and the girls think I should, of course, publish. I worked hard on this, and it was always a dream of mine to write a book. But in the end, is it going to be worth all this hassle? Maybe all the hassle has made it worth publishing? Hmm, something to think about for sure. If I don't publish, am I letting them win by telling me writing this book is wrong? Is that the lesson I want to make?

Chapter Eighteen

Bree

The days are barely dragging by. People continue to whisper behind my back. The faculty lounge is such a negative place that I eat lunch either in my room or with Reagan. I'm being pushed away from any type of parental involvement. I'm not supposed to communicate with anyone about school unless it's strictly lesson-based or need-to-know information for a parent about a student in my class. The bottom line, while I'm in school, I'm being kept at arm's length from any clubs, parents, or students. There doesn't seem to be an end in sight. It's starting to weigh me down and push me into a depression. Being an involved teacher is what I do, and who I am. Being told I can't be who I am is slowly breaking me down. I know I have a support system surrounding me, but they can't make this go away, and hoping that the school will back off and give me back my club and normal teaching routine doesn't seem possible these days.

The girls have tried to have a book club or meet up for coffee at Harmonious Bites, but being out in public hasn't been a very fun experience either. Looks and whispers are frequently aimed my way. At this point, I prefer to just stay at my place or Noah's.

Tonight, I'm heading over to Noah's with Franklin. He knows it's been a rough week with my in-class evaluation. Instead of going out for a date, it's another stay-at-home evening. I am too exhausted to deal with anyone siding with Melanie and the board right now.

I arrive at Noah's for dinner at six and notice a lot of other friends there. Huh? I didn't know we were having everyone over tonight. Did I miss a text? I pull my phone out of my purse and look. No, I didn't miss a text or voicemail. "Come on, Franklin looks like the whole gang is invading our quiet dinner." I grab the cat and head up to the house.

Before I even have a chance to open the door, Noah is there smiling at me and pulls us into a hug. "Hi, honey. Come on in. The gang's all here."

"I see that. Did I miss you mentioning that to me this week?"

"Nope. Just wanted to remind you that a lot of people love you and that we've noticed you slipping into retreat mode this week. So, Hillary called an intervention night, and well, here we are."

"Oh no," I say and look at him embarrassed and most likely turning red. I see the catering van outside. "Ugh. Did she happen to bring her big whiteboard?"

He just smiles, with a twinkle in his eyes, and gives me a kiss, "Come on. I'll protect you."

I put Franklin down and he goes looking for one of the toys Noah bought him. We walk into the family room where all my friends are with my mom, and even Gertie, and a huge whiteboard.

My mom smiles and walks over to me. She grabs my hand and turns me to look into the room. "Hi, honey. Before you say anything or retreat into yourself, I want you to look around this room."

I'm doing exactly that because I know my friends most likely have better things to do. But here they are and they're all smiling as if there's nowhere else in the world they would rather be but right here supporting me.

I look over at my mom. "I know I am very lucky to have these people in my life."

I say to the room, "I'm sorry. I guess I was starting to get overwhelmed again this week. Looking at all of you here..." I wipe tears away from my eyes that won't stop leaking. "Thank you. Thank you for reminding me I have all of you in my life and I'm not dealing with this horse pucky alone."

Noah puts his arm around my shoulders and kisses my temple. "We've decided it's time to act and fight back. We're going to brainstorm how we can support you and show the district that this stupid witch hunt against you needs to stop."

I look at each person. When I get to Gertie, she gives me a wink. I mouth, *Thank you.*

"Okay, guys, I'll put this in your hands. Please be gentle, and remember, this can't be a fight that gives them more ammunition against me."

Griffin grabs a marker and writes, TEAM BREE, at the top of the whiteboard.

Julia starts, "I think our best defense is involving the town in support of Bree. Let's not focus on the book itself. Rather, let's concentrate on her right to be an author. Fine arts are important in this community and they build character and life skills in the next generation."

Mom agrees, "Julia, I love that idea. Let's focus exactly on that. Where would we be if we couldn't use our abilities to expand our knowledge or create new things? We need to focus on using creative influence to push Team Bree."

Gertie stands up and puts her hands on her hips, "I use my creativity with Harmony Hears to share information that can influence the community, its opinions, and its actions. I will continue to do so in Team Bree's honor."

"Thank you, Gertie. That means the world to me," I say.

Garrett pipes up, "I'm going to be the devil's advocate here. Bree, is there any legal reason you can't be a romance author? Is there anything in the district rules or your contract that would prohibit you from writing a book? I would start there and make sure they don't have grounds to stand on."

"I don't think so, but I will make sure to check into that," I note.

Noah says, "Honey, can you get me a copy of your teaching contract and any ethics and compliance standards written by the district from Diane?"

"I can gather all that information. Why, what are you thinking?"

"Sometimes it pays to have a lawyer in the family," he says. "I'll call my brother, Hunter, and ask him to look your contract and any other material over and give us advice on how to handle things from a legal standpoint. I think Garrett's right. We need to know where you stand legally because it could make or break this situation, and I want to make sure we protect your job as much as possible."

My friends all agree. Griff is writing down our ideas: Creative Liberty, Lawyer to check contract and district rules, and Gertie HH Facebook posts.

I'm starting to feel back on solid ground and I squeeze Noah with the arm I have around his waist.
He looks down at me with concern etching his eyes, "You okay, honey?"

"I am now. Thank you for loving me so much and making sure I don't forget I have amazing people in my life."

He kisses my temple. "You make it so easy to love you."

Sam and Ellen point out that we should promote local book clubs, reading, and the library because reading is knowledge, a basis for creativity, and a means of personal escape, which quietly aligns with my being an author.

Rob raises his hand, "Hey, I think we need to show our support in a way that also reflects Bree's teaching personality. I vote crazy sock day!"

Some of the room is waiting for an explanation but my closest friends and family know that I love to wear crazy sock patterns. When I work with my kindergartners at carpet time, they always check to see what my socks look like.

Mom laughs, "I love that idea and that gives the students a chance to show you that they love and support you too. We could say the crazier the socks the better. That's an easy show of support and doesn't hurt anyone."

These people understand me and what is important to me. "I'd like to add to our list that we need to support the Drama Club. Even though I was asked to step down as the director, the kids are the ones suffering. I want them to understand that no matter who their director is, their individual dedication to the play is important. A lot of them are boycotting practice or quitting the club because they're mad at the district. I want them to understand that by being part of the play, their performance makes a *stronger* point than walking away."

After all our brainstorming, we head into the kitchen for the pizza and salad Noah ordered. The mood is light, and we're all laughing and joking around and talking about the next steps. Even Hillary and Garrett are behaving themselves, although never close to each other when in the same room.

After we finish eating, I say goodbye to most of my friends and my mom. It's been a long and emotional week, and they know I desperately need quiet time. I grab my glass of wine and walk back into the family room. I'm staring at the whiteboard when my best friends walk into the room behind me. We all just stand there, drink our wine, and look at the plan we worked on as a team. *Team Bree!*

Team Bree
Creative Liberty
Lawyer to check contract and district rules
Gertie HH Facebook posts
Promote Book Clubs
Wear Crazy Socks in Bree's Honor
Support Library-Check out a book
Support Theater-Buy ticket to Wizard of Oz

I take a deep breath and finally feel myself begin to relax. Julia puts her arm around me and squeezes, and Hillary tilts her head to mine and says, "This looks like a damn good plan. Man, that whiteboard has gotten a lot of good use with our group. It's like our *Board of Knowledge.*"

We all start to giggle, and I say, "Hill, I love you, but you're crazy. I can't believe you dragged this thing over here. How are we getting it back in your van?"

"Oh, honey, no worries. Griffin is still in the kitchen making googly eyes with Noah, Rob, and Jackson. He told them they can't leave until we say they can, and they need to move the board back into the van under his direction."

"Leave it to Griffin, and things get done," Julia says with a chuckle.

"Exactly bitches! I do get things done. Now someone take a pretty picture of that board so I can wipe it clean and get the gorgeous men in the kitchen to remove their shirts and load this thing into the van," Griffin says as he waltzes into the room.

We do as Griffin asks, and I take my phone out and take a picture, then we clean off the board and the guys take it back out to the van with their shirts on and Griffin pouting. Noah and I say goodnight and thank them for coming over. "Want another glass of wine? Then how about we relax in front of the tv?" he asks.

"Perfect idea." My phone buzzes in my back pocket with a text from Mom.
Noah looks up and asks, "Is everything okay?"

"Yes. It was my mom. She said to look at Facebook. Gertie must have posted something."
"Hmm, let's sit down so we can look together." He hands me my wine and puts his arm around me. "I don't know about you, but I'm exhausted but also relieved after this evening. How are you feeling about it?"

We sit on the couch, and I put my drink down, "I feel the same. I think it's in my best interest to not continue to play the victim. I didn't do anything wrong. I wrote a book. It's not any different than when one of our history teachers from the high school wrote a murder mystery a few years ago. I don't remember the board going crazy and threatening his job or activities."

"Does he still work for the district?" Noah asks me.

"He retired a year or so ago, but he's still local. I think I'll reach out to him and see if he'd be willing to speak on my behalf. First, I want to talk with your brother and make sure I'm not violating any of the terms of my contract with the district. Knowing I'm within my legal rights is our first step."

"You should definitely reach out to that teacher, Bree. Just because he wrote in a different genre doesn't mean it's not the same. A murder mystery could have been just as much of an issue as a romance. If they complain you write about sex why weren't they up in arms about murder? The same concept, if you ask me. If you get the contract and district info for us to send as soon as possible, Hunter should be able to review it for us this week."

"The soonest I could get that stuff will probably be Tuesday," I reply. "I don't want to bother Diane over the weekend. I'll go to her office Monday and ask her to get me copies of whatever we need. I know she'll be willing to do that for me. Oh, let's check Facebook before we forget."

I pull up the Harmony Hears page on Facebook. Mom said Gertie posted after the meeting tonight, so I know it's aimed at me.

TEAM BREE SUPPORTS THE FINE ARTS

Creative outlets help develop critical thinking, collaboration, and creative skills needed to be successful. How can you support this in your own community you ask?

Team Bree is happy to share some ideas:
Participation: Enjoy & Join Classes for Music, Dancing, Theater, Art
Support: Encourage others to use their creative outlets
Read: Visit the library and read - join or create a book club
Speak Up: Attend a school board meeting, PTO and voice your support for creative liberty
Lead by Example: Tell your teacher/principal/board how vital the arts are to a quality education
Local Events: Support your Drama Club-buy tickets to The Wizard of Oz
Be an Advocate: Speak with leaders and decision-makers in our community about the importance of the arts

139

Join the Cause: Wear your crazy socks to show support for our own kindergarten teacher who pushes our young students to reach for the stars

"Oh. My. Goodness. Noah, Look at this post! This may be one of my favorites."

He reads the post and smiles big. "See? I know I said Gertie is a harmless little old lady, but she sure knows how to throw a sucker punch when she wants to. If this post doesn't show the entire community that she supports you and shames them for their bad behavior, then nothing will. She loves you, Bree. Everyone that showed up here tonight loves you, and they are ready to fight for you." He whispers in my ear, "And you didn't even have to ask."
I lean my head against his shoulder, "I am so lucky to have such amazing people in my life."

"We don't have anything we need to do this weekend, do we?" Noah asks. "I mean like anywhere we are supposed to be or anything time-consuming for your lessons next week?"

"No, why? What's up?" I ask him.

Tomorrow let's go to your place and grab your overnight bag. I want to steal you for a night and head to the city. We haven't done much in town since this started because you tense up any time we try to go out for dinner. I want to give you a little overnight getaway. Pack something nice to wear for a semi-fancy dinner, and we'll set Franklin up for an overnight at your mom's. Sound good?"

I reach up and grab his face in my hands and give him a kiss, "Sounds perfect. Let's binge a little more Schitt's Creek and go to bed."

Chapter Nineteen

Bree

We arrive at the Waldorf Astoria in downtown Chicago and are quickly checked in and escorted up to our room. This charming hotel sits in the heart of the Gold Coast area and has a French-inspired décor with high-quality materials and soft tones throughout. Our room has a large king bed and a sitting area with a fireplace. I walk over to the windows and look out at a view of the Chicago skyline.

"This is beautiful, Noah. I always loved coming to the city and doing the architectural boat tours but looking out and seeing the skyline is just as magnificent." He walks up behind me, brings his arms around me, pulls me in tight against his chest, and rests his chin on my shoulder.

"I wanted to give you a romantic night away from all the nonsense. We have dinner with live music later, but we have time to go walking around the city if you want. Today and tonight are all for you to relax and get away from home and the upheaval caused by the school board."

I turn, wrap my arms around his back, and look at him. This man with his beautiful eyes and full lips, not to mention the strong arms he still has wrapped around me. He is such a kind man, and I am so in love with him. "In case I haven't said thank you yet, thank you. You always seem to know what I need, and I love you for putting me first and worrying about me. Let's go walk around. We aren't far from Navy Pier, and we can taxi back if we're running late. What time do we need to be at dinner?"

"I made reservations for eight o'clock, so we don't have to hurry. The restaurant has live music. I thought we could eat and then dance a little if you aren't too tired."

I smile so big that my cheeks are ready to bust. "You made us a romantic getaway tonight. It's a good thing I have a special surprise of my own for later."

"Bree, you can't say that to me and then expect me to leave this room and go walking around the city without a hard-on all day."

"Oh, but it will be your reward for such a romantic day. I promise you'll be very well rewarded." I push up on my tiptoes, kiss him, and grab his hand. "Let's go explore the city and get into some mischief." And off we go to enjoy the sunny, brisk, fall day in the city.

Navy Pier on Lake Michigan is a beautiful location for walking and people-watching. You never know what or who you may see. As a venue space for events, shopping, and restaurants, there is a revolving door of special happenings throughout the year. It also has a huge ferris wheel, and that's where I'm currently dragging Noah. Even after living in the city, he has never ridden the ferris wheel. I'm not sure if it's just not his typical type of adventure or if he is possibly afraid of heights. The Centennial Wheel, which is its official name, is two-hundred-feet off the ground but has the most amazing views of the city and the lake. He doesn't know what he's been missing.

"Come on, you big baby. I promise to keep you safe if you're scared. Look at the line. Women and children are going on the ferris wheel. It's perfectly safe."

Noah is already turning green. "I don't know about this, honey. I am not sure how I feel about dangling so high off the ground."

"You'll be fine, I promise. I will hold your hand the entire time. It has an enclosed gondola, so it's not like we'll fall out."

He takes my hand and allows me to drag him on the ride but doesn't release it until we're descending from the highest point. "You were right, this was worth all the fear and anxiety you've caused me."

I just look at him and bust out laughing, "You are ridiculous. Cute, and I am in love with you, but ridiculous."

"I'm glad you pushed me to do it. It really is amazing. Can you imagine being a little kid and being up here and seeing the world from this view? That would be so amazing."

"Are you saying if you were a little boy, you wouldn't have been scared to be up here?"

"Oh no, it would have been horrifying because Hunter would have been telling me that we were going to fall to our death and splatter on the ground and daring me to make it rock back and forth. My parents would have been calming Shannon down from crying and being angry with the both of us."

"Holy Guacamole. I hope your children never put you in that position because I don't think you'd survive."

"Oh, do you see children in my future, Bree?"

"Yes, at least a couple. Don't you think?"

"Whatever makes you happy, honey."

I'm still looking into his eyes as he smiles at me, talking about our children in the future as if it's a normal conversation. We haven't talked about where this is going long-term, but maybe it's something we need to do.

We enjoy the rest of the afternoon walking around the different areas of Navy Pier and going into some of the shops. I bought a Centennial Wheel magnet to put on the fridge, so Noah always has a reminder of how brave he was today. It still makes me chuckle to think about how green he was and how he nearly broke my hand with how tightly he was holding it.

We get back to the hotel in time for each of us to clean up and get changed for the evening. Noah tried convincing me that showering together would save time and water, but I know better. And I have bigger plans for him tonight. We need to get ourselves ready and out the door.

While Noah showers, I pull out my black cocktail dress and newly purchased red satin bra and panty set. I want to make sure to knock his socks off once we come back to the room. I decide to change and finish up in the bathroom while he relaxes out here. I don't want him seeing me before I have my dress on or our evening plans might change.

Noah steps out of the bathroom in only a towel draped low across his hips. The beautiful and defined vee from his hips and deeply lined abs are just waiting for my mouth. He's watching me take him in and knows I'd love to rip that towel off him and inspect him from head to toe. He chuckles, "Bree, stop looking at me like that and get in the bathroom or I can promise you we will not leave this room until we have to check out tomorrow."

I look up at his eyes and I know he'd be happy with whatever I decide but we need this night out. We need time out in public where I don't feel all eyes are on me and acting as though I have committed some horrible sin because I wrote a romance novel.

I lick my lips and give him a smile, "I just needed to get my fill of you before you get dressed. Go on now, put clothes on that I can strip you out of later, Dr. McHunky." I wink and sashay into the bathroom to get ready.

My hair is clean, so I tie it up and jump into the shower. After, I make sure to apply enough lotion so my skin feels like silk. Wearing the beautiful new red satin set I bought with Hillary last week makes me feel good under my clothes. Something about wearing sexy underwear always makes me feel good, no matter what nightmares are happening around me. I quickly apply the little makeup I normally wear to highlight my eyes, lips, and cheeks.

In the other room, my handsome man is standing in front of the big picture window in a black suit, white shirt, and black tie. He is wearing gold cufflinks and this man is dressed and looks delicious. *Shnookerdookies! Maybe we should just get naked and stay in?*

He hears me come into the room and when he sees me, he stops. Noah looks me up and down and his smile grows bigger. "You take my breath away. I can't wait to take you out and show you off. You are most definitely the most beautiful woman I have ever seen, and everyone tonight is going to wonder how the hell a shmuck like me was able to get someone as stunning as you."

I blush and begin moving toward him, "Thank you for your wonderful compliment." I hold my hair up and turn my back toward him. Over my shoulder, knowing he sees the red satin of my bra, I ask, "Can you please zip me?"

I hear him take a deep inhale then I feel his finger move down my spine and rub along the back of the satin of my bra and down to the satin of my panties, "As much as it pains me to zip you up, knowing that you have something special on for me has me in great anticipation for later." He bends forward and kisses the back of my neck, nips me, then runs his tongue against the same spot before pulling my zipper up. "You little vixen." I feel it all the way to my center and the heat and sensation tingle down to my toes. Maybe that tease wasn't such a good idea. Now I'm all hot and bothered too.

Noah spins me around and smiles, knowing he has me all turned on. "Ready, sweetheart?" I simply smile. He grabs my hand, and we head downstairs to the lobby.

***

We take a cab to our dinner destination — an upscale restaurant with a small stage where a bluesy jazz ensemble is playing. Noah says to the hostess, "We have a reservation for two under Mick Hunkey."

I put my hand over my mouth to keep from laughing out loud. *Did I just hear that right? Dr. McHunky made a reservation for Mick Hunkey.* He turns to look at me with the biggest smile on his face.

"You didn't!" I whisper to him.

"What? The Hunkeys are here for dinner," he says and winks at me. *Oh yes, he did.*

I just shake my head and laugh. "You are a nut."

Noah brings his hand to my face, "I just want to see you laugh and smile as much as possible. I love you."

"Love you too, you big goofball."

As the hostess leads us to our table we look around the room. The atmosphere at this restaurant is wonderful, and the food smells delicious. We are both in a great mood and looking forward to good food, good wine, and good music.

Once seated, we quickly decide on dinner and drink choices so we can dance a little to the fantastic jazzy blues quartet. It's so nice to be able to relax and laugh and put our worries aside for the night.

***

After we finish dinner, we dance again wrapped in each other's arms. We head back to the table. I take a sip of my drink, lean over to Noah, and whisper in his ear, "Thank you for making this the best day. I know my worries become your worries too, and I'm completely relaxed. But I have one problem."
He looks into my eyes with a bit of concern, "What, honey? What do you need?"

"We need to go back to our room so I can get you naked before I combust. I need you, Noah. I need you so bad." I look at him and lick my lower lip.

He already paid the bill, so we can go anytime. "Thank God. Let's go. What the lady wants the lady is going to get." He quickly gets up and walks around to my chair to help me up and leans down to whisper in my ear, "I've been hard all night since I saw that red satin and lace. Let's go."

We leave the restaurant with whispers and smiles. I'm sure everyone knows we're heading to our room to have wild crazy monkey sex, and I honestly don't give a hoot. This man took the time to bring me to the city to recharge my soul and not worry about anything except what brings me joy. Now I'm going to show him the reward he's earned for being so attentive and caring.

We rush from the elevator to our room. Noah digs out our room card, opens the door, and escorts me in. I walk over toward our bed area and stop in front of the window. I hear him come up behind me and stop with his hand on my hip. I look at him over my should and lift my hair, "Can you unzip me, please?"

146

He swallows hard and looks into my eyes. "Leave the shoes on," I hear in a husky voice. As he's unzipping my dress, he whispers in my ear, "Have you ever been made love to against a picture window?"

I inhale, "No," and I am so turned on. "I think we need to research exactly how that works. Will the glass feel cold on my naked breasts or will it warm up as you push into me from behind?"

I hear his breath change and I can feel his erection against my backside. He pushes against me so I know what I'm doing to him. "I look forward to finding out." I feel him lower my zipper and push my dress to the floor. He is still in his suit, but I hear his belt and zipper.

I am standing there in just my red satin bra and thong wearing my heels. He gently runs his hand down my side, then I feel a smack against my bottom. He leans forward and says, "Put your hands on the window, Bree."
I don't move as quickly as he'd like so he smacks the other side of my bottom. I am burning up inside, and I am so turned on.
He runs his hands down my crack and pushes my thong aside, "Mm...you are so wet for me. Is it me touching you and being almost naked in the window that's turning you on or my spanking you?"

"Both," I whisper. "Don't stop, Noah. Please, touch me, take me. I need more." I lean my forehead against the glass. It feels cool against the heat radiating off me. He's running his finger up and down my seam but not touching me where I need him to. "Please, Noah, more. I need you in me."

He slides my thong down my legs, and I step out of them. His finger starts moving in and out of me, still not touching my clit and giving me pressure where I need it. He adds a second finger. The pressure is building but it's still not enough. I turn my head so I can look at him and he has his penis out of his pants and is fisting himself with his other hand running up and down his hard length.

"Does it turn you on that I am touching myself?"

147

"Yes."

He smiles and continues to rub me, but it's not enough.

"Turn around," he says.

I turn and he walks me backward, so I'm up against the window, and he drops to his knees. I look down because now I'm half naked pressed back against the cool window. He's on his knees and leans forward and licks against my seam. He takes one leg and puts it on his shoulder. I'm open for him now and he continues to lick and suck me up and down.

I'm leaning against the cool window, but I can't feel it anymore. The sensations running through me are divine, and I'm so close to having an orgasm. "More. Noah. I …need…ohfuckinggod, more. Now." He starts sucking on my clit and adds a finger and the tingles start to form in my center. He is sucking and pulling on my clit his fingers hitting my special spot where I know it won't take much more before I orgasm. He groans and the vibrations added to what he's already doing push me over the edge. He continues to play my body until the last of the spasms stop.

He looks up at me and smiles, "Best dessert ever."

"Come here, silly man."

"Oh honey, I'm not going anywhere. We still have research to do. I love hearing you come. It's always interesting to hear the words that come out of your mouth."

I still don't believe I use cuss words when we make love and I orgasm, and I refuse to allow him to record us for proof. Noah walks over to the chair in the corner and removes his suit jacket, shirt, and cufflinks, then his pants and briefs. This beautiful man is standing in front of me completely naked and hard as granite fisting his length up and down.

"Come over here so I can touch and taste you," I tell him.

He walks over and slowly unhooks my bra and I watch it fall to the ground.

148

"Beautiful," he says then he pulls a nipple into his mouth. "Turn around, Bree."

I turn around, and he brings his arm around me. We are far enough from the window that it reflects us like a mirror but with the city skyline still shining through. I'm standing completely naked in front of it, thankful the lights are off.

He leans forward looking at me in the reflection and says into my ear, "Watch. Keep your eyes on us in the window."

He continues to tease me with his fingers, moving in and out of me and pinching my clit. It's hard to keep my eyes open but every time I let them close, he stops. I move one arm around me and reach for him, running my hand up and down his erection the way I know he likes. I can make him just as eager for release as he spins my body into a frenzy.

I'm watching him and getting so turned on. He sucks my earlobe while watching me in the window's reflection. He takes my hands and puts them up against the window. "I need your hands on the window."

I look into his eyes as I feel him begin to enter me from behind. Keeping our eyes trained on each other and seeing the intensity of our connection always turns me on even more.

"Bree, eyes on me." I watch us in the reflection as he begins to pump into me and pinches my clit and I am so turned on I am probably dripping. His other hand comes up to pinch my nipple and I gasp.

"Do that again. Harder."
Noah smiles and he pinches first my clit then my nipple. The sensations are coming at me from so many different directions I don't know where to focus.

"Oh my god, harder, Noah, harder."

He continues to pump into me and pinch rotating from my nipple to my clit. He leans forward and bites my shoulder, and I completely shoot off and climax, "Oh yes, fuck me, Noah, harder," and he follows right behind me. I hear him groaning and telling me how good it feels to be inside me as our bodies continue to spasm.

My head drops back against the window, and he is holding me up with one hand as my body continues to spasm around him. I've never experienced anything better than watching this big strong man completely fall apart and knowing I'm responsible for his pleasure. It is such a turn-on for me.

He brings both of his arms around me and looks at me through our reflection. We stand there having a silent conversation telling each other how much we love one another.

"Come on, let me clean you up." He grabs my hand and leads me into the bathroom. He turns on the shower and we wait for the water to warm. "I love you, Bree."

"I love you too."

We clean each other, make love again, and go to bed. I curl up in Noah's arms and fall asleep.

Chapter Twenty

Bree

We're on our way home from the city when my phone vibrates. I grab my purse and pull my phone out. "Huh, I just got a text from Gertie."

"What did she say? Is everything all right back at home?"

"I think so." I read the text to Noah, and we both wonder what was going on. With Gertie, you just never know if it's going to be good or bad. Let's hope for good.

Gertie: Bree, this is Gertie. I know this is last minute, but could you and Noah come to dinner tonight at 5:30. It is important so it's not really an invitation- you need to show up- no excuses sweetie. Don't bring anything-Peter is making a roast for us to enjoy.

"Noah, it appears we're invited to dinner at Gertie's tonight. Actually, it's more like a demand, not really an invitation. Is that okay with you?"

"Probably easier to just agree than to ask too many questions. Go ahead, let her know we're coming."

Me: Gertie, we will be there. Are you sure we shouldn't bring anything?
Gertie: Just yourselves. Don't be late.

"Looks like we have dinner plans. Is it okay if we head to my house? I need to grab Franklin from Mom's, and I have lesson plans to do for this week."

"That works. Do you care if I watch the game at your place or do you want peace and quiet?"

"I like when we're in the same place so, yes, please stay, and you don't have to ask me ever again. If I didn't want you over, you'd know it, buddy."

***

Noah

While Bree is working on her lesson plans for the week, I call my brother. I need to know sooner rather than later what we need to do on a legal basis.

Hunter answers my call and I can hear the football game on in the background, "Hey big brother," he says. "To what do I owe the pleasure of your call?"

"Hunter, I need your help."

"Oh shit, what's up man? You in trouble with work?"

"No. Bree is though, and I need your help with some legal advice for her. She still needs to gather her teaching contract and the district ethics and compliance documents to make sure she isn't in violation, but do you have time to look those over this week and just give us some idea of what we can do so she can fight back without losing her job?"

"Noah, you know I'd do just about anything for you. You don't even have to ask. What kind of trouble is she in? I know you're falling for this woman, but if it's something serious, I hope you're protecting yourself."

I'm a bit frustrated with where this conversation is going and say, "She didn't do anything bad, Hunter. She wrote a romance novel and some bitchy teacher, who has had it in for her since they were kids, told the school board she wrote porn. She hasn't even published it yet, but it's just a romance novel. We need you to look at her contract to make sure she isn't in violating any of the terms before we start to push back. She isn't even planning on using her real name to publish under. This would never have been an issue if this other woman hadn't heard about her book. Anyway, I appreciate if you can look at the documents this week as soon as I get them. I'll email them to your office, okay?"

"Are you fucking serious? Is this woman who turned her in still in junior high? Pretty vicious to attack a grown woman by ruining her career. Man, this really pisses me off. I'm on it. Not for you, but for the lovely Bree. It's about time to bring her to another family dinner don't you think? Even better, we'll come to you!"

"Fine. Call Shannon and see if she's free too, I'll give Mom and Dad a call and see what next weekend looks like. Let's shoot for Saturday because Bree uses Sundays to prep for her school week."

"Aw, you're such a good boyfriend, Noah. Can't wait! Send me those documents as soon as you can, and we'll get the ball rolling. Tell her once we have a plan, I'll send a nice letter over to the school board on my letterhead letting them know I'm representing her. That should scare them a bit seeing a big firm name from the city coming after them."

"We can hope! Thanks, man. Talk soon."

"Later," and Hunter hangs up.

***

Bree

We arrive at Gertie's at the requested time and are greeted at the door by her brother, Peter. I've known Peter for a long time. He's best friends with Mr. Stone, who is like a father figure to me, and he also owns the 1-Stop General Store in town.

"Hi, Peter. Thanks for making dinner. It's nice to see you outside the General Store."

"It's good to see you, kids, too. I'm sorry about Gertie, but you know, once she gets an idea in her head it's best to just go with the flow. Don't worry, though, I think this one will work in your favor. Come on in. I'll get you kids a drink while you talk to Gertie in the living room."

He walks us back to the living room where Gertie is reading a book and gets our drink order before leaving the room.

153

Gertie looks up, "Give me a minute. I just got to a juicy part, and I need to get through a couple more paragraphs. Have a seat."

I look at Noah who is lifting an eyebrow at me and trying not to laugh. "No problem, Gertie. No rush," he says to her.

I look at the book cover and see a Fabio-type man seducing a woman on the cover. *Oh criminy!* Thankfully, Peter comes back in with our drinks, looks at his sister, shakes his head, and sits down.
"Bree, how are you doing, kiddo? Gertie keeps me in the loop on what's going on around town. I'm sorry that the school district is in such a tizzy over this book thing. I don't see how it's any of their business, but I know once the gossip starts, it's hard to stop because it's like poking a hornet's nest."

Noah puts his arm around me. "I am doing okay," I say. "Noah and I got away yesterday and went into the city to just be able to be out and about and not feel like all eyes are on me. I'm tired of the gossip and people talking about me behind my back just because I wrote a romance novel."

"It's a damn crime what they are doing to you, sweetie," Gertie says while closing her book with a bookmark.

I guess she's done reading her romance novel for the moment. "Right now, I just need to focus on what I can control and see where things fall. It feels like I'm losing this fight, though, and I'm not sure what else I can do."

"That is exactly why you're here. This craziness needs to stop, and I think I have a way to make it go away. So, let's go over to the dining room table where I have my laptop."

Noah and I just glance at each other not sure what exactly it is we're in for with Gertie. She has us sit down on the same side of the table next to her, puts her laptop in front of us, and opens her Facebook. Noah grabs my hand under the table and squeezes it. Was that a squeeze for support or out of fear because this is Gertie we're talking about!?

154

Next thing we know, she's getting a Facetime video call from someone named JT, and she opens the video to a smiling Jax Turner. I smile back because Jax Turner was one of my favorite students, but Noah is staring at the screen with his mouth hanging open. To us, this may be Jax Turner, a regular guy who grew up in Lake Harmony, but to Noah, this is Jax Turner, Hollywood's favorite thirty-year-old star.

Once we're connected, Gertie starts the conversation off, "Hey, sweetie. It's so good to see you. I miss your face around here. When is Hollywood going to give you a break and let you come visit your favorite aunt?"

"Aunt Gertie, I know I'm due for a visit. I'm hoping to get away and come in this year for the holidays. It's about the only place anymore where I can go out without being surrounded by my security team. Anyway, hi, Ms. Daniels," Jax waves at me through the laptop. "It's great to see you. I wanted Aunt Gertie to get me in touch with you because, like everyone else, I've been following the whole school board issue through Harmony Hears. I think what they are doing to you is utter crap, and I want to know what I can do to help you. If it wasn't for your support and direction when I was in school and in Drama Club, I don't think I would be where I am today. I know that having the opportunity to have a career as an actor is all because of you."

Noah puts his arm around me because he knows I'm getting emotional. "Jax, it's so nice to see you. I appreciate your kind words, and it means so much to me to hear you say that. But buddy, I'm not responsible for your talent. I only guided you on how to use it, and I'm so proud of you. Also, please call me Bree. You aren't my student anymore, and you're a grown man. Noah and I just watched one of your movies last week. OH, golly. I almost forgot. Jax this is Noah, my boyfriend."

Noah is still a bit shell-shocked at seeing Jax in front of him, but he gets himself straight enough to say, "Nice to meet you. I had no idea you were from Lake Harmony but that's cool! I'm a little bit out of sorts right now talking to you on Facebook, but it's great that you want to help Bree."

"Good to meet you too, Noah. Next time I'm home we should all get together at Cooper's Corner. He does still have his restaurant, right?"

"Yeah, he still has his place. Since Bree is a little choked up right now, did you have anything in mind to help us deal with this problem? Maybe something on social media if you'd be willing to do something like that?"

"Absolutely. I just didn't want to jump the gun and do anything without asking my teacher for permission first," Jax laughs.

Bree wipes her eyes and takes a deep breath, "Jax, I don't want you to do anything you don't want to. Honestly, this will all blow over."

"But what if it doesn't, Bree? I can't let them attack your character and ruin your reputation like this and win. You don't deserve it. So, you wrote a romance novel. Hello! I pretty much live in romance novels and act them out. Why is that a bad thing? You educate and constantly support kids and writing a book shouldn't matter."

Noah looks at me and smiles, "Jax, oh man — I'm still a little shocked I'm talking to you. Sorry, but I wasn't prepared."

Laughing Jax replies, "No problem. Lake Harmony does a good job of protecting my privacy when I'm home. No worries, man, but I'm just a regular guy. I can't help I hang out with famous people."

Gertie pops back into the screen, "Stop showing off, Jax. You don't want me to come out there and stay with you to remind you that you still poop the same as the rest of us, do you?"

"Aunt Gertie, it's all good. I'm just teasing, but you're always welcome to come to see me. Want to be my date for a premiere? I'd be very happy to show you off."

Gertie is blushing, "We'll talk about that in private, young man. But maybe. I do always enjoy seeing your friends."

She sits back down, and Noah continues talking to Jax. "I spoke to my brother who's a lawyer. We didn't want to make a huge scene without knowing Bree's contractual obligations. He's going to look over her teaching contract and the district's ethics and compliance standards this week. Since she's using a pen name to publish under, we don't think she'll have an issue. Also, we don't want this to be just about Bree's book, but also want to promote the importance of the fine arts and allow everyone to explore their creativity. I'm thinking if you can support that same mindset with some posts while tagging Bree or the town that may put some pressure on the school board. It may also encourage the community to side with Bree if they see you're supporting her." Noah sits back from the table and looks at me. "Bree, are you okay with that idea?"

"I'm okay with whatever you want to do, Jax. I appreciate it very much, but it's not expected of you." I say to Jax and everyone around the table.

"Well, if you're leaving it up to me, then I have a plan. If at any time you want me to drop it or change direction, or it gets overwhelming, let me know. You're important to me Bree, and I think what's happening to you is wrong. Now it's my turn to support you the way you supported me. Deal?"
"Thank you," I laugh and wipe at my eyes, "Deal."
Noah wraps me up in a big hug, and we hear Gertie and Peter continue to finish up the call with their nephew.

Gertie looks at us. "That went perfectly. Jax is going to post something, then I'll repost it on Harmony Hears. We're going to show the school and this town of ours that they are picking a fight with the wrong person."

"Thank you, Gertie. I really appreciate you reaching out to Jax and doing this for me. Every little bit of support I get makes it a little easier to push through."

"Oh, sweetie, this was all Jax. That young man has been texting me all morning wanting your phone number. I didn't want him to harass you, so I told him to call us on Facebook, and I would make sure to have you here. I didn't want Hollywood getting your phone number and bugging you even more!"

Gertie, the silly woman, is all upset that Hollywood could possibly want my phone number to call me, but her intentions were good.

Noah looks over at me, "Did that seriously just happen? Was I just talking to Jax Turner, the latest Hollywood it-man, and making plans to see him next time he's in town?"

Gertie smiles big, "You sure did. He's my great-nephew, and I am very proud of him! Now, let's eat that roast Peter made for us and have another drink before Noah passes out from all the excitement."

Chapter Twenty-One

Bree

Monday seems to get the crazy train started. First thing this morning, I went to Diane's office and asked her to get me my contract and any other district documents that I need to send to Hunter. She completely supports getting help from an attorney and agrees it would show the school board that I wasn't going to just roll over and play dead. She said she would have the documents for me by tomorrow at the latest.

By lunchtime, my phone was buzzing from everyone I know that Jax Turner's social media is going viral with his support for me and that Gertie is reposting it all on Harmony Hears, along with her own post. Once the kids are at lunch, I close my classroom door, grab my own lunch, and pull out my phone to check.

WE MAY BE LITTLE, BUT WE ARE MIGHTY!

Our own Jax Turner from Hollywood has reached out to support his favorite teacher and Drama Club Director, Bree Daniels! Not only has he been sharing his support for Bree, but others in Hollywood are jumping on the #TeamBree Train! If you aren't already supporting her-you should be. See what the buzz is all about with #TEAMBREE.

Tweet: Jax Turner @JaxTurner
Fine Arts are where it's at! Support local Arts
#TEAMBREE #LakeHarmony

Tweet: Sophia Knight @SophiaKnight
My heart is with you! You got this girl!!
#TEAMBREE #LakeHarmony

Fiddlesticks! Sophia Knight! She's Hollywood's favorite leading lady right now. How in the world is this happening?

Things really pick up steam by evening. I have been informed through more #TEAMBREE posts that most of the kids have walked out of Drama Club and are boycotting the show until I'm back in charge and that they refuse to allow the stand-in director to smother their creativity.

Jax made another video post on his TikTok and Instagram accounts that went viral saying that I was the best teacher he ever had, that I encouraged him to become an actor, and that I am now being punished by my own school board for writing a romance novel that hasn't even been published yet. #TEAMBREE goes viral on Instagram with posts from celebrities, artists, and famous authors.

Geez, Louise! This is getting a bit crazy but also super cool! I have famous people talking about me because they also want to support my cause after Jax posted something on his social media.

Before my lunch period is over, Diane pops her head into my room, "Knock, knock. Got a minute?"

"Of course. Come on in, Diane. What's up?"

"Oh my goodness, Bree! My office has been getting hounded by calls and emails in support of you! Between Gertie and her Harmony Hears posts and Jax Turner posting and getting all kinds of Hollywood support thrown in, we now have parents and former students reaching out to see how they can help. I'm asking them to show their support without blocking all the lines and crashing our server," she laughs, "This is the craziest thing in the world. I've even had to run off reporters outside."

"Oh, shoot. Diane, I am so, so, sorry. I didn't realize that Jax posting something would turn the school and town into a circus. How can I help you?"

"Bree, don't even worry about it. I have some extra help answering the line that rings through so we don't miss parent calls, but I'm happy to see some positive movement on your behalf. I brought you the documents you asked for, so you can get that in motion. If reporters are already snooping around, you'll want to know exactly what you should and shouldn't say. For now, you should probably avoid commenting and avoid the reporters until you know exactly how to handle this. The school board and district office are most likely getting hounded just as badly, if not worse, as they deserve, so this little issue may just evaporate if the face of all the public support you're receiving. I'm looking forward to how things play out this week." She stands up and straightens her skirt. "Keep me posted. And if you need anything else, let me know. I better get back to the front office before my team walks out. I've already asked Tina and Marcus from our support staff to answer phones and man the doors instead of helping with the lunchroom and activities. They're happy to help and getting a kick out of telling the press to stay off school property."

***

My kids came back from lunch, and we finished the day out like a normal day. Thank goodness they're kindergartners and blissfully unaware of social media. Of course, they'll most likely get wind of what's happening once they get home and hear about it from their parents and siblings. Oh well, nothing I can do.

I'm home now and trying to relax, but my phone won't stop ringing and buzzing. It's starting to wear on my nerves. It buzzes again, and as I go to turn it off, I see it's a text from Noah.

Noah: Are you okay? My phone hasn't stopped buzzing from everyone worried about you or talking about all of Hollywood now posting about #TEAMBREE. You have probably gone into hiding again and I don't blame you. If you want, go hide out at my house, which is probably safer than staying home where they can find you. Take Franklin and clothes for the week. Garrett said reporters are snooping around town already. They have your school picture, so they know what you look like. Love

you, honey. I will be home as soon as my last patient walks out the door.

ME: OMG it is crazy! They overloaded the school office, and my phone is going nuts. Going to the park for some quiet yoga after I drop Franklin and my things at your house. Love you too! I'm okay-it's just weird. Have you seen all the famous people doing #TEAMBREE??? Crazy Noah!!! I am kinda freaking out, but I am okay. Promise *kissing emoji*

I say to Franklin, who's sleeping on the soft blanket thrown across my couch, "Hey, buddy. Looks like we're going to stay at Noah's this week. Go get packed up and ready to go." He looks at me like I'm crazy, then goes back to sleep. "Okay, guess I'll grab some of your things for you. I'm going to drop you off at Noah's, then I'm going to the park to try to relax with some yoga." Again, he just opens an eye staring at me like I should get moving and leave him alone to sleep.

I grab some clothes out of the bedroom to take to Noah's. He already has my normal essentials at his place, so I just need some clothes for the week. I still can't believe how crazy this is.

***

I dropped Franklin off at Noah's, and he went straight to the sunny window and settled in the bed Noah bought him. I'm attempting to catch my breath with some yoga and stretching in the park by the lake for an hour until Noah heads home.

As I'm walking to the lake with my yoga mat, I hear my name being called, "Bree Daniels, do you have a minute?" *Oh no!* I look back and a reporter and cameraman are following me. I start to jog away and a man I've never seen before comes toward me.

"Bree, keep going around the bend so they can't see you from here. I'll get rid of them," he says walking toward the reporter and cameraman. *Who the heck was that, and how does he know who I am?*

I go around the bend in front of some of the fuller bushes where there's a bench by the water. Maybe I should have stayed home after all. I didn't think it would be this crazy. Why do they even care about me? I'm just a kindergarten teacher for Pete's sake!

I'm still sitting on the bench trying to catch my breath and calm down when someone sits down on the bench next to me. *Fudge nuggets!* "You okay, Bree? I got rid of them. I told them you were my girlfriend, Sarah, and I don't know who the heck Bree Daniels is, but I'm going to call the sheriff if they didn't leave us alone."
I'm sure my confusion is clearly written on my face. "Oh, thank you. I appreciate that. Do I know you?"

"Maybe not, but I know Jackson and I'm somewhat familiar with the rest of your group since I'm from Lake Harmony. I'm Carter, by the way."

My new friend, Carter, has the kindest eyes, the biggest smile, a Rolling Stones lip t-shirt, and jeans. He looks harmless, and if he knows Jackson, that's good. Maybe he's one of Sam and Paul's veterans to whom they offered job and mentor programs.

"Thanks, Carter. I can't believe this day. I mean the last couple of weeks have just been weird, but today, today is completely surreal. Jax Turner made a couple of posts on social media, and it seems that his Hollywood people are supporting me too, and now reporters are trying to figure out why I'm so important."

He smiles, "I think you're important. You're a great teacher and always make the kids know how important and special they are. To me, that's one of the best qualities to have and is often rare. You deserve to be acknowledged, but you don't deserve to be harassed. I think you should call Garrett and see if he can come with his sheriff cruiser and escort you home. Why don't I stay and wait with you? I'd feel a lot better knowing you have him as an escort. The reporters are probably still lurking around."

"That's probably a good idea. Thanks for thinking of it. I'll send Garrett a quick text."

Me: Tried to go to park for yoga. Got harassed by reporters. Sitting here with Carter. Can you swing by and get me home to Noah's?
Garrett: On my way! Give me ten. Stay with Carter away from your car. I will text when I am in parking lot.
Me: thank you G *Heart emoji*

While I am at it, I'd better touch base with the girls.

Girls Group Text: Reporters found me trying to yoga @ park. Staying at Noah's this week *frustrated emoji*
Julia: Here for you if you want to hide at my place
Ellen: Avoid Harmonious Bites-Reporters in town!
Sam: Stick with Noah's and school or one of our houses
Julia: You, okay? Stay calm
Me: Okay now. Carter ran reporters off and Garrett is coming to escort me home to Noah's just in case *sad smiley emoji*
Hillary: Damn reporters. Should I send Griffin to harass them?
Me: LOL-Friday-Happy Hour @ Noahs?
Julia: Yes
Hillary: Absofuckinglutely!
Sam: Perfect
Ellen: I'm in
Me: C U @ 5:30-ish

Carter stayed with me until Garrett arrived.

"Hey, Bree, are you heading straight to Noah's, or do you need to go home first?" Garrett asks me.

"I already dropped the cat and my clothes at Noah's for the rest of the week. He was worried this would happen. I don't know why I didn't agree with him, but thanks for coming to my rescue."

Garrett runs his hand through his hair, "You know, until this blows over a bit with the reporters, do me a favor, and don't go out in public alone right now. You're like my sister, and I worry about you. Reporters can be aggressive, and I don't want to see you get hurt. If Noah or the girls can't get you from one place to the next, call me and I'll get someone from the station to escort you if I'm not free. If nothing else, we'll take turns until you aren't current news. Come on, let's get you home and out of here in case they come back."

Garrett follows me back to Noah's and waits until I have my car in the garage and I'm inside. I'm barely inside the house when my phone starts buzzing, "Ugh…enough already!" I'm about to turn it off when a friend group text comes through.

Garrett: Just escorted Bree to Noah's after reporters found her at the park. Carter was there and helped out too
Jackson: Love that guy! All ok now?
Bree: Yes, I'm home and not leaving until school in the morning
Noah: I've got her mornings to school covered. I will be driving her to school and getting her into the building this week. Can someone get her home?
Rob: I'll get her from school to home-no prob
Julia: Look at you guys go! Thanks for taking care of our girl
Griff: I love men taking charge *high five emoji*
Hillary: We know Griff, we know!! *laughing emoji*
Sam: Paul said he can be on standby if Rob is busy
Ellen: Scott too- avoid downtown Bree-reporters all over
Jackson: Stopped in 1-Stop General Store and Gertie was giving one hell just now
Noah: Go Gertie-thanks everyone. Bree, I'm on my way home w dinner!
Hillary: Aw so sweet. Relax you two-this will blow over too
Ellen: Exactly, tomorrow is another day *heart emoji*

Chapter Twenty-Two

Bree

For the rest of the week, Noah drives me to school and one of the other guys picks me up and drives me home. Franklin and I are still at Noah's house, and the reporters continue to try to get to me through the school or people in the community. It's Thursday night, and Noah has been called into the hospital for a patient, so he asked Mom to come over and have dinner with me.

I just finished making our chicken and rice casserole dinner when the doorbell rings. I look before answering the door. Noah wants me to be careful of reporters, but it's my mom standing on the porch holding a dish. Smiling, I open the door and let her in.

"Hey, Mom. I am so glad you can join me for dinner. I've gotten used to not eating alone, and with the current chaos, I really don't go anywhere but school and here."

"Honey, I'm sorry this has caused so much upheaval, but let's have dinner, do some catching up, and I can see for myself how you're doing."

"Come on back. I made chicken and rice casserole. Do you want a glass of wine or something else?"

"I'll have whatever you're having. I also brought your favorite butterscotch brownies for dessert."

"I just opened a bottle from the Harmony Winery, so I'll pour us both a glass and we can eat."

I put the casserole on the table with a salad I prepared earlier. "Come, sit down, and we can eat dinner. Before we talk about my situation, what's new with you, Mom? Are you still volunteering at the library?"

"Yes, because you know I get bored if I do nothing. Retirement doesn't mean you should sit on your bottom and be lazy all day. After working my whole life, I still like to be busy. I enjoy shelving books or helping out in the kids' section. It's nice to see everyone with their little children. But, come on. I'm here because I needed to see with my own eyes that you're okay. I've heard through Ruby that the guys have made it their responsibility to make sure you get to and from work. I'm glad you have so many people keeping you safe right now. I don't like that a reporter came looking for you at the lake when you were alone. Thank goodness you thought to call Garrett to get you home."

"Well, I ran into Carter at the lake, and he scared them off, then wouldn't let me stay alone. He's the one who suggested I call Garrett, which is what put my security detail in play with the guys. Between Noah, Garrett, and the rest of them, I don't think I had a say in the matter. It's fine. At least, I don't have to worry about keeping an eye out for reporters. It also gives me a break from the gossip and whispers."

"I'm happy they're driving you back and forth right now. It gives me some peace of mind. What's going on with school? Are they still pursuing some sort of action against you?"

"Diane and one of the school board members have been in my room for teacher observation. I knew they would be coming, but not when. I just did one of my regular lessons, and I was prepared because I always plan for my week. So that went fine. Diane also said it went fine and they aren't planning more observations for now. She thinks that with all the hoopla, including the support I'm getting from Hollywood, the board is reconsidering its position. They'll never admit they were wrong. Noah's brother, Hunter, reviewed my teaching contract and the other district documents, and he's sending a letter on his letterhead to the school and school board that lets them know he's representing me and hinting that this is borderline harassment, and I would have a case against them if the situation doesn't stop."

"Wow. A lot has happened since we met here with all your friends. When I was in the library the other day, the kids at our storytelling time were showing each other their crazy socks, Bree. It was so darling. I asked one of the kids about their socks, and she was a first grader that had you last year.

She kept talking about you being her favorite teacher and that the school office was being mean to you, so she was wearing her crazy socks for you every day. She was so cute and so serious. By the end of story hour, all the kids were going home to put on crazy socks."

"Oh my gosh, that is so sweet. I love my students. "I was also in the 1-Stop General Store. Do you know Gertie is selling crazy socks and t-shirts that say #TEAMBREE? She's donating the profits to the Drama Club to put toward the theater, costumes, and props. I guess Jax sent a huge order in all different sizes for her to sell."

"WHAT?! I had no idea." I'm completely shocked. "Mom, should I be doing something? I should let everyone know how much I appreciate all they're doing."

"You know, that may not be a bad idea. What about doing some sort of video on that Instagram or TikTok and have Gertie repost it on Harmony Hears?"

"Mom, I love that! Would you want to help me? We can do it right now. That makes my heart happy just thinking about it. I'm going to go change, and you get to hold my phone and record me, okay? This is so fun! Be right back."

I run to the bedroom, change my shirt, check my face and hair, and put on some crazy socks. Here goes!

I position myself in front of the big windows in my favorite reading spot, hand Mom my phone, and show her how to turn the video on and off. "I'm excited but nervous. I hate seeing myself on video, but this will be great. I don't really want to think too much about what I'm going to say so let's to wing it, and if it's bad, we can redo it. How about you count me down?" Oh, criminy. I am nervous. But this is a good idea, and I need to stand strong and show everyone I'm here, seeing their support for me, and I love them.

"Bree, I'm ready when you are." Mom begins the countdown, "Three, two, and.." she nods her head telling me she is recording.

Hi everyone, I'm Bree Daniels, and I want to thank you for your love and support. My entire life I've wanted to be a teacher who supports her students' learning and guides them to reach for their dreams and never quit. We should all be allowed to fight for our dreams without question. Please support the fine arts, allow creativity into your lives, and of course wear your crazy socks, like me, because they will make you happy!

"What do you think, Mom? Was that good, or should I say something else completely?" My mom looks like she's about to cry. "Mom, are you okay?"

"Honey, that was perfect. You couldn't have done it better. You were just... YOU. You showed the world in that video that you are an amazing, genuine person. I think you were perfect. Here, look at it, and tell me what you think."

I rewatch the video and smile. It turned out good, and I don't look horrible either. "Mom let's do a group call with the girls and see what they think about where to post it or what to do with it."

I get all the girls on the phone, and we discuss the video and the best place to post it. We decided that I should post it to TikTok and Instagram and add the hashtags #TEAMBREE and #LAKEHARMONY, which seem to have gone viral. Then, tell Gertie about it so she can add it to Harmony Hears.

We end the call and Mom looks at me and smiles. "Let's go back into the kitchen for those brownies while you get this video posted, honey. Then, I'll head out so you can go to bed."

"Mom, you don't have to leave so early. We could watch tv or something tonight."

"No, let's get the video up and enjoy a brownie before I go. Then you should take a bath, relax, and just crawl into bed. I don't know how quickly your video will be seen, but you may want to let Noah know, then silence your phone. If it's anything like when Jax did his first post about you, your phone may start blowing up again."

"Oh drats, I didn't even think about that. Let's get it posted and see how bad it gets in the first thirty minutes while you're here. We could be worrying over nothing."

We enjoy a brownie while I post the video and text Gertie to let her know so she can repost it. I also text Noah to let him know.

Me: Made a thank you video to everyone for their support and put it on social media. Not sure if it's going to create more chaos or not but if it does, I may turn phone off. Kiss me goodnight if you get in late and I'm already sleeping. Love you *kiss emoji*

Mom and I take the first couple bites of our brownies and my phone starts blowing up. We just look at each other and start laughing. "Oh criminy! What have we done? This could be bad, Mom."

"May as well see what the noise is all about while I'm here. I bet it's good news, though, so don't be so worried."

I have multiple texts from the girls that the post has tons of views already. People are reposting and #TEAMBREE is being used all over again. Jax has tagged my video and included a duet. This I need to see right now. "Mom, Jax did a duet with my video."

"What exactly does that mean? I'm not as hip with my social media knowledge, honey."

"That means he posted his video side-by-side with mine. Let's watch it." I pull up Jax's TikTok and while my video plays on the right side of the screen, his video is on the left side, and he has text flashing that says #BESTTEACHER, #RESPONSIBLE4MYCAREER, #TEAMBREE. I watch it run through a couple of times, and I wipe away my tears. It's silly, but I'm a little emotional about this video. He is so sweet. "Here, Mom. You watch. It will keep repeating."

My mom watches the video a couple of times too, puts the phone down, and looks at me. "That was very sweet of Jax. This isn't the first time that he has acknowledged that you've played a part in his success. Don't ignore that, Bree.

You make a difference in the lives of the students you teach. You make them stronger and eager to fight for their dreams, just like you said in your video. Be proud of yourself, honey."

"I know. It's just catching me off guard. It's a lot, especially coming from one of the most famous actors in Hollywood right now. I'm flattered, but I didn't do more for him than I do for all my students in Drama Club. I just gave him the tools for his toolbox. He's the one that knows how to use them."

"Honey, it's because you're an amazing teacher and have a huge heart. Your students succeed because you care and don't let them fail. Come on, this has been a long day for you. Let's clean up the kitchen together, then I'm going home, and you should call it a day too."

We clean up the few dishes and put the leftovers in the fridge. Mom leaves the rest of the brownies here for Noah and me to enjoy. She gives me a huge hug and heads home, reminding me to lock up tight after her.

Once Mom pulls out of the driveway, I head to the master bedroom and decide that a bath with a book is just what I need. I fill the large soaking tub with some of Stella Stone's lavender chamomile bath salts. Julia's little sister makes the most amazing essential oil bath salts and soaps. Noah has started keeping some here for me because he knows I enjoy relaxing with them in the bath. While the tub fills, I grab a glass of water and my current romance novel. I toss my clothes in the hamper and slowly slide down, letting the scent from the salts wrap around me, and lean my head back. Maybe just a few moments of resting with my eyes closed. *Why don't I do this all the time?* I should move in permanently with Noah so I can use this fantastic soaking tub every night. That would sure put a pep in my step to tackle my kindergartners. After about ten minutes, Franklin meanders into the bathroom. "Mew, mew," he calls out to me in his broken meow, like, *Mom, where are you*?

"What's up buddy? Are you ready for bed? Give me ten more minutes, and we'll turn out the lights. It's been another crazy day, huh?" He seems satisfied with that and walks out of the bathroom.

***

Later, I feel a kiss on my cheek and Noah says, "Love you. I'm home."

I open my eyes, "Hey, everything okay at the hospital tonight?"

Noah begins to shed his clothes from the day. "Yeah. Just a baby trying to be born too early. Mom is admitted and resting, and the baby is still in her belly and growing. She has a few more weeks, so she will be on bed rest for the rest of her pregnancy. I didn't want to leave until her contractions stopped. Sorry, I'm so late. Go back to sleep."

"It's been a crazy night for us both. How about coming to bed Dr. McHunky and snuggling with me."
Noah slides into bed and pulls me in close with a kiss. "That sounds like a great idea. You okay, baby?"
"Yeah. Just more social media chaos, but I started it this time, so I can't complain. I'm glad tomorrow is Friday, and I have nowhere to be this weekend, so we can relax a bit. Maybe go to the lake or out for a drive?"

"You, sweetheart, will be going to the city Saturday. Jackson gave me the info for the spa where he sent Julia. You're going to go relax, my treat, then we're having my brother and sister over for dinner. You need some pampering. As a matter of fact, let's start right now."

"Oh yeah. What do you have in mind?"

"I think I would rather show you than tell you." Noah pulls my nightgown over my head and starts to explore my body with his hands and mouth.

173

174

Chapter Twenty-Three

Noah

Bree's video on social media has created a stir again around town but in a positive way. Without realizing it, she put a face to the gossip. Those that didn't know who the gossip was about now do. Making that connection, putting a personal spin on it, and being a familiar face in the community have moved things in her favor. Patients are coming into the office wearing crazy socks. Every day, Gertie posts something on Facebook or shares others' social media posts with #TEAMBREE, including posts made by famous Hollywood stars. The community is starting to support Bree's prerogative to write a book, no matter the genre, and is recognizing it doesn't interfere with her ability to be a strong role model and teacher.

I let her sleep in this morning, brought her breakfast in bed, then sent her off for a day of pampering at the spa with Sam and Ellen.

My phone rings as I'm headed out to do some yard work. "Hey, Mom. Did you get my message about dinner tonight?"

"Hi, honey. I did but your father and I already have plans to go out with friends. I'm sorry about not seeing you tonight. How are things going? How is Bree holding up? Any good news to share?"

"A lot of things are happening. I told you Jax Turner was her student when he lived in Lake Harmony, and since his social media post supporting her and saying she is responsible for his success has gone viral, we've had reporters crawling all over town wanting to talk to her. We keep her company any time she leaves the house or school because she got tracked down at the lake this week by a reporter, and it spooked her a bit. Thankfully, a local guy was there to head them off. She's been staying here with me this week instead of her place so that she isn't alone at night."

175

"Goodness, Noah. That is a lot going on! How is she doing mentally, though? This must be a lot of pressure coming at her from all directions. Is she okay? Is there anything your dad and I can do to help?"

"Thanks for offering, Mom. That means a lot to me. I'm just trying to keep her safe and happy right now. Hunter sent a letter to the school district by certified mail yesterday, informing them that he is representing her and that they need to stop all action against her. They've never even seen the book, and it isn't even published. We're all hoping that his letter from the firm is enough for them to back off and drop it."

"Oh, I hope it does. I'm glad that you have Hunter there to help you with this. I am so sorry we won't make it tonight. I just want to wrap my arms around Bree and tell her it will all be fine and work itself out. We are worried about her."

"Mom, I appreciate that more than you know. I sent her off to relax at a spa today with her girlfriends. She needs a day of pampering. The whole situation is weighing on her, and she's being a lot braver than she needs to be. She isn't sleeping well, and I'm worried the stress is going to make her sick. I'm just trying to love and support her as much as I can and remind her that I'm in this with her all the way."

"Well, honey, I know you love this woman, so we love her too. We're here if you need us. Keep us posted on how Hunter's letter helps. Have fun tonight with your brother and sister. Love you."

"Love you too, Mom."

I hang up the phone and make my way outside. Hunter and Shannon are coming over for dinner, and I have some yard cleanup to do before they get here. I put my earbuds in and play music while I work outside.

***

Just as I step out of the shower, Bree comes home from the spa with a big smile on her face.

176

"Hey," she says. "Did you have a good day or did you just slave away in the yard the whole time I was getting pampered?"

Still a bit damp from my shower and wearing only a towel wrapped around my hips, I pull her in tight and give her a kiss. "I missed you. Did you enjoy your spa day with the girls?"

"It was wonderful, and I didn't want to leave. But I missed you and wanted to be with you. So, here I am, and here you are, Dr. McHunky, fresh out of a shower wearing only this towel."

I kiss her and step back. "The day got away from me. I didn't get a lot done with the phone ringing off the hook. Shannon called to tell me she was bringing a side dish and dessert, Hunter called to ask what he needed to bring, and I talked to Mom this morning. She and my dad have plans with friends, so they won't make it tonight, but she wanted me to tell you that she and Dad are both here for you if you need them. They're worried about you, and the stress you're under."

"I love your parents. They're so kind to me."

"You, honey, are very easy to love and support. Now, we don't have much time before Hunter and Shannon get here, and as much as I want to strip you naked and have my way with you for the rest of the day, we need to get downstairs and season the steaks and start the potatoes. Do you need to shower or are you ready to help in the kitchen?"

"Are you getting dressed first or prepping like that? That could help make my decision."

I pull her in tight and kiss her on the tip of her nose. "If I go down like this, I don't think you'll keep your hands to yourself, then I'll be naked when my brother and sister arrive. I don't think they'd appreciate that very much."

"Probably not!" Bree laughs. "Get dressed then. I'll start pulling food out of the fridge."

I quickly throw on some jeans and a cotton sweater and head downstairs. Bree has eighties pop music playing and is singing and dancing along in the kitchen. This right

here is what I want to see for the rest of my life. Her —
happy, smiling, singing, and dancing in our kitchen. Maybe a
few little ones running around our legs. *Man, I have it bad!* I
put my arms around her and whisper in her ear, "Move in
with me. Stay here with me forever." I feel her gasp and
stiffen. She slowly starts to relax and spins around to look at
me.

Her eyes a big and wide. "Noah, are you serious? Do
you really mean that? You want to move in together?"
This woman has no idea how lonely I am when she's not
around. How, when we're apart, I constantly think about her
and wonder if she's happy or sad, stressed or laughing. "I
am one hundred percent saying I want you here. I need you
here. I cannot stand to be apart, and after having you here
this week with me, I don't want it to ever stop. We've been
staying with each other every night for months, so why can't
we just make it permanent? I don't care where we live, as
long as we're together. I'll sell this house and move in with
you, or we can sell both houses and buy one that we both
like. Whatever you want. As long as you never leave."

I hold my breath. Bree studies me and then starts to
smile. "I'm sorry McHunky, but we are not giving up that
soaking tub upstairs. Franklin already feels at home here, so
let's figure out how to bring stuff from my house, and I can
sell my place or rent it out. When do you want to do this?"

"I want you here now, but the rest we'll figure out and
plan when we can get everyone to help move you. I want
you to bring whatever furniture you want, and I desperately
need you to bring some life into this place with your colorful
decor. Let's get through this current crisis first. Unless
moving you in will distract you and be a stress reliever? Up
to you. But you are sleeping in my bed, our bed, moving
forward."

"That sounds perfect. I love you, Noah, and I couldn't
be happier."

"Come on, let's get ready for my crazy siblings to
show up. They should be here any time."

We work together in the kitchen laughing and singing and dancing to the music. Soon, someone is ringing the doorbell and knocking. "Someone's impatient. Must not like not being able to walk right in. He better get used to it," I say, knowing it's my brother at the door.

I open the door to let my brother in and see Shannon pulling up. "Hey, what's with all the commotion?"

"Why is the door locked?" Hunter asks.

"Because I don't know if the reporters are going to figure out where Bree is, and I am not taking any chances," I tell him.

"Ah yes, that makes sense. Where is the lovely Bree? I'd rather look at her than your mug," Hunter says as he punches me in the arm.

"Kitchen. Go ahead. I'll wait for Shannon." Hunter goes in the house, and I head out to my sister. "Do you need help carrying anything in?"

Shannon answers as she steps out of the car, "Yes, grab the dessert box from the passenger seat. Don't tip it. I brought a chocolate silk pie. I'll grab the salad from the backseat."

I grab the pie, she grabs the salad, and Shannon asks, "How are things going here? Is Bree doing okay?"

"I think so. I sent her and some friends to the spa today so she looks happy. Plus, we have a surprise for you guys tonight."

Shannon stops immediately and stares at me, "Did you propose!"

"Not yet, but I did ask her to move in with me, and she said yes."

"Oh, does Hunter know yet? Did I get the scoop first?"

"He does not know unless Bree told him in the last five minutes. Come on let's go in, and you can tell him because I know you're dying to be the one."

***

179

The four of us are in the kitchen cleaning up our dinner and enjoying a drink. My brother and sister are ecstatic that Bree is moving in with me and have offered to help us move her. Everyone has avoided talking about the book and the situation with school, until now. But of course, my siblings like to know everything, so time is up on avoiding the elephant in the room.

Shannon and Bree sit down at the table and Shannon is fidgeting, "Bree, I know you and Noah are dealing with the fallout of your book with the district, but is it done? Are you going to publish?"

Bree and I have talked at great length about whether she should publish. We both feel that, in spite of the brouhaha, publishing is the right thing to do after all the support she's received, and her own push for others to indulge their creativity and support the fine arts. If she doesn't get her book out there, she'll feel like she let everyone down. To this point, though, no one else has asked her what she's planning...until my sister.

Bree looks at me then back at Shannon. "I'm going to publish the book. I've made the final edits, and it's ready to go. I'm publishing under a pen name so that it isn't tied to me in any type of school search, and because I'm not sure I want to go too public with the book title or pen name yet. I know writing this book wasn't a bad thing, but I'm still scared to put myself out there completely."

Shannon grabs Bree's hand. "I'm proud of you for following your dream. There's nothing wrong with using a pen name, and when you do publish your book, I want to help you. Since I work in marketing, I help authors all the time. I'd like to offer my marketing and branding services. We can do everything without your image or real name attached, but you need to get your book out there so people will find it."

"Oh, my goodness, Shannon! That would be so sweet of you, and I would love that!"

"Great, we can talk about it at a different time if you want. Give me your private email, and I'll send you a list of things I'll need from you. We can brainstorm together if you need help, or I can take what you give me, then make whatever tweaks we need. This will be fun," Shannon says.

Hunter and I bring the pie and plates to the table so we can continue talking over dessert.

"Bree, have you heard anything since the district received my certified letter yesterday?" Hunter asks.

"No, nothing. I went to my principal's office at the end of the day, and she hasn't heard a peep from them either. She thinks they're probably shaking in their boots!"

"They should be. This was harassment and completely inappropriate," Hunter says and takes a large bite of pie. With a mouthful, he says, "I have a feeling it scared them and they're going to back off." He reclines back in his seat. "Sometimes I love being a partner at the firm. Just a simple letter on our letterhead can be enough to make problems go away. Not that I don't like making easy money, but when people are out to just hurt others to make themselves look better, it ticks me off. This was a nasty, unprovoked, heartless attack on your character, and you are the kindest person I have ever met. No one is going to hurt you with me around, Bree. Not if I can help it. Or with Noah around. I think he kind of likes you too," he winks at Bree, and she blushes.

"I'm so lucky to have all of you in my life. Thank you for being so supportive through all of this. Who would have thought me writing a book would cause all this ridiculous blowback, get people in Hollywood talking about me, and find me being chased by reporters!"

"Seriously! I, for one, want to read your book," Shannon laughs. "So, when is book two coming out?"

I squeeze Bree's hand. "I think Bree has some more research to work through before she can start outlining the next story. Right, honey?" I wink at her, and she blushes.

Bree says, "Well, I do have a couple of ideas but, as Noah said, I need to do a little more research first."

Chapter Twenty-Four

Bree

Thankfully, the week begins without too much hassle, and I learn that my school parents, current and former, have organized an ice cream social at the Freeze Hut for Wednesday evening. Profits will be donated to the library to help build a new children's reading room. Everyone is asked to wear their #TEAMBREE shirts and crazy socks. Earlier in the week, Gertie put up a post to help support the ice cream social.

#TEAMBREE SWEET TREATS
Current and former parents of our sweetheart, Bree Daniels, are hosting an ice cream social in her honor and all profits from the Freeze Hut will go towards creating a new Children's Reading Room at our local library. A mural will be painted by a local artist to capture our town and our support of each other. Let your creativity shine!

Talk all over town is about the ice cream social night, and Nick, the owner of Freeze Hut, is getting worried he'll run out of ice cream. Since the season is coming to an end, the parents organizing the fundraiser told him to not order too much. When it's gone, it's gone. Just to be safe, though, he ordered another batch of vanilla and chocolate ice cream, as well as sprinkles for topping, since those seem to be the favorite among the kids.

I'm comfortable leaving the house these days without a chaperone, especially since Gertie advised in one of her posts for everyone to keep an eye on me while I'm out and about. She basically put everyone on town watch, which made Garrett worry, but has been a positive thing. I think he was concerned community members were going to go into some sort of law enforcement of their own. That did not happen. And bonus: they seemed to have run off the lingering reporters.

Once I posted that video, the town stepped up to protect its own. They made the connection to me and the gossip that had been going around, and if they hadn't personally had children in my class, they knew someone who had. The current talk around town is everyone's pretty angry this entire situation even occurred.

Somehow, the rumor mill, which was most likely Hillary and Gertie, let it slip that the one responsible for the character attack on me is Melanie, and now she seems to be getting hit with her own bit of karma. We continue to avoid each other during the school day, which is impressive since we both teach at the elementary school. It shouldn't make me happy, but I am enjoying the backlash she's getting just a teeny tiny bit. *Shh...Don't judge me! She tried to ruin my life!*

According to the same rumor mill, it doesn't appear Melanie is dating our school superintendent any longer either. Guess he felt jumping to conclusions about my book, without even reading it, put him in a pickle, and now he has some serious backpedaling to do with added pressure from the school board.

Noah and I stay busy trying to figure out when exactly to move my bigger items to his house. The minute the girls found out we were moving in together, they came over with Hillary's catering van, and, with Griffin's help, we moved all my clothing and food to Noah's. Now, we need to coordinate the furniture and other household items.

Have you ever sat down with a man and tried to explain the importance of kitchen gadgets? *Criminy, he just doesn't get it, but he will.* I'm not giving away my KitchenAid or my French press. Yes, we have two coffee pots, but we should keep the better of the two, not just the newest.

Noah has come to the compromising conclusion that anything we have a double of will be donated to either the town center or our local thrift store. Honestly, that man thinks we need a double set of pots and pans. Why?

Since he didn't have a bedroom set for his spare bedroom, we'll move my set into there for a guest room. My couch will go into another spare room with a desk and become my office where I can go to write or read. He calls it my Femme Den because I'll be writing steamy books there. Since Noah has only been living in his house for six months, he hadn't had a chance to furnish it completely, which works out quite nicely for us both. My "colors," as he calls all my artwork, pillows, and throws, have given his home a warmer, welcoming feel, which he tells me every day makes him happy. He also tells me that Franklin and I have turned his house into a home now. *How sweet is that man!?* He warms my heart with those types of comments. Franklin has settled in easily enough since we'd been staying over a lot. He has now figured out how to sleep around Noah's head at night. It cracks me up when I wake up and Noah is wearing a Franklin crown on his head. Those two boys love each other so much. Noah has taken it upon himself to teach poor Franklin how to meow correctly. It isn't working because you can't teach an old cat a new trick. *Ha! I'm funny.*

Chapter Twenty-Five

Bree

"Good morning, pretty ladies," I say, as I'm the last to arrive at Harmonious Bites for a Saturday morning coffee chat with the girls. "How's everyone today?"

"Girl, your face just screams that you are completely orgasmed out," Hillary says in a singsong voice.

"Don't embarrass her, Hill. It's nice to see Bree in love and glowing," Julia adds with a wink.

Ellen leans in, "Are you and Dr. McHunky still getting your research on?"

"Um, yes?" I reply, blushing.

"Bree, I decided to follow your lead, and Paul and I have been doing some research AND experiments ourselves," Sam says with a huge grin. "In fact, I think I hurt my back from him rolling us off the damn bed last night."

"Oh my god! Are you serious?" I ask.

"Yep! But I'll gladly take on the aches and pains of doing what your book recommends and add to my sexy times," Sam says.

Ellen whispers, "Ditto, girl. Dit-to!"

Everyone looks pretty happy to me — except Hillary. I know she's still looking for her special someone. If she and Garrett would just figure out their love-hate relationship, we'd all be a lot happier. Ugh!

Julia grabs my hand, "So, lady, what's the latest with school and the book? Anything new? The ice cream social was a huge success. I can't believe Nick ran out of all that ice cream in two hours! He said he's going to do that every fall before he closes and donate the profits back to the community. He said it was better than having to close shop and take a loss for anything that didn't sell."

"It was so much fun. Noah and I were there the whole time talking to my students and their parents. Did you know that Jax had Gertie set it up so he paid for all the ice cream?

No one was allowed to pay for a single thing. So, we put a donation bin out. We ended up collecting double what we expected with Jax paying for all the frozen treats and everyone else putting their money in the donation bin instead!"

Ellen's eyes get big. "Wow! No, I hadn't heard that Jax paid for all of Nick's ice cream ahead of time. That's wonderful! It's so funny because I still see Jax running around in the 1-Stop General Store with Gertie when he was a little kid and not this Hollywood heartthrob. Wasn't she his babysitter when his mom worked?"

"Yes, because she's his great aunt. I think she helped out a lot because she never had her own kids. So, the fundraiser was a huge success, and rumor says it was the final breaking point for the school board. I just found out that they have a closed-door board meeting Monday night and are deciding how to move forward with my book, my position at school, and whatever else is involved with this mess Melanie started," I tell my friends.

"I hope it just goes away; they have no ground to stand on, anyway. Has anyone even bothered to ask you for the book or talk to you directly about what the book is about or if you are publishing?" Julia asks.

"No, they haven't," I answered. "Diane is the only one that has bothered to ask me, and I am not sure if they're going by that. They certainly never bothered to ask me about it. All I know is that between the letter from Hunter to the board and district, Hollywood's social media outpouring, and the community now backing me, they're spooked and don't want to look like the bad guys. At least, that's what Diane shared with me yesterday."

"All a bunch of assholes! How the heck could they go after you without even having the facts?" Hillary asks. "I guess, if Melanie was sleeping with the superintendent, he didn't really care what the facts were. He was more worried about keeping her in his bed."

"Probably. Which sucks. But, Bree, you're stronger now. Through it all, you've had Noah and all of us right behind you. I hope you finally recognize how important you are to all of us. We wouldn't be the same without you," Julia says.

"This crazy experience has made me step outside my comfort zone for sure. And, yes, I realize I'm not alone and have all of you to support and love me. Thank you," I say. "I couldn't have gotten through this without all of you!"

Hillary says, "So what's next with the book? You are publishing this baby, right?"

"Yes, and as a matter of fact, I wanted to have you guys help me with one of the most important things. I need to think up a pen name. I'm not publishing this book under my name. After all this, I want to separate my real name from my writing to be safe. To me, it doesn't make much difference if I publish under a pen name. It's still my work on those pages. But if a pen name protects me and my career, then that's what I'll do.

"Is this like a hooker name? First pet and street name you grew up on. Like Blondie President?" Hillary asks with a devious smile.

"Um, I guess? I mean I don't want to be embarrassed by it. It can be some random name. So how about it? Want to help me think up a pen name?"

My friends all lean in and get excited. Ellen jumps up and runs to her office to grab a pen and paper. "Here. Now we can jot down our ideas. What do you have already? Anything?" she asks.

"Nope. I've got nothing. I'm at your mercy," I say.

Hillary is looking at her phone. "Hey! There's a romance author pen name generator app! Let's see what it says. Do you want the initials to be the same as your name? Do you want to use your birthstone? Do you want to use a certain day, month, or season? Jesus, Bree, no wonder you want help. Did any of that crap sound good, or should we start from scratch?"

"I don't think I can go through my writing life being called something weird, so how about we pick two normal names that I like? I don't think the initials should match my name. And we can't really do a play on names like Jules did with her business."

Ellen says, "Why don't we just start jotting things down and see what happens? Let's focus on first names. Is there anything that comes to mind that you like? A favorite girl's name or something? Then we can do the same for the last name, and we can mix and match until we get something you think is a good fit."

"Oh, I love that idea, Ellen. Okay. Everyone start sharing names you think would be good, but they also need to fit me. It's hard because I teach and so many names are ruled out because of a certain student I've had. So, I may veto things you love but it's because I have my reasons."

Hillary starts first, "Amber, Violet, Gloria, Savannah."

Ellen is busy writing all the names down.

Julia adds, "Kendal, Gwen, Maddie, Rachel."

Sam has her turn, "Belle, Victoria, Blair."

I throw in, "Valerie, Marlow, Lyla."

Ellen finishes the list. "Okay, that's a good start. Now, shoot out random last names, then we can cross-check to see if anything works. Hill, you go first again."

Hillary says, " Black, Love, Edwards, Cullen."

Julia laughs and includes, "Grey, Quinn, Richards, Chambers."

Sam says, "Wood, Marrow, Tate. Bree, you're up."

I think for a second and choose, "Taylor, Austin, Ray, Kelly. I think that's all I have. What've we come up with so far?"

Ellen scoots the list to the middle of the table so everyone can see.

First Names	Last Names
Amber	Black
Violet	Love
Gloria	Edwards
Savannah	Cullen
Kendal	Grey
Gwen	Quinn
Maddie	Richards
Rachel	Chambers
Belle	Wood
Victoria	Marrow
Blair	Tate
Valerie	Taylor
Marlow	Austin
Lyla	Ray
Valerie	Kelly

I stare at the list. I immediately cross some off for one reason or another, leaving me with a couple of first and last names.

First Names	Last Names
Kendal	Quinn
Valerie	Richards
Lyla	Tate

I ask my friends, "Do I look like Kendal, Valerie, or Lyla?"

Everyone looks at me. Hillary silently calls me by each name, which is hilarious. Julia stares at me, tilting her head back and forth. Ellen chews her thumb and looks down at the list then back up to me. Sam makes a squishy face and bites her lip, deep in thought.

"Jiminy Crickets, you guys! You're making me nervous!" I whisper-yell to them. "Is this really that hard? Do any of them fit me?"

Ellen finally says, "I like them all. Are you leaning toward one more than the others?"

"No, I like them all. But I'm not sure which one I like best or which first name to mix with which last name."

"I have an idea," Julia says. "Why don't you ask Shannon? You said she's going to help you market your book and author pages. Why don't you see what she thinks since she lives in the marketing world? It would also be good to Google all these name combinations and make sure there isn't another person with the same name, especially another author. That was the best advice Jackson and I got before we officially named Harte of Harmony."

"Oh, smart! You don't want to compete with another author with the same name," Hillary says. "It's important to make sure your brand and name identify with only you. I had to think about that when naming my business. I did a business and Google search on *A Matter of Taste* before naming the catering business too."

"Okay. Thank you for helping me. I feel better having a short list and some ideas. I like them all. I don't want a name that associates only with sex. I want it to be classy. Just because I write steamy love scenes doesn't mean I want to have a hooker name."

We gather our things and I tuck the list into my purse. "Thank you again for meeting with me today so I could get out of the house and just do something normal again. I hated dealing with all the reporters hiding around every corner. As much as I needed Jax and his support I also want to smack him! But don't ever repeat that — I'll deny it!"

As we leave *Harmonious Bites,* Julia reminds us, "Don't forget the BBQ at my house tomorrow." She stops and quietly says to Hillary, "Behave tomorrow. My brother will be there, and I've already warned him too."

Interesting. I guess everyone feels the tension building between those two. We hug goodbye and get in our cars.

***

Noah

Bree is back from coffee with the girls, and we're discussing her list of pen names and the next steps. She's going to call Shannon to get her help with choosing the right name from a marketing perspective.

Bree seems happy and, finally, the worry seems to have lifted. I admire her and the closeness she has with her friends. They are quite an admirable team of women. To cross one is to cross them all. Not to mention, they also have a handful of men that are just as bold and willing to stand up for each one of them.

I sometimes stop and think about how my life has taken such a different turn. A year ago, I was part of a huge medical practice and felt no connection to my patients. I was single, and my friend group consisted of my now-engaged ex-wife and former friend. Weird doesn't even explain where my life was at that stage. Now, after six months in Lake Harmony, I have new friends, and I feel like I've been here all my life. Hunter is so jealous of it that he has even joked about moving to Lake Harmony himself.

"Noah, Shannon just texted that she's home and has time. Do you mind if I work on my pen names with her now, or did you have plans for us?" Bree asks.

"Go ahead and brainstorm. I'm going to relax and check out what's on tv. Franklin and I will chill while you talk on the phone. We don't have any plans for later, so take your time. Do you want to go out to dinner, or do you want to stay in tonight? If it doesn't matter to you, I could go for some Italian food at Bella Roma's."

"Oh yes! That sounds delicious. Let's do that," Bree says. She gives me a kiss, "I'll be back when we're done talking."

"Say hi to my sister for me and take your time. We don't have to rush to get there. We have time before the food runs out."

Bree walks out of the room, and I say to the cat, "Come on, Franklin. Let's see if we can find some sports or

Die Hard on tv. While we watch, you can practice your meows."

As soon as I get the movie started and settle in on the couch, I get a text from Hunter.

Hunter: Any kickback from my letter?
Me: No but heard through the grapevine the district and school board members have a closed-door board meeting Monday night. We're pretty sure they're shaking in their boots. I appreciate you stepping up and helping Bree out.
Hunter: I was happy to put some pressure on them to drop it. You're my brother and Bree is good people. She didn't deserve this bullshit
Me: No, she didn't. Thank you though
Hunter: No Prob. Here to help you, man.
Hunter: Keep me posted with what happens
Me: Will do!

Franklin and I watch tv and take a short nap. A bit later, Bree comes in wearing a smile. "Hey, you look happy. What's up? How'd the chat with Shannon go?"

"I officially have a pen name! Want to hear it?" She's full of excitement as she bounces on her toes in front of me.

"Absolutely. What's it going to be?"

"Shannon and I worked through all the names, chose a combination we both liked, made sure there wasn't another author with that same name, and even Googled the name to see if that combo linked with anyone else. Since it didn't, it's the one we picked. My pen name is going to be Lyla Tate!"

I wrap her in my arms and say, "Lyla Tate sounds sexy as hell and perfect."
"Simple and easy to remember too. Shannon and I spent so much time mixing and matching each name to the other and double-checking to make sure we weren't picking something that was already out there. If it is, it isn't a very popular name right now, so I feel good picking that one."

"Are you happy?" I ask her.

"Yes, I am very happy, Noah. I love you," she says.

"I love you too, honey. Are you hungry? If we get to Bella Roma's at five when the doors open, we can bring our dessert home and eat it in bed tonight."

"Perfect. Let me clean up, then I'm all yours," she says.

"I'll give Franklin his dinner. No rush, though. We still have time. I wish Maria would take reservations, but I know she doesn't have time to answer the phone."

Chapter Twenty-Six

Bree

Noah and I are heading over to Jackson and Julia's for a group BBQ with our friends. I got all next week's lessons done early so I'll be able to relax and enjoy being with my people. We're having ribs and all types of southern sides. I brought jalapeño cornbread with whipped honey butter. Hillary made stuffed poppers, and Ellen and Sam brought their own sides to add to the feast.

We get there, and Garrett is pacing back and forth in the driveway with Cooper and clearly pissed off about something. I wonder what happened and hope everything is okay. I say to Noah, "Oh no, this doesn't look good. We better go see what's going on before we go in."

Noah calls out, "Hey, Coop! I didn't know if you were going to make it over today or not, but I'm glad you did."

Cooper says something to Garrett then comes over to us, "Hey, guys, good to see you. The bar is under control tonight so I'm able to be here. I hired a few more people to help me cover the manager role so I have more time to do other things outside the bar. How's everything going? I hear bits and pieces about the book and school thing at Coop's Corner, but are you okay Bree?"

"I'm better now than when this all started. Everyone has been so supportive the last couple of weeks and that helped get me through it. So, what's up with Garrett? Everything okay with him?" I ask.

Noah chimes in too, "Coop, what's going on man? He looks really upset. Anything I can do?"

"Guys, I don't like to meddle, but Hillary came into the bar last night with another one of her online dates. Garrett was at the bar with Rob. The guy was all over her. To the point that she dumped both her drink AND his drink in his lap, then stormed out and left. I didn't know the guy, but Garrett was pissed. Now, she's here talking about it like it was no big deal. We all know there's something brewing between those two, but neither of them wants to discuss it. I just hope that they don't blow when I'm around."

"Oh lovely," I roll my eyes. "Well, I haven't heard about her date, but let me see if I can help keep the conversation from heading in that direction while they're both here. Come on, we better get inside before they tear each other's heads off."

The girls are in the kitchen putting the food together, and the guys are out on the porch or by the grill. "Hey," I say, "I brought some of my spicy cornbread and honey butter. Where do you want it?"

Julia gives me a hug. "I love that cornbread and dibs on any leftover butter. It's so yummy on my toast in the morning."

"Then it's all yours if there's some left." I pull her aside, "Hey did you know Hill and Garrett are at a boiling point again?"

"Yeah. Garrett stormed out of here earlier, and Coop went after him. It's getting old watching my brother and best friend always ready to kill each other. What the hell is going on between them? No one seems to know what happened to make them like this. One thing I know for sure is they need to figure out a way to work through it because I hate seeing them both hurting each other all the time."

"I know, Jules. It breaks my heart. If they could work through it, I think they, and the rest of us, would be happier. We're always together as a group and them being at odds is no fun for anyone."

She replies, "Agreed."

***

All through dinner, Hillary and Garrett steer clear of each other. Oh well. Better that than them at blows and dragging us all into it. We're sitting around the fire outside on the deck relaxing after cleaning up the leftovers and having a last drink with each other when Sam asks Hillary what she ended up doing last night. Noah squeezes my hand. Garrett's reaction to the question is to clench his jaw tight.

Hillary laughs, "Oh my god Sam. I had a date at Coop's. It was so ridiculous. Why do men lie so badly on their profiles? If they expect to meet in person these exaggerated lies are pretty easy to spot. The guy last night had all the right things to say through messages and texts but come to find out he was just looking for a romp in the sheets because his wife found out he cheated and won't touch him."

"Oh, gross," Sam replies.

"Yeah. So once I learned he was married, a cheating loser, and couldn't keep his hands to himself, I accidentally dumped both our cold drinks in his lap and left. I am so over these losers," Hillary says.

Noah and I watch Garrett's reaction. If you can imagine watching a pot beginning to boil over, you have a pretty good image of what's about to happen.

Garrett jumps out of his seat, and Hillary immediately looks over at him with her eyes squinty and mouth pulled tight, "What's your problem over there?"

He takes a deep breath and says to her, "You, Hillary. You are my problem. One of these days you are going to get yourself into a situation you can't handle by yourself. You need to either stop this online dating or learn how to vet your dates better."

Hillary gets an evil smile on her face, and I think we collectively take a deep breath, afraid to move, "What I do, whom I date, and how I do it is absolutely none of your fucking business, Garrett."

He replies, "One of these losers is going to make it my business! Jules, Jackson, I need to go. Thanks for dinner."

Garrett storms out, and, before we have time to even exhale, Hillary shouts after him. "Screw you, Sheriff! Stay out of my life! What a dick head."

Not one of us replies, but we all know this needs to stop. Sooner rather than later because none of us wants to deal with this every time we get together.

Julia and I share a look.

Chapter Twenty-Seven

Bree

Tuesday morning, Diane is in my classroom as I walk in for the start of my day. "Good morning, Diane. Please tell me you have news for me from the not-so-secret closed board meeting last night."

"I do indeed. Why don't you put your things down and come sit with me," she says, but she's smiling so I am not nervous for the first time since this all began.

"I don't have it in me to beat around the bush. Give it to me. What's happened?"

"Let me start with what has been determined first. The board dropped all actions against you and is allowing you to resume your normal activities, including parent volunteers in the classroom and directing Drama Club. They ask that you discontinue posting negative content about them through Harmony Hears, soliciting Hollywood support, or pursuing legal actions. They acknowledged they have no right at this time to punish you for your unpublished book. They did request, however, if you do publish, that you use a pen name, as suggested in the legal document from your lawyer."

"Wow, really? They are going to totally back off if we stop pushing back too? And I already decided to use a pen name so that's an easy fix. I guess this is finally over?"

"Yes, Bree," she says. "It's over, and you can have your life back. I took the liberty to notify the parents of students involved with Drama Club that you would be resuming director duties next week. I wanted to give you a week to catch your breath and prepare. If you have any other questions, go ahead and ask. You can notify your classroom parents that they may come back in to assist you. Things are back to normal."

201

"This is great news! Thank you for coming in to tell me. I'm going to call Noah before my day starts so I can let him know too. Thank you again, Diane, for having my back. I don't know how I can thank you for all your support."

"Bree, you thank me every day by just being the amazing teacher you naturally are. I hope you have a good day. If you have any other questions, just let me know," she says and leaves my classroom.

I shut the door and call Noah. I should be able to get him before he sees his first patient.

"Hey, honey. Are you okay?" he asks.

"Yes! Noah, the board basically dropped everything! If I don't fight back and if I publish my book under a pen name, this all goes away. I have Drama Club back, and my parents can come back into my classroom. I feel like a hundred pounds have been removed from my back."

"Oh, honey, I'm so happy for you. Now, take a deep breath and have a good day. Let's plan on going out to celebrate tomorrow night."

"I love you, Noah."

"I love you too, baby. Have fun with the munchkins, and I'll see you at home later." We end the call and, being the dork I am, I punch my fist up in the air and yell YES! *So what? Nobody saw me.*

Then, I text the girls. I know they're on pins and needles too.

Me: Not so secret board meeting decided to drop everything. I have drama club back, and parents back in my room. If I just stop any negative comments towards them and use a pen name. Done and Done!!! *Happy Smiley emoji*
Julia: SO SO HAPPY for you
Hillary: Finally they get it right-yay you!
Ellen: So glad you got good news
Sam: Because you did nothing wrong Bree! Proud of you
Julia: What she ^^ said
Ellen: Ditto ^^^

Hillary: ^^^Absofuckinglutely

***

Noah

I'm in my office about to begin my day, and Jackson pops his head around the door. "Hey! I just talked to Jules, and she said Bree is clear. The board dropped all their bullshit, and she is good to go like nothing happened."

"Yeah. As much as I want to get back at them for putting her through all this, I am just glad her job isn't in trouble, she has her Drama Club kids back, and life goes on like it didn't happen. Pisses me off that Melanie was able to get away with a character attack on Bree," I grumble

"Well, I don't think Melanie's getting out of this unscathed. I know she got dumped by the superintendent of schools, and she created her own set of nasty gossip. I think the mean girl got justice, and we didn't have to get our hands dirty. Trust me when I say I was having a tough time sitting back and watching Bree get hurt. I think all the guys were, so if something needed to be fixed, you weren't alone, Noah."

"Thanks, Jackson, that makes me feel better. By the way, I have a new patient coming in this morning. I'm happy to see the practice is still growing, and I haven't scared anyone off yet. You aren't the 'it man' anymore." Jackson laughs, shakes his head, gives me the finger, and walks out of my office.

My first patient of the day is new to the practice, and I better get a move on. The nurse pops in to notify me that he's already in exam room two.

"Good morning," I say as I knock and walk in, "I'm Dr. Roarke. How are you doing today?"

"Hello, I'm Dan Jordan. My wife and I took over the winery from her uncle, and I seem to have hurt my hand over the weekend. I was happy they squeezed me into your schedule."

"Well, let's have a look. I'm going to remove the bandages. What did you do?"

"We were cleaning out the dead vines and trying to get the grounds ready for winter. My wife's uncle had a small crew, but he couldn't keep up with the maintenance. We moved here to take it over for him, and I slipped and got myself with the pruners somehow. I cleaned it out really well and it doesn't look like it needs stitches, but I want to make sure it won't get infected. It's been feeling warm."

"The winery, you say. Which one?"
"Harmony Winery. We're on five acres outside of Lake Harmony. We took it over this summer, and we're still cleaning up certain sections and making new wines. It's been quite the adventure."

As I clean his hand up, I say, "My girlfriend loves your wine. Anyway, you did a great job cleaning this up. Even if you needed stitches, which you don't, it would be too late to do them. I'm going to have the nurse clean it up one more time and put some butterfly bandages on it. I also think we better give you some antibiotics to help fight off any infection that could start. Since you work outside on the land, you have a bigger chance of infection, so better be safe than sorry."

"Thanks, Dr. Roarke, I appreciate it. My wife and I just opened a small tasting room, and I don't want to let her down and not be able to use my hand. We're handling the tasting room ourselves now to see what sort of interest there is before we hire staff."

"Are you open tomorrow?" I ask Dan. "I have a celebration and that would be a fun night."

"Right now, we're usually open only on the weekends, but since you squeezed me in and I have to be there anyway, come on out. Can you come at seven?"

"That would be great. I appreciate it." I shake his hand. "I'll have the nurse come in and give you a prescription for a five-day course of antibiotics to make sure we keep your cut healthy. See you tomorrow."

"Sounds great! I'll make sure my wife, Margo, has a small charcuterie board of cheeses, berries, and olives for you. We have a small selection of wines, so we can do a tasting of all or just a bottle of one."

"I would enjoy trying all your wines if we can. If we find a new favorite, we can buy a bottle to take home with us. See you tomorrow and keep that hand clean."

***

That evening Bree and I are relaxing on the couch when her phone rings. "Oh, Jax is calling me. I asked Gertie to tell him I'm in the clear, so I hope he isn't causing me more trouble." "Better answer and find out why he's calling, honey," I say. "Hey, Jax, what's up?" she says. "Let me ask him. Hold on a second," she says, then looks at me.

"Noah, do we have plans for next weekend? Not the one coming up but the following?"

I answer, "Not that I know of. This weekend we finally have time to move your furniture over so we can clean out your house, but the following weekend we don't have anything on the calendar. Why?"

She smiles really big, "Jax invited us to go to his premiere."

"Okay, that sounds great. I'm in if you are," I tell her.

"Yes, we're in Jax. Are you sure? No, you don't need to do all that. Yes, okay, we accept, but that's too much. I am not responsible for your career, but I am very flattered that you feel that way. Yes, email me the details, and we'll see you then. Thank you. I'm excited too. I've never been to a premiere. Yes, I'll make sure to tell him, although he may not believe me." She starts laughing, "Yes, you may want to send him that note. Okay, see you next week!"

She gets up and does a little dance and is bouncing around the family room. "Bree, as adorable as you are, what in the world is going on?"

"Oh my god, Noah! This has been the best week. Jax just invited us to go as his guests to a movie premiere in HOLLYWOOD! And, Sophie Knight, his costar, asked that I get ready with her in her suite, and you're hanging with him and his guys while you get ready. He wanted me to tell you to send him your measurements so he can have a tux waiting for you. I need to send Sophie mine, and she's picking out a dress for me! Can you believe this? I am so stinking excited!"

"Wait. WHAT? Are you serious? The premiere is in Hollywood. I thought it was like here in the city. Oh man, that's kind of cool. I am fanboying again, aren't I Bree?" *How silly do I feel that I want to get up and dance with her right now*? We start dancing and twirling in the family room together until we both bust out laughing.

Bree wipes tears from her eyes. "We are ridiculous, but I wouldn't want to be ridiculous with anyone else. Oh, my goodness, Noah — we're going to be among Hollywood stars! This is absolutely crazy, but I am so excited."

I'm smiling just as big. "I wonder who the heck he refers to when he says I will be hanging with him and his guys? I'm going to make an ass out of myself aren't I honey?"

"Not any more than I am. Let's just smile, be excited, and enjoy ourselves. I haven't even told you he's flying us out on a private jet and putting us up at the Chateau Marmont for the weekend so we can enjoy ourselves."

I give her a kiss. "This is not my life. It is so strange, but I am excited too. I may not sleep at all tonight."

"I don't think I will either," she says, as she grabs my hand and starts pulling me toward the bedroom. "Come on, I need some help with all this excitement."

"Lead the way, sweetheart, I am here for whatever you need."

Chapter Twenty-Eight

Bree

Noah has promised a celebratory night out for the two of us. I'm wearing a beautiful new dress I bought for a special occasion. When I went shopping with the girls, I saw this pretty dress in the window of the boutique. It's made with a flowing skirt in a soft, silky fabric that swirls around my legs with a form-fitted bodice and heart-shaped neckline. The color is gorgeous turquoise with an ombre effect. When I twirl it almost appears like moving water is swishing around my body. It is divine and sexy, and I feel powerful wearing it. Not to mention the garter set I have on underneath. That will be my surprise to Noah for supporting me through the last couple of months. He is truly an amazing man, and I am so lucky he is mine.

I walk into the family room where Noah is and take a moment to look at my gorgeous man. *Yummy*! He's wearing dark charcoal slacks and a grey dress shirt with the cuffs rolled up. He is a beautiful man and has the kindest heart I have ever encountered. He hasn't realized I am standing here yet, "You look very handsome tonight."

He spins around to face me and looks me up and down. "You take my breath away," he says to me before he pulls me into his arms. "My god, how did I ever survive without you in my life? When I look at you it's like you fill this void in my heart that nothing could touch before. You, sweetheart, make me a whole man, a better man than I ever thought I could be."

I am fighting my tears. I could go all sappy on him, but it's time to head out and celebrate. "That was awfully romantic, honey. You make me a better person too. You stand by my side and fight with me and show me how to be strong. I love you."

"Love you too. Are you ready to go celebrate?"

"Absolutely, what's the plan?"

He smiles at me and winks, "I'd rather it be a surprise. Let's go!" He pulls me along to the garage and we get in the car.

We drive away from the house, make our way through town, and go past Cooper's Corner. We're clearly leaving Harmony Shores, and I have no idea where we're heading. Maybe we're going the long way around the lake up to the Golf Club for a special dinner? No, he just went west. Now I really have no idea where we're going. We are in the countryside, and I don't think there's anything out this way.

"Noah, do you know where you're going? I'm not sure if there are any restaurants in this direction unless we're heading into the next town?"

"We're going the right way. I promise. Just a few more minutes. Trust me," he says with a smirk.

We're approaching a farm, and I see a small sign up ahead. "Oh my god! Is this the winery? Why are we going to the winery at night? Isn't this a working vineyard, which means they're probably closed now?" *What in the world does he have planned*? I didn't think there was anything here to do at night.

Noah grabs my hand, "I met the new owner this week, and he told me they're starting a tasting room on the weekends. He wanted us to come out tonight to celebrate your victory."

"Oh, my goodness. Are you serious? I didn't realize they were doing a tasting room. This is awesome!"

We drive down the winery entrance toward the building with the tasting room sign. We go slow and admire the rows of vines and the pretty white farmhouse.

"I wonder if they live here on the property. That would be like living in a Hallmark movie, wouldn't it?"

"Dan didn't say anything about that, just that he and his wife, Margo, had taken over the winery from an uncle." He slows the car to a stop. "Looks like we're here."

We park in front of a cute outer building that's painted white with black trim and has large windows with an overhanging patio. There's a big wine barrel next to the door with lush greens planted in it and a beautiful hand-painted sign: Welcome to Harmony Winery. "This is so charming," I say to Noah. "Thank you for bringing me here tonight."

"It seemed like the perfect celebration, and I love knowing that it's something new for the both of us. Ready to go in?"

"YES! Let's go celebrate."

I'm probably bouncing more than walking because I love this! Noah pushes open the door to the cute tasting room. There's a beautiful wood bar along one side, and the room has small sitting areas with couches and chairs in rich gem colors and dark wooden tables. The artwork seems to be done by local artists. The large, west-facing windows provide a sunset view. Soft, romantic music is playing on hidden speakers at a low level. We just stand there and admire the beautiful setting.

"Oh Noah, this is absolutely beautiful and very romantic. They have a goldmine with what they've done here. I can't wait to bring the girls!"

The owners come in from the back. Both are wearing big smiles. "Welcome to Harmony Winery."

Noah grabs my hand, "Dan thank you so much for opening for us tonight for our special celebration. And since we pulled up, I don't think Bree has stopped radiating her excitement. This is quite a great space you've made here."

We introduce ourselves, and Dan and Margo tell us a little bit about taking over the winery from her uncle and how they want to bring life back into the place. They sell their wines well locally, but they want to try to tap into a larger market.

Margo says, "Bree, it is such a pleasure to meet you. Dan talked about Noah when he came home from his doctor's appointment, but I didn't realize that the two of you were a couple. I should probably admit that I feel like I know you through Harmony Hears. I am so sorry for everything you had to go through."

"Oh, Margo, thank you. It was pretty awful, but the board had a meeting Monday and determined that they jumped before thinking. I have my life back. That's why we're celebrating tonight. Thank you again for opening. Noah said you usually only open on the weekends. What a special treat for us tonight. I love your red wine, so I'm excited to try whatever else you have."

"Perfect, why don't you both have a seat, and I will bring the wines out in order for you to try with a cheese board," Margo says as she gestures around the room.

"After you, sweetheart," Noah says.

I look around and decide to take the area by the window, so we can watch the sunset. "This is awfully romantic."

"I wanted you to feel special. I think this place is perfect. Don't you?"

"It is. I love it. I'm going to tell Gertie to bring the Widow Crew here too! That'll give them a lot of free advertising because you know she'll post about it in Harmony Hears."

"Oh see, Gertie IS a benefit. I knew I liked her the minute I met her," Noah says rather smugly.

"Oh, okay, Dr. McHunky," I say with a giggle.

Margo and Dan put four glasses in front of each of us on a wooden tray with the names of wines written underneath them.

Margo says, "These are the four main wines we always have here at the winery. We have a chardonnay, named 'Drink Wine, Feel Fine.' It is an unoaked wine with layers of peach, pear, and floral aromatics of honeysuckle blossoms. Our cabernet, 'Age Gets Better with Wine,' has notes of cocoa, red currant, hints of cracked white pepper, and baking spices. Then we have our two table wines. The red is 'I'll Clink to That,' and it has deep flavors of black cherry, blackberry, strawberry, cedar, and orange zest. The white table wine, named 'Time to Wine Down,' has citrus blossom, pear, peach, and apple. The names are under the glass and here is a paper with the descriptions that I just shared with you. Please enjoy yourselves. Dan and I will be here all night working on things so there is no rush. I'll be right back out with some artisan cheeses, berries, crackers, and olives. If there's something you don't like, please don't feel you need to finish it. If you want a glass of something, I'm happy to bring you one. Enjoy."

Margo and Dan leave us and walk into the back room. "These look amazing," I say. "I love their cab, but now I'm excited to try all of them. The names of the wines are so fun! I always smile when I buy a bottle of the Age Gets Better with Wine Cabernet."

"I think between the vibe of the tasting room, their wine names, and the setting, they will be quite successful," Noah says. He picks up the first wine, I do the same, and we clink glasses, "To good things to come!"

We sip, nibble on the charcuterie, and talk about each wine. The cabernet is still our favorite wine of the four, but they all taste delicious.

Noah leans forward and gives me a sweet kiss, "Would you like anything else? A glass of one of the wines? I'm going to go find Dan or Margo and let them know."

"Why don't you surprise me, I do love their cab."

"Be right back," he says.

I start to snap some pictures with my phone so I can send them to the girls.

Girls: OMG you guys. Noah surprised me with a date at the winery. They have the cutest tasting room!! *image* *image* *image*

Hillary: I heard they were going to open that but wasn't sure it was already opened.

Julia: Oh, the pictures you sent are lovely! When are we going just girls?

Ellen: What are their hours?

Me: Weekends only but they opened privately for us tonight to celebrate

Sam: It looks so romantic *heart emoji*

Me: It is SOOO romantic. Someone is getting lucky tonight as a big thank you

Hillary: You go girl! Get you some sexy times *wink emoji*

Noah heads back toward me. "They will be right out. They have something they want us to try."

"Oh great. Did they say what it is?"

"No, just something they're hoping to offer as a new selection," he says.

Just as soon as Noah is seated, Margo and Dan walk out with two glasses in their hands. Margo smiles and puts them in front of us, "This is something new we're working on. Dan and I have always been beekeepers and now with the winery, we decided to try our hand at making mead. Have either of you ever tried mead before?"

"I haven't but it always reminds me of the Vikings."
"Exactly," Margo answers. "Ours is a honey mead named 'Is It Mead You're Looking For' and has an earthy spice with honey with cinnamon and vanilla sweetness."
I start laughing, "Oh my goodness, Margo! That's my favorite name of all of them for sure! Although, I feel like I would have to sing it each time I read the label. I for sure need a bottle of that to go so I can share it with the girls at book club. They will all crack up! You are so clever with your names. It makes your marketing so easy!"

"We hope so," she answers. "Although we haven't even started to think about marketing the new wines or moving into a bigger market."

"My sister is in marketing and would probably be happy to help you. She's been a huge help to Bree with marketing her book and author branding. I can give her your business card and ask her to touch base with you if you'd like."

Margo asks Dan, "What do you think? It would be nice to get an idea of how to move forward and grow the business. That is not in my wheelhouse, or yours, honey, so I would really like to talk to her."

Dan nods, "I think we better get whatever help we can. I'm too busy trying to keep the vines healthy."

"Great. Before we head out, make sure I have your contact information, and I'll pass it to Shannon," Noah says.

"Thank you, Noah. The other glass I put down in front of you is our sparkling wine, 'Drink Happy Thoughts,' which has a pineapple, peach, pear, and lemon finish. Since you're celebrating, we thought you should start with the mead, and you can take the sparkling wine and walk through the vines as the sun sets. Go. Enjoy yourselves. Just bring the empty glass back in with you. If you need anything else, let us know."

"Thank you so much. Both of you," Noah tells them.

"Yes, thank you both. It has been a lovely evening here, and we'll be back for sure."

We enjoy the little sample of mead, then Noah says, "Come on. Let's walk down into the vines and watch the sunset."

"Okay. It is a beautiful evening, and I know you'll keep me warm."

We walk hand-in-hand into the vines and away from the tasting room. "This is so beautiful and peaceful. Don't you think?"

Noah stops walking and turns me so I'm looking up at him. "It is very beautiful, but not as beautiful as you, Bree. I have never loved someone as deeply as I love you. I am so happy that your work seems to be back on track, and you don't have to worry about the chaos that the district caused. You deserve to have nothing but the best in life."

"Noah, I have you, and that is all I need. I'm surrounded by people that love and support me when I don't even think I need it. Thank you for loving me as big as you do."

"It's so easy to love you, sweetheart. As a matter of fact, I would like to love you for the rest of my life. I want you to be my wife, the mother of our children, and grow old with me laughing with all our friends. Marry me, Bree. Make my heart whole forever."

Of course, I'm crying because that's what I do. He gently wipes the tears as they fall. "I would love to marry you and grow old together. Yes, YES!" I throw my arms around him, our glasses falling to the ground.

He reaches into his pocket and pulls out a beautiful engagement ring, "I wanted to get you something special and since you spoke about Princess Diana being someone you would have loved to meet, I went with that idea."

He slips the ring on my finger. It is like the beautiful sapphire ring with diamonds Princess Diana wore, but mine is a diamond with sapphires surrounding the center stone.

"Noah! This is gorgeous. Oh, jiminy cricket, look how it sparkles even in the low light." I look up with more tears blurring my vision. "I am NEVER taking this off."

*****

Later that evening…Noah and I send out a group text.

Me: *image* I said YES!
Noah: *gif of a fist in the air* She said yes!
Jackson: Congratulations to both of you
Julia: SO SO HAPPY 4 U
Hillary: Woot Woot *heart eye emoji*
Sam: Paul and I are so happy for both of you
Ellen: Scott and I are too! Yay-a wedding!!!
Julia: I know the perfect place to have your wedding *wink emoji*
Cooper: Congrats guys-come in for a drink to celebrate
Garrett: Great news!!
Rob: Aw sweet Bree is off the market *sad emoji* U R a lucky son of a bitch Noah!
Noah: Yes, I am! *smiley emoji*
Me: we will have everyone over to celebrate soon. Thank you for all the love. We are very happy *heart emoji*

Chapter Twenty-Nine

Bree

Noah and I arrive in Los Angeles for the movie premiere and are whisked away in a limo to the Chateau Marmont. We are so excited and t and are looking forward to the movie tomorrow night. The brief overview that Jax shared with us so far has us both starting with preparations early in the morning and then getting together again just before we leave for the premiere at the Chinese Theatre.

We pull up to the hotel and are greeted by the valet. He speaks to the driver, and they gather our bags, "Your bags will be brought to your room. You can go ahead and check in at the desk. Enjoy your stay at Chateau Marmont."

"Thank you, we are looking forward to it," Noah says.

Once inside, we both stop and stare at our surroundings. "Wow! This is amazing. I didn't expect this. So much character. I guess I was expecting the typical hotel lobby, but instead, it feels like we walked into a chateau in France."

The décor is distressed, with faded oriental rugs, velvet couches, brass candelabras, and beveled mirrors that provide a decadent atmosphere. We both just stand there, looking around, wondering how in the world we ended up here. Noah squeezes my hand, and we head to the front desk to get our room key.

The surprises continue as we walk into our suite. Again, it's more than we expected, and, upon our arrival, we were informed that Jax instructed the hotel staff to treat us as his personal guests.

"Holy Smokes! This is too much. Jax didn't have to go all out like this." The room screams old-style Hollywood and is beautiful. The bathroom and kitchen area have all the old fixtures, the carpets are thick, and the furniture is beautiful.

"Honey, come here," Noah holds his arms out to me. "Jax wanted to make sure this is a special weekend for us.

We're going to enjoy ourselves and make sure to thank him. Let's just continue our celebration of your life being back to normal, our engagement, and Jax's new movie."

"When we checked in, they said Jax made reservations for dinner with us at the restaurant on the patio. I feel like I'm dreaming. Did you see who was sitting in the lounge area when we walked in?"

"I was trying not to geek out and fanboy, but was that Jeff Goldblum sitting with that group?"

I laugh, "Oh my goodness, I think it was. This is so bizarre, but I think we better get used to all this. And fast. Because we're going to be surrounded by it tomorrow for sure."

There's a knock on the door and Noah goes to answer it. I'm guessing it's our luggage, so I walk around the main sitting room. I find a small tray with fruit and a handwritten note.

Dear Bree and Noah,
It is such a pleasure to welcome you to the Chateau. I hope you have a lovely stay. As personal guests of Jax Turner, please reach out to us for anything you may need. Enjoy your stay!

"Hey, what's that?" Noah asks, pointing to the note in my hand.

"It's a welcome note with some fresh fruit for us."

"Nice. Let's take a look at the envelope that they gave us when we got our suite key," Noah says. "It looks like a note from Jax."

Welcome to LA you two! I can't wait to see you for dinner at the restaurant here on the patio. Food is delicious and you never know who you may see. It's also a place I can eat and not get harassed. I don't want to hear that this is "too much" either. You both deserve some fun and happiness after the last few months and that is exactly why I asked you out here — to have a fun weekend. Premieres are typically a lot of work for actors that star in the film, so I am unfortunately busy with interviews and photo shoots until dinner. I made reservations for us at eight so that gives you plenty of time to go out and enjoy the day. I left you two tickets for the Hop on-Hop off tour bus. Mom said it would be the best way to get the most out of a one-day tour experience. The concierge can get you to the starting point. Have fun. Tomorrow's schedule is attached, and you will both have cars waiting in the morning to take you to different destinations. Remember — Have fun! Jax

SATURDAY/PREMIERE
NOAH-
CAR PICK-UP AT 9 AM-TO JAX'S HOUSE
HANG WITH THE GUYS, HAVE LUNCH, AND GET READY HERE
TUX HERE FOR YOU

BREE-
CAR PICK-UP AT 9 AM GOING TO SOPHIE'S
YOU DO NOT NEED TO TAKE ANYTHING
SHE HAS A DRESS, SHOES, HANDBAG, MAKE-UP/HAIR STYLISTS
CAR TO MY PLACE AT 3 PM

ALL OF US-
5 PM- HEAD TO PREMIERE AND AFTER PARTY

After reading the note and seeing tomorrow's schedule, we at least have an idea of what's in store for us. "I say we hit the road, mister. Our flight got us in early enough that we have the day to enjoy ourselves. Let's go get our Hollywood fan geek on! We can grab lunch somewhere along the route. Sound good?"

"Yep, let's go. We have at least six hours to go run around the tour. I love doing these in new cities I visit. It's the best way to get the most out of a short trip," Noah says. "Let's head out."

We grab our things and head back downstairs. "Keep your eyes open. You never know who may be in the lobby area now!"

We both laugh. Noah asks the concierge, "Can you point us in the direction of catching the Hop on-Hop Off tour?"

"I can ask a driver to take you to the starting point, so you get the full tour. Head out to the valet, he'll call the driver. On your way back just take it to our stop, and you can walk back. Enjoy your day."

Within five minutes, a hotel car is taking us to the tour starting point. I could get used to this first-class treatment. Well, maybe not. But its fun feeling special for a day.

Since we only have one day, we decide to do the Hollywood tour with sixteen stops that include the Hollywood Walk of Fame, Rodeo Drive, Sunset Strip, LA's Farmers Market, LA Brea Tar Pits, and some famous shopping areas. The tour operator said if she sees anyone famous, she'll make sure to point them out.

As we go to the different stops along the tour, she shares stories of all the sites and films that have been made in certain areas. So far, our favorite stop is the Hollywood Walk of Fame. To see so many famous names and to think about their accomplishments is awesome.

It's been a long day, and we tire out quickly. I'm leaning my head against Noah when he says, "We're almost back to the hotel. Why don't we catch a quick nap before we clean up and meet Jax for dinner?"

I can barely hold my head up, "That sounds amazing. I don't know why I'm so tired, but I can't keep my eyes open."

"Honey, we have been on the go all day. If it makes you feel any better, I'm completely wiped out too."

We get off at the tour's last stop and slowly make our way back to our room so we can collapse. Neither of us notices anyone sitting in the lobby this time because we are both dead on our feet.

Once we're back in our room, we tear off our clothes. I ask, "Should we set an alarm or ask for a call from downstairs, so we don't oversleep?"

"That's probably a good idea," Noah agrees. "Jax isn't coming until eight. What time should I tell them to call up?"

"I'd like to shower and freshen up. How about six?"

"Sounds good, I'll make the call. Why don't you crawl into bed? I'll be there in two minutes," he says.

Before Noah makes it to bed, I'm already under the covers, barely keeping my eyes open. With my eyes closed, I feel him slide in beside me.

"Come here, honey, let's rest for a little while," he says before kissing my temple. "Love you."

"Love you too."

***

A quick one-hour nap and shower make all the difference, and we both feel refreshed and ready for dinner.
"I don't know about you, but I am starving. I hope we get to eat right away," Noah says.

"Me too. I'm completely famished, and I'm so excited to see Jax. I haven't seen him in person for at least a year or two. He doesn't always make it home, and when he does, he sticks close to his house on the lake. The last time I saw we were on Rob's boat and he was out on the lake. We ended up tying up together and catching up with him. He'd just finished a movie with an actress who was hard to film with. He came home to try to unwind because she was such a diva. Are you nervous to meet him, Noah?"

"No, I'm excited. After talking to him and getting to know him a little, I don't think I'll embarrass myself tonight. Oh god, is he coming alone or is he bringing someone that I may fanboy all over?" Noah stops and looks at me.

"You'll be fine. No matter whom we meet this weekend, they're all normal people and not the characters they play. Just do me a favor too, okay?"

"What's that, honey?"

"Don't let me make a scene or embarrass you, either."

We both laugh. "Oh my god, we are both ridiculous. But I can't wait. Let them be warned that we may both lose our shit."

Walking hand-and-hand out of the elevator we hear our names and Jax is walking over to us with a big smile across his face. "Am I happy to have you both here!" He shakes Noah's hand and pulls me in for a hug. "It's so good to see you both. Did you have a fun day?"

"Jax, thank you so much for flying Noah and me out here. It's been so much fun already. We did the tour today and saw so many cool things. We're both a little giddy and nervous about tomorrow, but we're looking forward to it. How are you?"

"Starving! I hope you guys are hungry," Jax says.

"Yes, we're starving too."

We are seated on the patio in a semi-private area of the restaurant. Those who are already here dining, watch us walk by with their mouths open. I get it – movie star in the building. As we walk to our table, I also see some rather famous actors and musicians enjoying a meal. Jax just nods at those he must know. At least, he can enjoy himself and not be harassed by fans here. At least, I hope.

Jax waits for us to sit then takes a seat and stretches back, "I hope you like your room. I wanted to make sure you got the most out of Hollywood while you're here. Honestly, I just wanted to show my appreciation, Bree. There's no room this weekend to tell me I did too much, or I don't owe you anything. I do. So many times, when I was building my career, I thought about techniques you taught us, or how to approach things with tricks of the trade. You may not think those things made an impact on me, but they did." He leans toward the both of us and whispers, "Can I share a little secret with you?"

"Of course. I have your back. What is it?"

"Any time I have a crying scene, I still use the technique you taught me in high school. I think about my

220

favorite dog from childhood that died, or a family member and how much I miss them. Does it every time."

"I really appreciate that, Jax," I say. Then continue, "Noah and I had a talk on our way down from our suite earlier. We decided we're going to accept your generosity and enjoy this weekend with you as a continuation of our celebration. Anyway, I still think you give me too much credit for your success but thank you. See...I accept the acknowledgment and I thanked you."

Jax and Noah just laugh, "I am glad you accept it because it's true. Like you say, Bree, 'you gave me the tools for my toolbox.'" Jax sits back and winks. "No arguing, I will win."

"And THERE, is the student I remember. Stubborn Jax!"

Jax laughs. "I know you are celebrating the mess with the district being done but anything else?"

I smile and bring my hand up to show Jax, "Noah asked me to marry him last week, and I said yes."

Jax beams his famous smile, dimple, and all, "Well, now we really need to celebrate. Let's have some champagne with our appetizers. I'm so happy for you both!"

The server comes over, and we order appetizers and our dinner, and Jax orders champagne.
We talk about the new movie and what tomorrow will look like. Noah and I are excited and Jax still hasn't spilled the beans on who his buddies are.

"I appreciate Sophie going through all the trouble of me getting ready with her," I tell Jax.

"Bree, Soph is cool. This is our second film together, but her first as the lead opposite me in a rom-com. She's from a small town in Iowa, so we have a lot in common coming from small Midwest towns. She has become one of my best friends out here in LA."

"Oh, that's nice. Are you dating?" I ask.

"No, Soph's more like a sister, nothing romantic. We thought about it and both of us busted out laughing because she said it would be *gross* to kiss me."

"Oh my goodness, that is funny. I don't know much about her, but I trust your judgment. I know how hard you work to stay grounded here in Hollywood. I'm looking forward to getting to know her. I know she was very supportive of me and #TEAMBREE."

"Yeah, about that, Bree." Jax leaned in a little closer, "I want to warn you that once people make a connection, it might bring that nonsense up again, and there may be some more tabloid fodder about everything. I talked to my agent and PR team today when we were doing some prep work for the premiere. They're going to handle it since you're here to support me. I hope that's, okay. I know you're trying to stay out of the news now as part of your deal with the district."

I nod. "It's fine. As long as I have Noah here with me," I give his hand a squeeze, "I'll be okay."

Noah gives me a quick kiss, then takes a sip of his drink and asks, "Jax, while Bree is getting pampered with Sophie, what are we doing all day?"

"You and I have a little more play time because we just need to throw on a tux. Some of my buddies are coming over, and I figured we'd relax by the pool or whatever."

"Sounds good to me. Are they also from the movie-making industry?" Noah asks.

"Nah, my buddies are in a band. Have you heard of Brick Row?"
Noah's eyes bug out and he nearly chokes on his drink, "The rock band?"

"Yeah, Devin, the lead singer, and Josh, Mattie, and Jeff are my buddies. I've known them since I came to LA. We've kind of figured out Hollywood and becoming famous together."

Noah looks over at me nervously, "Bree, I am going to make an ass out of myself. I apologize to you now."
Both Jax and I start laughing, and Jax says, "Nah, they're cool. Sometimes when they come by, we have a jam session. Sound good?"

"Yep, cool sounds good. Jax, you know this is kinda weird for me, but I will try to relax and enjoy myself. This is completely weird, and I'm waiting to wake up from a bizarre dream."

After dinner, we head our separate ways until morning. Jax refused to let us pay for dinner, giving me the evil eye for even asking.

"I don't know how we're going to get any sleep tonight," I say. "Tomorrow is going to be surreal. I'm so excited to be part of this special night with Jax, but it feels like I am not here."

"I know, honey. I'll be hanging out with one of my favorite rock bands. How in the world am I supposed to just chill? Should be quite interesting for both of us. You better share all your details with me, and I'll share mine. We'll have a lot to talk about on the flight home."

"That we will, honey, and when we get home, you know the gang is going to be beating down our door for all the details."

"Do you think we can hold them off until Tuesday Trivia at Coop's?"

"We can try, Noah. We can try, but I doubt it."

Chapter Thirty

Bree

We both wake up at seven and order a light breakfast. We're enjoying our coffee, chocolate croissants, and fresh fruit, and we are running on nerves in anticipation of the day ahead.

"Jax said to just shower and head out without doing my hair or makeup. Whatever we wear there will be brought back to our rooms. I guess the only thing I want to have on me is my phone. There is no way that I am going anywhere without being able to text you all day," I say.

"Honey, I have to have my phone. I know I promised I wouldn't fanboy, but I'm not dumb enough not to ask the band for a picture. I need something as proof this is happening. Jax will be okay with that, right? He won't care if I have a few minutes of geeking out on them?" Noah asks while bouncing in his chair.

"I feel the same. No one would believe in a million years that I'm spending the day getting ready with the famous Sophie Knight! I am so excited. I know she must be down to earth if Jax is so fond of her. He's always said he tries to surround himself with non-divas in Hollywood. I'm looking forward to the day even though I have no clue what to even expect. All I can envision is what you see in the magazines or on Entertainment Tonight."

We finish our breakfast, get dressed, go down to the main lobby area, and check in with the concierge who lets us know the valet will come to get us when our car has arrived.

While we wait, we drink another cup of coffee and watch a few Hollywood A-listers walk in and out of the door. We say nothing to each other, instead just have a silent conversation with our eyes, telling each other we can handle this, and we aren't totally gawking at the famous actors and musicians we just saw who casually walked by. Noah is the first to get picked up and is hesitant to leave me sitting here alone. As I sip my coffee, another person walks by and takes a seat across from me. I try to not stare, but this person looks familiar to me, but I can't place him. A few more people come in and call out for him. Of course! He was the lead singer of a very popular band. *Man, this is so bizarre!*

My car arrives and takes me to Sophie Knight's home. She lives in a gated mansion up in the hills. We pull up to the front, and she comes out waving, wearing shorts and a t-shirt with flip-flops. *Jiminy crickets, this is so surreal!*

I take a deep breath and the driver opens my door. Before I am completely out, Sophie is pulling me in for a hug. "Bree, I'm so happy you're here and that we have the day to get ready together. I know we haven't met before, but from everything Jax has shared about you, I feel like I know you already. Are you having a fun weekend so far? What did you guys do yesterday? Jax was trying to think of something fun for you. Oh my gosh, I will stop talking and let you answer. Come on in, we have about thirty minutes before hair and makeup arrive to start putting us together."

What the hell-o is happening right now? Is she excited to meet me? I am in Oz right now. Where are the munchkins? Will I see flying monkeys next? Instead of freaking out, I just smile, "Thank you so much for today. It's lovely to be here with you Sophie. When we got in yesterday, Jax had left us tickets for the hop-on-hop-off bus. It was so much fun. We only did the Hollywood tour, then went back to take a nap before we met Jax for a late dinner."

"Oh, I loved doing those when I visited a new city. One of my favorite places for that was in New Orleans. Make sure if you haven't gone there, you do their hop-on-hop-off bus tour. It takes you all over. My mom and I used to do those, and we'd do the whole tour first and figure out where we'd want to get off and tour on the second round. Savannah is another city for that type of tour."

"Oh, thank you for the recommendations. I haven't been to either place but would love to. I'll mention it to Noah for future long weekends away."

Sophie loops her arm through mine and pulls me through the house. We head into the back of her home

226

towards the terrace and pool. "We can wait out here until the stylists arrive. I have some dresses and shoes inside you can choose from. The designers know you're also picking a dress for the premiere and that we're the same size, so they sent extra."

"Thank you so much, I feel like I'm dreaming. This has been such an interesting and crazy weekend so far."

"Bree, trust me when I say sometimes, I feel the same. Sometimes I look in the mirror and ask myself if I'm dreaming. Living in Hollywood's bubble can make it hard to stay normal. When you have people giving you clothes and jewelry so you can be seen wearing them is fun, but when you have to go out to a simple dinner in secret or have security keep you safe, it's a bummer. I know, I'm famous, and I have the recognition and opportunities others don't, but sometimes I still want to throw on my sweatpants, put my hair in a messy bun, and not worry about who may see me. You know?"

"I'm sure it's hard not having privacy. I can't imagine not being able to just run out to grab a coffee with my best friends on a Saturday morning. Dealing with the reporters after Jax's social media post supporting me was intimidating and felt like an intrusion in my life. Sophie, I do want to thank you for all your support through that crazy stuff with the school district. You didn't know me, but you put yourself out there and supported me. That was nice. I appreciate it a lot."

"Bree, if I can use my status to support someone who's trying to pursue their own dream but being harassed because someone else is jealous, then it's what I need and want to do, not what someone tells me to do. Does that make sense? Jax was so upset they were trying to hurt you and destroy your reputation in the community. Once he made sure with you that he could voice his support, I wanted to support him and you. He's my family out here. That's just what you do."

Someone from Sophie's staff comes out to the terrace and lets us know the stylists are here and in the master suite waiting for us. Sophie stands up, loops her arm through mine again, and says, "You ready for some Hollywood-style pampering?"

"Probably not, but let's go get pampered." We walk into the house laughing.

***

Noah

The car pulls up to a huge mansion and the driver gets out and comes around to open my door. "Mr. Turner said to go ahead and go inside. He's expecting you." I exit the town car I, look around, and at least four other expensive vehicles are in the driveway.

"Oh, thank you." I head towards the door. I can't just walk in, so I knock first, then open the door, "Hello, Jax?" No answer so I start walking through the house toward where I hear talking and laughing. Holy shit! Jax is in jeans and a t-shirt lounging in a big family room with two huge leather sectionals. *Oh, my fucking god.* Devin, the lead singer of Brick Row, and three of his band members are sitting around the room shooting the shit with Jax.

"Hey man, I'm so glad you get to hang with us today. I hope Bree got off to Soph's okay." Jax stands up and puts his hand on my shoulder, "Noah, I'd like you to meet some of my good buddies. This is Devin, Josh, Mattie, and Jeff. Guys this is Noah, Bree's fiancé, and my friend from home." *His friend from home!* They all greet me, and Jax grabs me a drink. We sit around and just converse with each other like normal people. One of the guys is talking about his wife, and another is talking about how he's so tired of being harassed by the paparazzi every time he goes outside his house. Another guy is talking about his kids and how they all had the flu and one of the kids puked all over his bed in the middle of the night. Huh, these guys are cool, and it really isn't much different from sitting around at home shooting the shit with my friends.

228

I'm relaxed and enjoying myself. I say to the flu dad, "Next time your family is down with the flu, make sure you have some popsicles. The trick with the little ones is to freeze Gatorade or Pedialyte so when they're sick, they still get the electrolytes they need."

Mattie, the drummer of the band says, "Oh man, that's a great idea. Trying to get them to drink when they have tummy issues is brutal. Thinking they're getting a popsicle might do the trick. Do you have any other doctor tricks you can share? Jax, man, make sure you have Noah's number. We may need to text him next time. That'd be okay, right? I don't want to harass you more than your normal patients."

"That's fine. I'm always happy to help a frazzled parent when their kids are sick. I'll make sure you have my number. I can't imagine how I'll feel when my own kids get sick."

Jax smiles, "Noah and Bree just got engaged last week. They came out to celebrate, and I'm taking them to the premiere tonight. Bree is with Soph getting ready."

Devin says, "Cool. Sophie is good people. Jax said Bree has been through the wringer lately with her job and her book. Who knew writing a romance novel could become such a crazy crisis? I was happy to support her."

"Oh, did you post something on social media too? I know Bree was so floored that Jax and others were supporting her."

Devin looks at me, "Team Bree all the way, Noah. My background is a bit like Jax's. Small town kid, and an awesome music teacher that told me to reach for the stars. I was a geeky choir boy in high school, but I enjoyed being on stage and singing my little dorky heart out. My music teacher hooked me up with someone and that helped me get my start. Sometimes it's the people back at home that get you to where you are before you land in the spotlight. They're the real people in your life, not the shiny new ones that tag along for the ride."

It's about lunchtime, and Jax has a big spread brought in. Bree texts me throughout the day about how she's doing and how nice Sophie is. I tell her I'm enjoying myself too and not acting star-struck. It's easy to forget these are just normal guys and that it's their job as singers or actors to provide entertainment. In their downtime, they're just as regular as anyone.

Late afternoon comes around, and the band members all slowly get up and head out. They know Jax and I need to get ready for the premiere before Bree heads back over. It was so cool hanging with them, and I can't even believe this is happening to me.

"Hey Jax, I wanted to let you know that Bree and I are really flattered that you've gone through all this trouble for us. For supporting her and helping her keep her job, bringing us out here this weekend, and sharing the premiere with you. Obviously, it's not in our regular routine, but it's been cool as hell. I loved meeting the guys and please make sure if they ever need my doctor's advice, have them call. I know they all have their own doctor, but if they want a second opinion or whatever, I'm happy to help. This whole experience has been great. I'm so glad I got to meet you. When you come home to Lake Harmony, please stop by, or let's have a drink. I can't imagine there are too many places you can go where you can't just sit and relax and put the Hollywood hat away."

"Thanks, Noah. That means a lot. I'm glad Bree has you. She deserves the best, and that's what this weekend is all about. I wanted her to see the value she offers her students and to know that what she does for us means a lot! You don't have to thank me, though. Honestly, I'm getting a kick out of having you guys here. It's like you brought me a little piece of home. Now, are you ready to go put our monkey suits on?"

"Yep, lead the way."

Jax heads towards the master suite, "I hope it's okay with you, but I got us both Armani to wear."

"Sure, no problem. I wear an Armani tux all the time." We laugh at the same time.

Bree

Jax, Noah, and I are all in the back of a limo. Jax wants to make sure we get out first, before the explosion of lights from the cameras. Once the press and reporters figure out who's in the limo, things get a little crazy.

Jax says with a laugh and a wink, "Remember, have fun. This could get crazy. If it's too much on the red carpet, just stand back. If you're okay sticking with me, that's fine too. This is your night, so only handle what you can."

Noah squeezes my hand, and we pull to a stop outside the theater. There is a red carpet and the press on each side. There are so many people standing across the way, and I think I even see bleachers full of people. "Oh my gosh, Jax, is this how each premiere is for you?"
"Pretty much," he says. "Depends on the film, the location, and how much press I do. This one is the big guns because it's a rom-com with me and Soph. They think we are the next big romantic love story. Sorry to disappoint them that neither of us feels that way. Okay, you two, ready?"

The door opens and Noah steps out, grabs my hand, and I follow him. Before we get two steps away, Jax gets out of the car, and the crowd and lights go crazy. Noah and I slowly move a few feet away so our eyes aren't blinded by all the lights and Jax can have his moment. Before a minute goes by, he's looking around for us. He lifts a brow, silently asking me if I'm okay. I nod, and he smiles. Noah and I walk back up to him, and we walk as a group up the red carpet.

Pictures are being taken, Jax's name is being yelled from the crowd of onlookers, and a reporter along the red carpet stops him and asks him who we are. Before he answers, he looks our way for approval, and I smile. *I can do this. I am freaking Bree Daniels a kindergarten teacher and zookeeper of those monkeys.*

He gestures to us to walk up beside him. "This is Bree Daniels and Noah Roarke from my hometown. Bree is the one responsible for my success. She was my drama coach and you've maybe heard about Team Bree."

The reporter must have done her research and said to him, "What a great night to share with her, Jax."

He gives her his best Hollywood dimple smile, "Yes, this is the person we have all been supporting. Team Bree."

We slowly walk up the red carpet, Jax bringing us both into the pictures occasionally. Word spread about who we are so that puts more interest in us.

We finally make it into the theater and are waiting to be escorted to our seats. Looking around the room Noah and I see other key members of the cast and probably crew from the film and other recognizable Hollywood talent whose publicists thought it would be good for their careers to be seen with the current Hollywood romantic it-couple. The media is still allowed into the premiere for this portion of the night. The movie screening and the after-party are invite only with no media allowed.

Sophie walks over to us. She isn't here with anyone but her assistant and close team. She said once she arrived, she would be sitting with Jax and spending the evening with us so she didn't need to bring her own group in when her best friend would already be here. We were able to get to know each other, and she feels like a little sister to me. I told her if she ever needs to get away from the Hollywood chaos, she should come to Lake Harmony, and the girls and I would make sure she isn't lonely but still has her privacy.

The lights begin to flash, announcing that we are to take our seats. Our rows are reserved so we can take our time. They'll show the movie, followed by a brief Q and A session with the actors. Then, we'll make our way to the private after-party.

The movie finally starts. Noah and I are sitting next to Jax and Sophie. We are surrounded by the film's producers and writers and other A-list actors. It's a cute love story where the billionaire character Jax plays meets the quirky girl who's a coffee barista and spills the drink down his suit then tells him off for standing in the way. Sparks fly along with their murderous looks and sarcastic dialogue. The audience laughs along with the film and claps loudly at the end.

Sophie, Jax, and the producers head to the stage for the Q and A session. Most questions are directed to Jax or Sophie; a few are for the producer about how the film was made. Eventually, the questions seem to be slowing down. Before anyone can stand and leave the theater Jax leans into the mic one last time. "Sophie and I would like to thank you for coming to watch our film tonight. We enjoyed making this story and sharing it with you. On a personal note, many of you may be aware that I have been supporting someone very special to me. Her name is Bree Daniels, and you may recognize her if I put it together with the hashtag Team Bree. She was my drama coach in high school. I tell everyone that she's responsible for me standing before you tonight and for putting me up on that screen. She mostly denies her role in my success, but at least she's beginning to willingly accept my heartfelt gratitude." The crowd chuckles and Jax continues, "she tells me she is only responsible for giving me the tools to put in my toolbox, but that I am the one responsible for knowing how to use them. We will have to happily agree to disagree. She has been through some trying times over the last couple of months because she finally took the time to pursue her own dreams and wrote a romance novel. She is a teacher, and a role model and the school district was misinformed about what she was writing and attacked her character. Even then, she didn't fight for herself. Instead, she continued to fight for anyone else wanting to pursue their creative dreams and their right to do so. She continues to teach us that reaching for our dreams is possible if we have the right people guiding us and telling us we can succeed. Thank you, Bree, for always believing in me."

I am wiping away tears, and Noah has his arm around me. The clapping gets louder, and Jax jumps down off the stage and comes towards me. He comes right up to me and gives me a big hug. The audience's clapping seems to get louder. He lets me go and shakes Noah's hand. "Come on up here with Soph and me. We are going to sneak out the back instead of going through this big crowd," Jax says, and we get up and walk with him to the stage.

We take the limo to the party. Noah and I lean back against the seat. We're about to pass out from nervous energy and exhaustion.

Noah squeezes my hand, "Are you okay, sweetheart? That was a pretty big and emotional speech Jax just made. Do you still want to go to the party?"

"I'm good. I didn't know he was going to do that. Wow. Here I am a little kindergarten teacher from the Midwest being honored by Jax in front of his Hollywood peers. That is crazy, right? I mean did that really just happen?"

"Oh yeah. That happened. He really admires you. Now, everyone in that audience knows why, and you deserve it. Just think of all the students you have had during your years teaching. If you made even a fraction of a difference with them as you did with Jax, you need to admit you're making a difference in a lot of lives, Bree. Just being yourself and sharing your joy with the students you teach, makes such an impact on their lives. You don't even try, it's just who you are, and you are amazing."

"I love you, Noah."

"I love you too, sweetheart. Now, let's go have some fun before we pass out. We can sleep on the flight home tomorrow. Did you see all those actors and musicians at the theater tonight? So cool."

Epilogue

Bree

Tonight is Tuesday Trivia at Cooper's Corner, and the gang is all coming. We haven't had time to talk about the premiere, and they are all dying to know what famous people we saw. There were a few cool pictures in some online articles of Noah and me with Jax and Sophie that included a small mention of #TEAMBREE. Nothing to be too concerned about with my job, thankfully. Of course, Gertie reposted everything she could find so the town knew we were in Hollywood celebrating the movie premiere with Jax.

#TEAMBREE GOES TO HOLLYWOOD
Celebrating in Hollywood with our own Jax Turner, Bree Daniels and Dr. Noah Roarke, take to the bright lights as one of Tinsel Town's 'It Couples,' proving that following your dreams and letting your creativity shine can lead you to the stars!

Slowly, our gang trickles in for dinner and trivia. Griffin is still the host announcer and Stella still comes to help. Jackson and Julia arrive at the same time as Noah and I do and we head in to grab our table.

"Looks like your weekend trip in LA was a blast. I can't wait to hear all about it," Julia says.

Cooper sees us and walks towards us from the bar. "Hey, good to see you guys. I have that table right in front of Griffin reserved for you. I figured twelve of us if I have time to join you."

Noah and Jackson are busy talking so I look over at Julia, "I think that's everyone. I haven't heard someone isn't coming. That should be good Coop. Thanks."

We sit down and everyone else starts to wander in. Cooper drops off some water for the table and a couple of pitchers of beer with glasses. "I'll grab some wings and fries and keep them coming."

Once we're all sitting around the table, Hillary claps her hands, "Alrighty, tell us all about your glamorous weekend. Who did you see, what did you do, and were there any scandalous moments?"

"Hmm, let's see." I muse. "We saw Jeff Goldblum in the lobby of our hotel, Noah hung out with Jax and his buddies from the band, Brick Row, I got ready and pampered with Sophie Knight for the premiere, and you name them, they were at the premiere. By the time, Noah and I got through walking the red carpet with Jax, we were a bit numb to the rest of the A-listers that were there."

Noah adds, "It was super cool. I was hanging out with Jax and the guys from the band all day. They were down to earth and deal with the same kind of crap we do when they aren't touring or doing a show. They acted more impressed that I was a doctor. Same with Jax and Sophie. They are all cool people."

Rob laughs, "Is it just me or does anyone else think this is so crazy? I mean Noah and Bree are talking about celebrities and rock stars like 'hey it's cool, we hung out with Hollywood stars and rock stars but like we all sat around the room and sang campfire songs and shared nachos.'"

"Sorry to burst your bubble, but it was normal outside of the premiere. I mean okay, Bree and I both laughed at each other and did geek out and fanboy a bit but after getting ready and getting to know them all it was like they didn't belong on some fancy pedestal. They were just normal. We even felt it was as normal as being here with all of you."

Hillary, "Well, some of us are normal. Not all of us."

Julia and I see her direct a dirty stare at Garrett. *Here they go again! Ugh.*

Sam asks, "Who was the person that surprised you the most?"

"I think Sophie surprised me the most. She comes from a small town, and she is closer to Stella's age. She seemed a bit lonely, though. She was so sweet, and she had all these designer dresses, shoes, and bags for us to pick

236

through to wear for the premiere. I told her not to tell me how much the dress was worth because it was probably more than my car. She was so nice, and I told her if she ever needs to get away she should come here and stay in Jax's lake house and that us girls would keep her company."

Julia says, "That would be so cool. I bet it does get a bit lonely if you're single in Hollywood. It would be hard to know who to trust. Are Sophie and Jax a couple?"

"No, everyone assumes they are, but both of them said they are like best friends, that there's no chemistry between them."

"That's good news for me, then! Let me know if she ever comes to Lake Harmony, and I'll make sure to keep her company so she doesn't get lonely," Rob says in his lady-killer personality.

Griffin joins us at the table, "So how are we doing this thing tonight? Girls versus boys again or couple versus couple? Team winner versus team loser? Figure it out boys and girls, and let Mr. Griffin know."

Jackson looks around the table, "Why don't we couple up then?"

"I'm out!" Rob stands and walks over to the bar and sits by Cooper.

Julia and I look nervously at each other, biting our lips, because that leaves Garrett and Hillary teaming up.

"Fuck, I can't team up with the mighty Sheriff. He isn't going to compromise on answers, and we all know he isn't always right even though he thinks he is," Hillary says and folds her arms across her chest.

"Fine with me. I don't want to deal with your temper tantrums anymore, Hillary. You and your bitchy attitude need to go. I am sick of it, everyone is sick of it," Garrett says.

Again, Julia and I look at each other. She exhales with exaggeration and stands up, "Listen up you two. We have been listening to you bitch and moan at each other for months now." She looks at Hillary then Garrett and continues, "We don't know what the fuck happened between the two of you, and honestly, I don't think any of us give a

237

flying rat's ass anymore, BUT…you are both getting on our nerves and, to be honest until you both can be in the same space TOGETHER like we all used to be just leave. Don't come back until you can peacefully hang out with all of us. I think I can speak for everyone sitting here, your best friends by the way, that we are exhausted by your behavior toward each other, and we don't want to be around it anymore. So, go. Both of you. Just. Go."

Hillary and Garrett stare at her then look at all of us. We're all looking back at them like, *Yeah you two drive us crazy and it sucks.*

Jackson grabs Julia's hand, "Okay, sit down, honey. You said what we were all thinking."

"SERIOUSLY. Do you all fucking feel like this? That Garrett and I are getting on your nerves. Fine. Fuck it. I'm out too," Hillary says before storming off.

Jackson looks at Garrett, "Listen, man, I don't want to know what happened between the two of you, but we all know something did. You two need to work through it. Obviously, Hillary's hurting, and you are too. Go, talk to Hillary and figure your shit out. You will be better off making peace with Hillary than continuing this personal war against each other."

Garrett runs his hand over his face, "Talking things out with Hillary is like putting me in front of a shooting range. I know. I'll make an attempt to talk, but she has to want to listen. You know Hillary, and she's stubborn as a mule, especially if anyone suggests she isn't right. I know it's gotten out of hand." He stands, "Sorry we ruined the night. I'll try and track her ass down. She is either slashing my tires outside or already home throwing things."

Garrett heads out the door looking a bit defeated. "Does anyone know what the heck happened between them that has escalated to this point?" Sam asks.

"Whatever it is, they need to work it out because it is at a boiling point. Underneath, whatever is going on I know they care about each other. Somewhere along the way they ran into a hiccup, but it's time they figure out a solution together," Julia says.

Noah squeezes my knee under the table. I look over at him, "Is it so terrible that I just want Hillary to have her happily ever after too? She needs to stop fighting her feelings and just work through whatever chaos is brewing between them. I hope that Garrett can get through to her and she realizes that all the online dates she has are not working out because the man she's supposed to be with has been by her side protecting her since childhood."

Noah leans forward and kisses me, "Sometimes the best things are worth fighting for. Let's give them the time and space they need so they can work this out. Sometimes it's all about the timing."

Dear Reader,

Thank you for reading Bree and Noah's story-**Sexy Secrets**. Want more of this hilarious group of friends? The series continues with Hillary and Garrett's story **Covert Entanglements**, the third book in The Lake Harmony Series.

Not ready to leave Bree and Noah yet? Click here to get an exclusive BONUS scene or use the QR code!

If you want to start at the beginning and fall in love with Lake Harmony and all its characters read Julia and Jackson's story-**Five Dates**.

Binge the rest of the series Free in Kindle Unlimited!

The Lake Harmony Series:
Five Dates (Julia & Jackson)
Sexy Secrets (Bree & Noah)
Covert Entanglements (Hillary & Garrett)
Star Obsessions (Rob & Sophie) *coming soon!*

242

About the Author

Tanja Waltrip was born and raised in the 'burbs of Chicago and now resides in sunny Florida. She has a daughter, Emily, who lives in the Maryland/D.C. area. Despite the tumultuous nature of chasing the sun, one thing has remained the same—her voracious reading habit. She always knew that she would one day turn this passion for the Contemporary Romance genre into her own writing pursuit.

Please sign up HERE for my NEWSLETTER to receive news about upcoming releases and giveaways.

I love to interact with my readers, whether it's a plotline critique or a desire to see one of my characters live in infamy, so please don't hesitate to send me a message. Tanjawaltrip.com

Book Links and other content:

www.ingramcontent.com/pod-product-compliance
Lightning Source LLC
Chambersburg PA
CBHW051946220626
47052CB00004B/813